A Touch Of Happy

by Andrew Kanago

A HellBound Books Publishing LLC Book
Austin TX

**A HellBound Books LLC
Publication**
Copyright © 2019 by HellBound Books Publishing LLC
All Rights Reserved

Cover and art design
By Carlos Villas for
HellBound Books Publishing LLC

www.hellboundbookspublishing.com

Acknowledgements

To Dave Hudson for giving me valuable feedback and even more valuable friendship.

To my amazing children. You give my days meaning and give my nights less sleep.

To Heather, my first reader, my N, S, E, and W, my butterfly.

A Touch of Happy

Andrew Kanago

1996

"Your handcuffs are loose," the voice said. "You can get out."

I pulled against the cuffs; it hurt to move my arm even a little. Maybe the right hand one was a little wabbly. "It's not loose enough. I can't do it."

The voice, it sounded like the voice of God, whispered back, "It's going to hurt to pull your hand out. It's going to hurt a lot."

I could hear the groan of the water pipes. The angry man had finished his shower. "I hurt all over."

"I know," the voice said.

"He's been hurting me."

"I know."

"I hurt too bad."

"I know. You can do this. You can take the pain. All the pain. Pull now."

"I can't." The sound of footsteps.

The voice no longer whispered. It screamed, "NOW! NOW! NOW!"

Chapter One
Saturday, October 8, 2016

"Why are you trying to kill me?" Mark Peter asked. He gestured toward a purple stuffed bear sitting against a small mountain of those small pillows wealthy people pile upon their beds.

The person he was speaking to, an FBI agent named Bill Mallory, looked up from his phone. He appeared annoyed. Not annoyed at any particular thing; it was more like annoyance was the natural default setting for his long, dark-skinned face. "Would you like me to call a doctor?"

Mark looked back at the bear with its head cutely tilted to the side, almost mockingly so. "You know what I mean, Bill."

"What you mean is that you don't want to touch a harmless itty-bitty stuffed animal." Bill's voice had a slight tinge of weariness to it.

"I mean that I want to be at home listening to my stereo and eating a frozen pizza." Mail order, brand new CD's, and frozen pizza defined an awful lot of Mark Peter's private life. He'd like to own actual records, but buying used ones from

Kanesville Kollectables in Council Bluffs was like a game of Russian Roulette.

The third person in the room spoke up. She said, "You always pull this shit, Mark. It's getting old." She did not like frozen pizza and felt that listening to old-ass CD's on a 1970s cabinet stereo lo-fi was the height of lameness. Dylan (pronounced Die-lan, not like the folk singer) Mannion had been with the FBI for only a few years and had been working with Mark and Bill for just over four months.

In that time, Mark had been called in on three cases (two custody case kidnappings and one business executive held for ransom in Uruguay). Both kids on the custody case had been found safe, but only the head of the business executive had been discovered, delivered to the local police station in la Ciudad de Guichón in a cardboard box.

Pictures of the girl, three days gone, covered the room's walls. Photos of her on a horse, with her father, petting a dog. Eight years old, hair the color of sunflowers. Quinn had the face of a pretty little girl who would someday be a beautiful woman.

Mark shrugged his rounded shoulders, plaintively, at his oldest and best friend. As a matter of habit, Mark wore leather driving gloves whenever he left his house. Otherwise, he might touch something with a bad history and his whole day would be shot.

"I need a few minutes," Mark said. "This is something I got to build up to. I don't need you shitting on me right now."

Next to the thick door sat a pair of gray equipment containers. Despite the "Forensics Unit" labels, however, the containers did not contain swabs, measuring tapes, or biohazard labels.

Playing for time, Mark pointed at the stuffed animal. "So, the bear was her favorite?" The purple bear was the kind that, if squeezed, would sing a song, tell you it loved you, or even giggle.

Bill nodded. "According to Mama, and Mama always knows. Apparently, Quinn got it for Christmas a few years ago from Grandma," he added. "Grandma is not doing so well either, what with her heart and the stress of Quinn's disappearance."

Mark turned toward the bed once more and leaned over toward the bear before quickly pulling back. "Bill, I can't do this. I just can't. The girl's probably dead anyway."

Bill sighed. Mark captured spiders and released them outside rather than kill them, but he also was not the kind of person who suffered in silence. Mark complained about the temperature, pondered ad nauseum why God had given that particular gift, and so on.

He tried to keep the annoyance out of his voice. "What you are saying? All hundred percent accurate. Quinn might be dead, that's true. If she is, she deserves to be found, to allow her parents to at least know what happened. If she's alive, then we can do something amazing. Just… just do your thing, man, that's all you got to do. When you think about it, you're already here, so why not touch the teddy bear?"

"That's your pep talk?" Mark asked. "You have the worst people skills, Bill. 'You're already here.' Damn. It's not like I'm dragging my feet about getting a root canal or something. This..." Mark pointed to the purple bear sitting on the pink duvet, "is going to stay with me for the rest of my life."

"So does a root canal."

Mark rolled his eyes and put a hand to his buttery tummy. "Dental work doesn't cause you nightmares."

"You didn't know my childhood dentist," Bill's face looked even more annoyed than usual.

"You're smiling," Mark said. "You're laughing at me. Inside, I know you're laughing."

"I'm not smiling," Bill replied with another cough into his sleeve, "it's just that you are the Old Faithful of whiny crap holes. Every time, you whine like a two-year-old not getting an ice cream cone, and then every time you end up using your gift and helping out. For once I would like to skip the opening act."

"This time, I'm not. I'm leaving," Mark got off the bed. His hair ran on the wispy side and possessed a growing bald spot, as if his cranium couldn't decide how to rid itself of hair and decided to pull every lever at once.

He took a step toward the door. As he did so, Bill slid in front of Mark's path, blocking him.

"I thought I was free to go."

"You are," Bill answered, "but you need to remember two things before you leave."

"What's that?" Mark asked.

"First, in order to exit the house, you're going to have to go past Mama Bear in the living room. She's going to be watching you and asking you questions."

"About forensics. She doesn't know what I really do."

"You're still going to have to talk to her. Maybe the dad too," Bill replied, adding smugness to his annoyed expression. "There's a younger brother, not yet three years old. He's probably wondering where big sister Quinn is right now."

"I can handle all that," Mark said.

Bill snorted, which turned into a cough. "No, you can't. But that's not even the most important thing."

"I'll bite. What is it?"

"She might be alive. And if she's alive, Quinn is far from home and very, very scared. You know about being far from home and you know about being scared. Better than anyone I've ever met." Bill's deep voice softened, remembering how they'd met years before. "You can help her. Alive or dead, you can help Quinn. Please, Mark. Help the child."

After a moment. "Crap."

"I'm saving you some time."

"Do you have to keep saying her name?"

"Quinn's?" Bill asked. "Yeah, I do. Because Quinn is eight years old and Quinn loves horses."

"Shut up, please."

"Her mom told me that Quinn's horse is named Brownie. Brownie the horse likes apples."

"You're making that last part up." Mark ventured a small smile.

Bill held up his notepad. "It's all right here, pal."

"Just stop. Please." Mark searched his friend's face for laughter, found none, and turned toward the purple bear. "Okay. Fine. Well, fine. Okay, set up the easel," he said. He took off the driving gloves, stuffed them in the pocket of his blue, unfashionable windbreaker.

Dylan placed a chair next to the bed and positioned an easel to a spot where a left-handed person could reach it. She strapped a thick pad of heavy drawing paper to the easel. Then she positioned herself behind the easel, ready to rip sheets of paper from the pad.

Bill strapped on a pair of blue latex gloves and picked up the purple bear.

Mark chose a Faber-Castell graphite sketch pencil from a blue plastic pencil box and weighed it in his hand. For a few seconds, he stared at the blank paper. "This would be a lot easier if I wasn't going to remember any of this," he said. Mark tried to swallow but found he couldn't. This happened a lot whenever he worked a case.

"Yeah, I know." Bill shrugged, as if to imply that he had thought the same thing many times. "What fun would a gift like yours be if it came without strings?"

"Shut up, dickhead." Mark reached out toward the teddy bear with his bare right hand. The fingers hung in the air, inches away from the toy.

He braced himself and touched the bear.

Nothing happened.

Except the bear said, "I love you" in a dreamy voice.

"That's weird," Mark said after a moment.

"You're not getting anything?"

Mark shook his head, confused. "Nada."

"Damn," sighed Bill. "I could have sworn with the bear… Well, this happens sometimes. Even you don't bat a thousand. Dylan, get another one of those stuffed animals from the bag."

"I don't know," she said in her deep voice, "the mother said the teddy bear was Quinn's favorite."

She handed Mark an Elmo doll. He winced as his bare hand touched it.

A moment later, Mark slumped, looking even more tubby. "Nothing."

"You feeling okay?" Bill asked.

"Some allergies maybe. It sucks in the fall. Anyway, it's never mattered before." Mark reached out and grabbed, in succession, a black dog with large glass eyes, a brown teddy bear, a stuffed horse, a plush Dora the Explorer, and a story book (about Pete the Cat, who apparently liked baseball).

"Do you have to touch them a certain way?" Dylan asked. She spoke to Mark with a patronizing and disdainful tone, as if he were a con man not yet caught. The previous agent to work with Bill and Mark had retired, and she had only been with them a few months.

Mark's expression grew incredulous. "What, like do I have to rub them against my privates or something?"

"No, uh, maybe you have to hold them, I don't know, upright or something," Dylan replied.

"Dylan, it doesn't quite work like that," Bill tried to suppress another cough.

"Nothing," Mark spat after going through several items of costume jewelry. Frustrated, he asked, "Are you sure that Quinn existed? I mean, this isn't some kind of test?"

"Quinn Hughes. Missing three days. She's real." Bill's narrow face glowered, "You think we rented out a mansion to test you? We all know what you can do. Look, let's think this out. You've had problems before. I can think of a couple of times you couldn't help us. Like that time in Santa Fe."

"It's different," Mark said. "I always get something. In Santa Fe, it was like… I don't know, maybe being in a dark closet and there were people outside whispering. Maybe I couldn't give you anything to work with, but I always got something."

"I didn't know that," Bill said.

"Now, with the talking bear and all of her other toys, I am literally getting nothing. It's as if I'm touching a park bench or my own phone. There's nothing there."

Dylan, still angry, asked, "You been drinking again, Mark? I've heard you had some issues in the past."

"I have not been drinking," Mark shot back.

"Whatever you say." Dylan got up and stretched. "Maybe we should pack up?"

"Wait," Bill said. "Not yet. I'm curious what's different about this girl that you don't get anything. Look at the pictures. Does she remind you of anyone from your past or anything?"

Mark walked over and sat on the bed. The girl looked like a million other little girls. Blond hair and a serious expression for the camera like she'd been told to smile and didn't like being told what to do. Another picture showed Quinn and her father on the front porch of the mansion. He was smiling; Quinn stared distractedly off to the side.

"Serious girl," Dylan said. "She likes animals, though."

One picture, the one nearest the bed, was of Quinn and a black and white border collie. She knelt next to the dog, her arms around it. "She's smiling in this one," Mark said.

Mark and the FBI agents began to look through the room. Gloves off, Mark let his hands drift through the clothes neatly folded in drawers, on the unused science kit sitting up on a closet shelf, over the shelves of apparently unread books.

After a few minutes, Bill deep voice pierced the silence, "Anything, Mark? Anything at all? Again, time is of the essence."

"Zilch. This is messed up." He knelt on the plush pink carpet, his hand resting on the Disney princess blanket draped over the bed. "Maybe there's something under here…" He spotted something shiny near the rear leg of the bed. Mark leaned forward and saw a tiny metal crucifix, half-hidden in the carpet.

"How many maids do these people have? There's not a speck of dirt here." Bill said.

"Maybe, just this," Mark grabbed for it with his right hand. When his fingers touched the thin metal, his mind reeled away. Mark's body fell over, and his left hand began to twitch.

Dylan looked over her shoulder, saw Mark's arm convulsing. "Bill! He's got something. Help me get him in the chair."

The senior FBI agent rushed over, grabbed Mark under his armpits and lifted him into the chair. Dylan forced a pencil into Mark's palsied hand and directed it toward the paper.

Mark hand shaded some indistinct figure and made a motion with his right, non-drawing hand. Dylan ripped the page away.

The drawing continued. Mark and Dylan stood silent, intent on the paper.

A window appeared in the upper left corner of the drawing, a tree in the distance. Bill turned around and checked.

"It's this room," he said.

A figure appeared in the center of the drawing.

"It's the mother," Bill said after another minute.

"Look at that expression," said Dylan, her voice hardening.

Bill made a sound of agreement. "She looks pissed."

A little girl's hand, Quinn's hand, appeared in the lower right corner, clutching the crucifix. The mother's face flushed ugly with splotchy anger. Barely seen is a length of broomstick the mother was holding in her hand.

"No, mama, no," Mark said in a little girl's voice.

Dylan grimaced. "I hate when he talks like the vict…"

"Shut the hell up," Bill whispered.

"Is that a broomstick?" Dylan murmured.

"It's the Stupid Stick," Mark answered in Quinn's voice.

Mark waved his hand away for another drawing. Tear of the paper. A new drawing. The wall, no posters. The drawing is blurry and half-done.

"What is that?" Dylan asked.

"Hurting me," Mark answered. His head jerked to the side, as if it had been hit. Again.

"That motherfucking bitch." Dylan hated, absolutely hated people who hurt their kids.

"Dylan, keep your cool," Bill hissed.

A wave of the hand. A new sheet of paper.

The pencil began to draw Mama's face again, half hidden.

"What is that?" Dylan asked. "I can't tell."

"A… pillow?" Bill responded.

Mark's legs began to jerk. "No mama! Mmmmmmmm."

The drawing ended with, at the moment of Quinn's death, the graphite pencil breaking heavily against the drawing pad, a thick line trailing from a strand of Mama's hair away to nothing.

He fell from the chair, twisting. Mark arched his back and heaved in breaths. The thick walls muffled the sound, as if he were once again trapped in some small, windowless room.

Several minutes passed as Mark, on all fours, gasped for air. It felt like some part of his brain had been bored through. A wall tumbled in. His head felt like it had been split by an axe. "Can I get some water?" asked Mark at last, his words almost inaudible. "And a Tylenol?"

"Yeah, I'll take care of it." Dylan ran to the bathroom, holding Mark's thermos. Bill had the painkillers. By the time the junior FBI agent returned, Mark was sitting up. He accepted the thermos with shaking hands.

After a few tentative sips, Mark looked up at Bill's kindly face. "Did I get anything?"

"Yeah buddy." Bill looked at one of the drawings, held it in a way that Mark couldn't see it. "It was the mother. One of your pictures showed the room. Totally bare. She kept the kid up here without the bed, the carpet, the stuffed animals, anything. Smothered the kid with a pillow."

"Jesus."

"I don't know how the crucifix ended up here," Bill continued, "The dad has to be an accessory. No way this goes on without him knowing. The bed and furniture didn't magically transport themselves here, you know."

"Mark, you want to see what you drew?" Dylan asked. She knew what she was asking.

Bill spoke up testily, "Go make yourself useful. Pack up. We got what we need." When she began to pack the art supplies, Bill sat next to his friend and spoke low. "Don't pay any attention to her. Dylan is an ass and doesn't like that you can do what you can do. It doesn't make sense to her worldview."

"Doesn't matter. I'm going to see all of it anyway," Mark replied and tapped his broken head. "Maybe not tonight, but soon."

"Thanks for doing this. They weren't suspects. I mean, they were because the family always is in these kinds of cases. But we didn't really suspect them. That's going to change in a hurry. I need to call Parmero," Bill said, referencing the head of the Omaha field office from whence they came. Mark's information had to go through the proper channels.

"I can't do this anymore." Mark closed his eyes and groaned. "It's so hard."

"You know," Bill said, his expression less than annoyed, "even though I make lots of jokes, I really admire what you do. I don't know if I could, were our positions reversed. I'd like to think I'd try, but I don't know. You're a strong person, Mark. And if you decide not to do it anymore, that's up to you. I thank you for all your work. But if I think you might be able to help, I'm going to ask."

"Please don't," Mark said, "I mean it. I'm done. Forever."

Chapter Two
Sunday, October 9, 2016

Megann Artis had the phone to her ear when he found her.

"That party was cray-cray," Megann said to her friend, a friend who would in a few hours recount the conversation to the police. "I mean, you think that Lexi would have known not to come. It's not like a big secret that Jake was not that into her anymore."

The friend, also named Lexie but spelled different, said something about how everybody in the basement stared at Lexi when she came down the stairs already drunk as shit. Megann laughed as the dark van spotted her and began to slow down.

Megann said that the longer that Lexi stayed at the party, the dumber she got. "No one ever told her that if the boy she's flirtin' with ain't trying to get in her after half an hour, she needs to stop trying."

The dark van pulled to the side of the road about half a block ahead and a man opened the door and got out. Two in the morning, a dark van, and a man in a baseball cap. Megann should have torn her shoes off running away, but Lexi and her quest to get with Jake made her blind (having smoked weed didn't help her reflexes).

Lexie the friend said that Megann missed the best part. Lexi puked in Ashley's lap and Ashley wasn't having any of that shit.

"In Ashley's lap?"

Right on that skirt she loves, Lexie the friend said as the man positioned himself next to the sidewalk. He pretended to look at his rear tire but the excitement made him distracted. The girl continued to walk toward him, talking about some stupid party she had been at. She didn't see him; she didn't even look up. He stuck out his tongue and tasted the air; no one watching them. He could always tell if someone was paying attention, he tasted something bitter, the taste of sour beer. Tonight, his tongue only felt salt and sweet. No one noticed his van.

Over the phone, Lexie heard something, a man's deep voice, something about a lug nut. Then Megann's scream, cut off when a hand karate chopped her throat. The next day she would try to describe the voice but knew not the words to do so.

Six minutes later, the next person saw a cell phone in the grass, and heard the thin sound emerging from it of a girl's voice screaming "Megann" over and over again.

Mark came awake in a flutter of movement. He felt his gloved hand knock something away. He swung his eyes to the left and saw a woman recoiling.

"You hit my hand," she said. The hand in question held a crumpled Kleenex. "You were drooling in your sleep. And talking."

"Did you touch me? Did you touch me?" Mark demanded. When the FBI flew him to a crime scene (he always went to the crime scene; bringing the objects back to Omaha never netted so good a result), Mark had two absolute rules.

One: Mark took with him his own sleeping bag and pillow. Most hotel beds and sheets did not trigger his particular ability, but Mark didn't like to take chances. Besides, hotel beds were nasty, especially the bed covers. Under a UV light, most hotel rooms looked like a Jackson Pollack painting composed with human fluids. Mark also carried a police flashlight to help check for bedbugs.

Two: Mark required, absolutely required, two seats on the plane. The window seat for him to sit, the middle seat so that he could suffer through the flight alone, certain that his last seconds on earth would involve trying to figure out how to put on that stupid oxygen mask amidst a din of screaming and the sight of solid earth approaching at sickening speed.

In addition to an extra seat, Mark always flew while wearing long sleeve shirts, pants, and gloves to expose as little skin as possible for accidental contact.

There had been some computer screw up this time, or else United Airlines sought to make a little more money by canceling Mark's safety seat. Either way, the Atlanta-to-Omaha flight consisted of 257 minutes of shoulder-to-shoulder goodness with a woman named Stephanie Gerrold, who liked mystery novels, one or two drinks ("to loosen me up, ha ha ha"), and torturing introverts with inquisitive and non-stop small talk on long domestic flights.

The plane had been aloft nearly an hour when Mark began to wonder if Stephanie Gerrold had been, in fact, flirting with him. The woman, who looked to be in her early thirties, had a tinkling laugh and a tendency to lower her gaze as if to convey seriousness when in fact she only declared that she would be getting another white wine.

Mark felt reasonably certain that he'd been flirted with before. Once, in college, by a drunk woman at a Burger King after Mark and his friends had completed a seven-hour game of Axis and Allies. That woman's name was Gwen and she smelled like perfume and sour beer. Her voice squeaked like a pet toy but she seemed to like Mark's face.

Luckily, she only brushed her hand against his cheek, not full contact (or, God forbid, gone in for a kiss). Everyone else at the Burger King thought the woman had just passed out and hit her head. There were a few others: that woman who cleaned his teeth, that sad-eyed teenager on one of Mark's cases.

Now, Mark never knew for certain that these women were flirting with him. He'd read about flirting in books and online, and Stephanie Gerrold's actions seemed like flirting. However, he tried hard not to dwell on the subject. What good was flirting when it could not possibly go further?

"I didn't touch anything. I was trying to be kind," Stephanie Gerrold said in an affronted tone. "You looked like you were having a nightmare."

"I don't like being touched." Mark wiped the drool away from his lip.

He must have sounded apologetic because Stephanie Gerrold only harrumphed and looked in another direction. However, after a moment, she turned again toward him. "What were you dreaming about? It didn't sound very nice. You were talking in a not nice way."

Mark hesitated. He hadn't known he talked in his sleep. "Just a nightmare."

"You sounded mean." Stephanie Gerrold gave Mark one final, inscrutable look (maybe… sadness? Or disappointment? Maybe she was mad. Emotions + Mark = Confusion) and turned toward the center of the plane. *She was actually pretty cute*, Mark thought.

Only when the person in the last row had passed by did Mark get up. Only when he exited the terminal did he turn on his phone.

To his surprise, he had three messages. Mark barely knew three people.

"Hey friend," Bill's deep voice always softened when he talked to Mark, "be glad you're in the Big O. It's a real snafu here in Atlanta. It's not our case, technically, but Dylan went and started asking the father some hard questions. Naturally, Dad clammed up. Now Mom is on the warpath. It's going to be in the papers tomorrow; she's giving a sob story about how the FBI suspects the parents instead of going after the real kidnapper. How their little girl is still alive. All that bullshit. Never mind that it's not even our case. The mom is very telegenic, by the way. Anyway, I wanted to check, see how many weird looks people gave you on the flight. You know, the usual. Text me when you're in."

Mark looked at the phone and thought about the other messages. Decided to wait and call his best friend instead. Bill answered on the second ring. "How bad is it going to be?" Mark asked.

Bill coughed through the receiver. "Craptastic. I'd like to strangle Dylan. The FBI wasn't out front on this; we were brought in to advise, to assist. And our little team, of which Dylan is a member, does not talk to suspects. The public is never to know that you even exist. But Dylan couldn't help herself and she started talking to Dad. Damn it."

"You think Dad would have talked?"

"Yeah, I do. I saw the bastard. Man looked guilty as sin. If the police had approached him right, he'd have sung. Once his wife got wind that we suspected, she shut his ass up. He'll never confess now. She's got him under her thumb. Parmero," Bill added, referring to the Special Agent in Charge of the Omaha Field Office, "is pissed at me. Basically, he let me know what he thought of our continued use of you in kidnapping cases. It was not a pleasant conversation."

"Luckily, that's not a problem," Mark said.

Bill coughed a second before answering. "Damn allergies. Yeah, of course."

"I'm done."

"I know."

"I am," Mark insisted. "Anyway, can't you get rid of Dylan?"

"Her? Nah. She's not incompetent, but she's got some real issues with child abusers. This case set her off. Besides, not too many people in the office want to work with you."

Mark sighed. "Nice to know I'm loved."

"Screw 'em. You still on the plane?"

"On my way to the car. The flight was hell and I have a killer headache." The headache seemed to sneak up, ninja-like, on Mark somewhere between the plane and luggage claim, where he stood next to the spot where the luggage would go back into the terminal. "If you were here, I'd probably ask you to go and put me out of my misery."

"Is it the after effects?" Bill asked. "Headaches aren't uncommon."

"This one is worse," Mark replied after a moment. "Thank God I'm done with the FBI."

Bill didn't say anything for a second, clearly choosing his words with care. "Thanks again for coming out, even if it turned into a world of shit." Bill pointedly did not say anything about Mark wanting to quit the FBI, and Mark did not press it.

It took until he reached his car in the long-term parking lot for Mark to will himself into listening to the second message. Stacy, his sister, sounded as if she was doing three things at once.

"Mom's birthday is tomorrow," Stacy said amid the engine sounds of her old, noisy car. "That's a Wednesday. That's October 12. That's tomorrow. So, you'd better come to dinner. We'll eat at six, but try to be there by five. It's KFC, which I know you hate, but Mom likes it. So, you'll just have to deal. Do NOT bring your own dinner. If you do, Mom will feel all guilty and she'll do that thing where she sighs before saying something. I know you did not get her a present, so I did your shopping for you. It's a really nice robe. Pink. Soft.

You can pay me later. It's forty dollars. You're welcome. Bye. Love you."

Mark deleted the message and started the car. The headache stabbed and slashed. While the motor idled, he opened the glove compartment to see if there was any Tylenol. Out of luck.

He hadn't forgotten about Mom's birthday. He'd bought a card. He even remembered that Mom would want KFC for dinner, but families had their own unspoken traditions, slots into which each member was locked into.

Mark did not buy his mom presents because he knew that Stacy wanted to feel like the hero of the family. Stacy thought that little brother Mark needed rescue, even as an adult. Sometimes he wondered if Stacy was looking for a way to even the score for that thing that happened so long ago.

In contrast, Mom needed blindness, the absence of any clouds in the Peter family sky. To pretend that all was well, that Stacy lived with her because of choice. To pretend that Mark was normal and just waiting for the right girl.

Mom would complain about how much money they spent on the presents, even though she wanted them to spend too much. If they didn't spend enough, or get KFC on her birthday (even though Mom always said "you should get what you want. Pizza, hamburgers, whatever."), then Mom would start crying in the middle of dinner. But it would be "for no reason, no reason at all."

Isn't that what families were for? To pretend that everything was normal and everyone led amazing lives? No matter that Stacy had a daughter at twenty; that Skylar's dad had never wanted to see his daughter; and that Mark would never get married, have children, or even be able to shake hands without having to wear gloves. Everything was normal.

Once, Stacy complained about not being able to be honest with Mom anymore. She'd even used the word "mendacity" and compared the Peter family to a decades-long game of emotional Twister. Mom sighed before every sentence for nearly two months.

And what, Mark wondered, *did he need?*

People who didn't see him as a freak, perhaps.

Oh, how his head pounded.

Sunday traffic was light. Mark whizzed by the abandoned grain elevators that passed for Omaha's public architecture, turned off at the 42nd Street exit. Once, he'd wanted to move away from his family. Somewhere in the desert: New Mexico or Utah. It would never have worked.

The headache redoubled its efforts. He decided that the pain would not allow him to cook a meal. Mark turned left on Farnam, stopped at Don and Millie's for drive-thru. He ordered the Double Don, hold the mayo. Something about mayonnaise, its sickly viscosity, always bothered him.

Food in the bag on the driver's seat, the smell somehow scaled the headache back from raging surf to rough waves. He turned left onto Dodge, momentarily believing that he would get on top of the headache, that he'd be able to ride it out without falling under the waves. He passed by a block of apartments and saw a young woman in the window talking on the phone while staring out into the gloomy weather. The car turned onto 49th Street. And Mark remembered.

An image of Quinn's mother, her face distorted in rage, filled Mark's eye. For a split second, he felt himself be Quinn, felt the sharp pain across her right forearm where Mama hit her with the stupid stick, and felt the pee run down her panties because she sometimes dribbled when Mama got into one of her moods.

Mark's face jerked around as Mama slapped Quinn in the face. "Look at me when I'm talking to you," Mama screamed, not an inch from Quinn's face. The car passed the place where they'd torn down a lovely building to build a hideous CVS pharmacy. Mark's car lurched to the right on Capital and he jerked the Toyota to the side of the road. Stopped.

A honk. The sound of a man's voice screaming at Mark. He tried to put the car in park as Mama slapped her again.

"I'm sorry, Mama," Mark wailed. Somewhere, not far away, the sound of tires screeching sounded faint in his ear, as if a wall of water were between them.

Mama slapped her again and again, and Mark whipped his head from side to side. He heard his voice screaming "No, Mama, NOOOO!"

Then Mama disappeared. The bedroom disappeared. Mark came back to himself. His little Toyota idled across from a pair of white, anonymous houses, and Mark whispered a quiet thank you to the universe that he managed to park the car in a safe place, and that no one else seemed to have seen an episode of what Mark privately called "My Own Private Horror Show."

"You're okay. You're in your car. You are okay," Mark said to himself, a habit he'd been meaning to break since his teen years. "There is nothing to worry about. It was ugly but it's over now. You are going to go home and eat your food. It's okay. It's okay."

Mark was blinded by the headlights of a car, one that had stopped behind him. He squinted at the rearview mirror for a few seconds. A cop? If so, then an undercover one. Then the dark sedan slid to the left and passed him. Mark looked at the passing car's window and saw only the shadow of the driver looking back at him.

When he got home, Mark had no desire to eat.

The one saving grace to his evening happened when Mark opened the door. When the door opened, Mark heard his cat surprisingly loud meow echo from his bedroom. Frodo, a massive gray feline came bounding out from the hallway a second later. Mark almost fell over from the feline rubbing against his legs.

"Hey, Fro," Mark said in a quiet, affectionate voice. "How's my Frodo-doh?"

While his house nearly sparkled through frequent and thorough cleaning, Frodo the Cat brought into it chaos: a layer of stray hair, globulous hairballs, and the occasional dead bird or mouse. For Mark, the cleaning of mouse-laden blood pools or lumps of unidentifiable foulness were worth it. It helped that Mark could afford three self-scooping litter boxes which he arranged in the basement, each beside an air purifier.

God, in Mark's opinion, was finicky and spiteful, random and cruel. But he was never absolute. Mark's ability made human contact impossible. Most animals could sense this. Dogs, even studded collar throat-rippers, slinked away from him. Mercifully, however, cats did not mind his touch.

After petting and playing with Frodo (a feline fond of laser pointers), Mark ate his food and got ready for bed. Frodo hopped into bed with Mark, the cat arranging its poky body between Mark's legs.

"Goodnight, my little friend," Mark said. Frodo didn't reply, but he communicated his affection for Mark through kneading his human's leg and curling into a ball and falling fast asleep. Mark tried to follow suit.

The afterimage of Quinn's final few moments played on his eyeballs when he closed them, his head propped up by new pillows (he threw out his pillows ever two months). He'd painted his bedroom blue and had hung large photos of space constellations from the walls. Aside from his books, Mark's remaining shelves were filled with intricately painted figurines of dwarves, bugbears, and other magical creatures from various role-playing games. On the bedside table sat a lamp, a flashlight, and a .38 caliber pistol.

There was something calm and impersonal about space. During his bad times, Mark imagined himself in the infinite expanse. He imagined a spaceship bound for some distant star, Mark the lone conscious human amidst thousands in cryogenic sleep. A mission to some remote planet, perhaps, to plant the flag of human society on a new world.

They would think Mark was sacrificing himself for the good of all, the man who would stay awake to monitor the ship while everyone else slept. The endless games of chess against the computer, the regulated schedule, and the predictable food. A willing prisoner in a gulf of nothingness.

It would be no sacrifice; it would be a pleasure.

Mark imagined sitting in the chair at the front of the ship, the view screens fixed to a black void nearly infinite in scope. Bach playing in the background. His breathing slowed. In space, no one touched you, no visions of looking at a pillow clamping down over your face. Just the dark emptiness of space.

He slept.

Chapter Three
Monday, October 10, 2016

The morning arrived too early after a night of fitful, crimson-violent dreams. Consequently, Mark's Prius screamed down Underwood Avenue as he wanted to avoid the more crowded Dodge Street. Of course, the scream of a Prius is more like a high-pitched warble. Either way, Mark was running late to work.

"Crap, double crap. Crap, crap, crappity crap!" He shouted at the dashboard, unable to keep the 7:46 from turning to 7:47, then 7:48.

Drops of rain began to plop onto Mark's windshield, almost innocently. Unsullied blips of water just happening to find their way onto the glass. Oh, terribly sorry, but we just chanced to end up here.

7:53 happened as Mark screeched into the parking lot of Eastside High School, almost taking out a freshman who was crossing the lot and staring at his phone. The kid looked up; his eyes widened a micrometer. Then the kid lifted up his middle finger and screamed that Mark better look where he was fucking going.

Eastside was that kind of school.

Mark pulled into the farthest-from-the-door employee lot stall (marked with green lines), the rain changed from "Oh, why fancy meeting you here" to "Sweet God Almighty, I'm a coming!" A wave of rain charged from the west, drenching Mark as he left his car.

"Perfect," Mark said in an undertone.

The 5-minute bell rang as Mark opened the front door, a shopping bag holding his lunch in his left hand, his damp computer bag in his right (also gloved). He looked at the scene before him with bile rising into his throat.

Students filled the main hallway, a loud and slowly churning mass heading toward first period class. The air around the student body reeked of sweat, perfume, aerosol deodorant layered upon underarms, minty gum, and a curiously piquant odor of blue cheese.

Most days, if he arrived late, Mark would invent some excuse to avoid the crowds. The faculty bathroom in the main office offered a safe space, as did the copy room (where Mark could look at the Omaha World-Herald for a few minutes until the students thinned out. However, that day, he had an 8 a.m. meeting with Shit the Principal, and Shit hated tardiness. And the meeting was in the counseling office on the other side of the school.

So, he swallowed and waded into the maelstrom.

Visions of his own high school experience flashed before his eyes. Four long, difficult years.

Mark walked with his hands held stiff at his sides, walking with as quick a step as he could. Most gave him a wide berth. No doubt the students regarded Mark as some kind of weirdo, but so long as they didn't touch him.

"Hey, it's Mr. Peter," a voice called out from somewhere behind him. Mark turned and saw Kyler Rankin and a couple of his bros brushing through the crowd.

The muscles in Mark's neck contracted as his shoulders rose. The classic bullied kid defense of going rigid. Mark forced himself to relax, repeating that he was 34 years old. *I'm an adult*, Mark whispered to himself. *I'm an adult. They are children. They don't matter.*

"Going to class?" Kyler called out, followed by a quick snigger. The kid was a monster, tall and heavy, dressed in clothes that Mark supposed were fashionable. He played football, probably as a way to express his violence without repercussion.

Mark had heard the football coach complain about Kyler's practice efforts. "He's great in games, though," the coach had said with a tired shrug, "he mauls whoever's in front of him. He could get a scholarship if he tried."

Certain kinds of kids were able to detect weakness, a predatory sixth sense for the kids who spent their passing periods trying to get from one end of the school to the other without getting hassled. The kids with extra thick glasses or bodies that looked goofy even by the standards of adolescence. The ones who avoided certain bathrooms.

"What can I do for you, Mr. Rankin?" Mark asked when Kyler and his posse caught up.

"I didn't know it was so cold today? Is there a storm front moving in?" While Mark's eccentricities were well known in the school, most kids were content to make jokes and laugh behind his back.

Kyler Rankin saw weakness. Since the beginning of the year, Mark had found himself the occasional victims of harassment from a bunch of youths who could not yet vote.

"Go to your class," Mark said, his voice straining for credibility. "Let's continue working on your world-class education."

"Hey," Kyler said, "is there something in your hair?" He reached a hand toward Mark's head, which cause Mark to jerk his head to the side. "What's wrong? I'm just trying to help."

Somehow, despite the fact that he wore a staff ID around his neck, Mark felt his psyche crawl all the way back to seventh grade. If he reported Kyler to admin, the kid would deny it, say he was joking. And Mark would look like a weakling.

If he tried acting assertively, the kids would laugh at him.

If he let Kyler touch him, Mark would probably end up fired.

"Oh, Mark, just the person I wanted to see," a voice came from behind.

Kyler looked back and his expression darkened. Ms. Hapke, a first-year history teacher, limped up, holding her computer. "I'm having a problem with this."

Mark exhaled. He hoped his relief did not show. Computers, he knew. "What seems to be the problem?"

Ms. Hapke didn't respond right away; instead, she fixed Kyler with a stare that pinned him to the wall. "Mr. Rankin, I just finished grading the quiz you took. Three out of ten. A phone call home, I'm afraid…"

Kyler's demeanor flipped. "Ms. Hapke, c'mon. Let me retake it. I didn't know about the quiz. I was absent the day before."

She raised a thin eyebrow. "While you were indeed absent last Wednesday, I had sent the entire class an e-mail, shared what was due on ICW, and posted it on the board outside my room. The quiz grade stands. Now, run along. If you are late, that will be mentioned when I call your dad later."

Kyler muttered under his breath and turned away toward his class. As he did, the two-minute bell rang.

"I make it a point to love all my kids," Ms. Hapke said as she watched Kyler melt into the rushing waves of students, "so I may have to redouble my efforts to find something lovable about Kyler. Because I have not found much yet to build on."

Mark smiled. "You mean that Kyler is not a paragon of intellectual achievement?"

Barking out a laugh, Ms. Hapke asked, "Can I walk with you? I really do have a problem with my computer and I sense you are in a hurry."

He held out his hands and she put the opened computer in them. "What's wrong?" he asked.

"The screen isn't right. It's like I centered it wrong somehow." She ran a hand through her blond hair. Streaks of purple and blue ran through it, as if they'd been placed there by accident.

He tapped open the settings folder and began to click away. The flow of students had thinned, and the ones remaining in the halls hurried toward class. "Don't you have to teach?"

"First period plan," she said. "So, is my computer salvageable? Or should I just shoot the thing through its heart and be done with it?"

"To begin with, the heart of the computer is called the central processing unit, or CPU. And no, you somehow mangled the display. What were you doing to this thing?"

"I sat around on Saturday night and purposefully messed it up so I could embarrass myself in front of the IT guy. Duh." Ms. Hapke shook her head. "I don't know. I go online, read the news, put in grades, pretend that I'm turning my master's thesis into a best-selling history book. All that."

They arrived at the conference center and Mark handed her back the computer. "All fixed. You have a… way with computers, Ms. Hapke."

"I've only been here a few months. Just wait," she said. "Most people call me Happy, by the way. Ms. Hapke is what my students call me, and it makes me sound like a German nursemaid who slips the baby a thimble of schnapps so that the kid takes a good nap."

"That's… a really detailed simile. Most people would have stopped after nursemaid."

"I tend to over-metaphor," Happy said. "My students think I'm weird."

"I have a bit of a reputation too, it seems," Mark said. "Anyway, Kyler is scared of you."

She gestured as if Kyler were just over her shoulder. "A psychologist might argue that I teach from an angry place. Probably my parents." Her hand wavered through the air. "Anyway, I don't let Mr. Ranken get away with anything. He knows I follow up. It's not like I don't know some of the things they say about me outside of class. They call me a freak, of course. They also call me Miss Gimp." Happy gestured towards left foot, which was pointed inward more than her right. She looked at Mark very intently, expectantly. Not that he had any idea what she expected.

"I wonder what they say about me." Mark said. "Not that I care, of course."

"Same as me, probably. A freak. It still stings. Being teased, I mean, even by little twerps like Kyler." She shrugged. "So, you have a meeting?"

Mark looked up. The late bell had already gone off. 8:01. "Shit. I have a meeting with Shit."

"Is this a person?" Happy asked. "Or do you need to use the restroom?"

Mark took a few excited steps toward the counseling center. "Susan Hamrick-Thompson. SHT. Me and the other IT guy, Lawrence Chang, call her Shit. We have a meeting at eight. I'm on the Staff Development Committee."

"Shit the Principal." Happy fingered a purple strand of hair. "You just made my day. You'd better get going. I'm looking forward to Thursday."

Mark cocked his head.

"Staff development day. You're leading a class on using the new interactive chalkboards."

Mark felt his eyes widen. "Thursday. Right. Are you in my class?"

"Given how little I know about computers? Wouldn't miss it."

A small feeling in Mark's stomach erupted in something very similar to a yelp. Perhaps the feeling was surprise. Happiness? Hope? He couldn't decide, except that it felt unfamiliar. Like a distant relative, maybe, one you haven't seen since forever.

Chapter Four
Tuesday, October 11, 2016

"Mark…" Bill's voice from the other end of the line sounded scratchy and thick. Rolling his eyes, Mark stood up and cracked his back. He'd been painting the horns of Orcus, Prince of Undead, when the phone rang (one of Mark's hobbies involved painting miniatures for Dungeons & Dragons). Mark told himself that he needed to work out more.

The way Bill said his name suggested the conversation would turn toward dark subjects.

"I'm really hoping that you don't mess up my day."

"Maybe I wanted to talk."

"I'm actually in a good mood today, Bill. Do you want to know why? One, my headache is gone. Two, I had this incredibly horrible meeting at work because this one woman is evil and tried to make us redo the entire staff development day next week. But I figured out a… What is it?"

"Mark, this is all good and everything, but…" Bill said, a few light coughs followed.

"No, no, no. You probably have some murder to tell me about, but I want to say my piece first. Okay?"

"Shoot then."

"Thank you, Bill. Anyway, this woman, we call her Shit the Principal…"

"Shit the Principal?"

"Not to her face. Shit probably got a POP call, a Pissed Off Parent. Apparently, the parent probably complained about some teacher not knowing how to post assignments online. The result of this is that Shit felt every teacher in the building should receive a thorough training in our class website software, which we've already been using for the past three years. Now the committee that I'm on had to readjust the staff development day."

Bill laughed. A hoarse, weak chuckle. "Let me get this straight. One parent calls about one screw up, and now every teacher in the school has to waste a chunk of time on something they already know how to do?"

"Welcome to modern education," Mark said. He walked upstairs, into his spotless kitchen and turned the oven on to 450 degrees. If Bill wanted to talk about dead bodies, then Mark would at least treat himself to a frozen pizza. Frodo had not yet put in an appearance. The cat, which could leave via a cat door converted from a basement window, ranged far and wide in Mark's neighborhood. Also, Frodo did not seem to care much for Bill, avoiding the older man whenever he came over. Bill liked to call the cat a feline racist.

"Why doesn't this Shit the Principal have you give the teacher in question a one-on-one tutoring session? Wouldn't that work?"

Because he had no dependents and in possession of a good salary, Mark didn't have to eat cheap-ass Tostino's anymore. He pulled out a Red Baron pepperoni and answered, "That is an excellent question, Bill. However, what if Shit gets another angry phone call about a teacher not knowing the software?"

"Mark, fuck me if I'm wrong here," Bill said, now almost jovially, "but it seems more like Shit is more interested in not getting a phone call from an angry parent than in not wasting everyone else's job."

"That about covers it."

"So, why do I hear a smile in your voice? You hate idiots like this Shit the Principal. Wait, is this Mark Peter? Did aliens kidnap you? Develop a new personality? Create a clone?"

"I am happy because Shit never mandated how long or thorough the class needed to be. So, I created a two-minute presentation. We also put it right before lunch. No one's going to ask any questions."

Bill asked, "You're not going to get in trouble?"

"Well, Shit's got no squeeze with Chester." Mark threw the pizza onto the pizza stone, not waiting for the oven to pre-heat.

"That sounds wrong coming from your mouth," Bill said.

"Anyway, that's why I'm happy. I have helped pull one over on incompetence. You don't get to do that every day."

"Well, then, I am happy for you."

"Okay, now that I've told you my story. You tell me yours. What tale of woe do you have for me today?"

On the other end of the line, Bill closed his eyes and softly coughed. "I'm sitting in my car here in Council Bluffs. North end of town. Nice area. The Council Bluffs Police are examining a crime scene. Some dog walker spotted a body at nine a.m."

Silence from Bill's friend.

"Mark?"

"Bill, I'm retired. Re-tire-d." Mark looked at the ceiling.

Silence for a second, followed by the slamming of an oven door. "Is it a kid?"

"No, a young woman. Natalia Chavez. A student at Iowa Western. Wanted to be a nurse. Lived with her sister. Went missing some time yesterday, we think."

"Okay…"

"She's very pretty," Bill continued.

"Wait a second," Mark said over the phone. "With all due respect, Bill, but why are you guys involved? Why are you calling me?" The FBI generally stayed out of local homicides.

"It's where she was found," Bill said, hearing the sound of a truck horn in the distance. "There's a park up here, near I-29, called Big Lake Park…" He let his voice trail off.

"No," Mark said, his voice faint over the phone. "Nope. No way."

"Some early morning dog walker saw her floating in the reeds."

"No," Mark repeated. "Uh, uh."

"No clothes. We're checking her background but Natalia appears to not have been involved in any illegal activities. No boyfriend. By all accounts, a model student. It's very suspicious."

On the other end of the line, Bill could hear Mark's breath grow heavy and jagged.

"Mark, you okay?"

"He's dead, Bill. He died four years ago."

"I know," Bill said. He coughed. "I know. We were both there. We saw him fall off the bridge. He's dead."

Some of the local news vans remained in the parking lot. Bill could see their spotlights. Natalia's murder would probably be the top story at ten o'clock.

"Do you think it's a copycat?" Mark's voice sounded so distant, almost child-like.

In his most reassuring voice, Bill said, "I'm sure it is."

"It's not like Vandergeest's M.O. would be that hard to duplicate," Mark continued, "It's not uncommon for people to dump their victims in water."

"I know, I know," Bill said, "It's a good way to destroy evidence."

"Exactly." Mark's words fell away. A silence. "There's more, isn't there?"

Bill could hear his voice, it sounded like a man about to jump off a bridge. "The killer used disposable handcuffs. White ones."

In the definitive book written about Eric Vandergeest, The Hunter in the Heartland, the author mentioned that the serial killer secured his victims by "plastic handcuffs." The book never mentioned the color of the disposable restraints. Nor had any of the magazine or newspaper articles.

Bill and Mark knew every detail about the manner in which Vandergeest chose, subdued, humiliated, tortured, and ultimately killed his victims. For each of the nine known victims, Vandergeest used white double-loop disposable handcuffs.

"That doesn't necessarily prove anything. It's not like white cuffs are so out of the ordinary. Right?"

Bill didn't answer. Mark sat at his kitchen chair, feeling as if the world had closed in upon his chest.

"We don't know anything for certain at this point," Bill said. "If you want to come down…"

Mark shook his head, a gesture his friend obviously could not see. "I can't, Bill. I'm retired. I can't do this again. Not with anyone, especially Vandergeest. I'm done with all this."

Bill said, "I know. I'm afraid that Vandergeest, if it is him, might not be done with you."

Chapter Five
April 23, 2012

It's raining outside when I hear the car pull up. We live in Springfield, a few miles outside Omaha, so we don't get a lot of traffic. We don't have a paved driveway neither, just gravel, so I hear the crunch of the tires. Car's quiet, so I figure it's folks from the police. The papers and TV people park down the street. They're gone right now but they'll be back soon. Andrea is a big story around here.

The rain is being blown by the wind a little bit, and it hits the window pretty regular. The drops run down the window and collect on the sill in little puddles cause the sill got dinged to hell from a hail storm a year ago and I figure Dad probably wanted to save a little money from the insurance by only getting the new roof. He's been unemployed for a while now although sometimes he works at Mike's Garage when one of the regular guys don't make it in.

Mom works at an office in Omaha and makes good money. She hadn't been there long, but her work is real nice about everything. She sometimes gets emotional and talks about how they say that she needs to take care of things here and that her job's gonna to be there whenever she gets back and everything. Then Mom starts crying like she does about everything else.

"Janelle," Dad says from the living room, "come on in here, now." He sounds quiet, like he just woke up and his head is all muzzy from his pain pills.

I give up watching the rain fall down the window and go out into the living room. Even though it's a Monday, I'm tired of being at home and I'd rather be at school. I went Friday but I'm not going today. I've always hated school. Now it's creepy with all the kids walking around being… not mean. They give me space in the hallways and the teachers are paying attention to me, acting like I'm about to start crying. At least no one is making fun of my hair and my clothes and that I'm fat and the way I walk butt-clenched down the hall. I'm kind of like invisible now but also everyone sees me and gets out of my way.

There's three men in the living room when I open the door and walk down the hall. I pass by Andrea's room, but I don't look at her door. Two of the men look alike: both big and strong and wearing dark suits and ties.

They all wearing sunglasses too; It's raining out so it ain't like they need them. Some folks, though, got to make themselves be something in front of other people so I guess that's why the two FBI agents wear them. It's the same thing I do when I have to wear the same sweatshirt three times in one week and I can't even wash it because Mom says that's wasting water. I know that the other kids know I'm wearing the same sweatshirt but I have to pretend in my head that it's not. Sometimes it's hard to pretend.

"Honey, this is Agent Bill Mallory." Mom is standing by one of the men, the tallest of them. He's tall, black, and looks like he works out a lot.

I say hi. He's not from the Sarpy County Sheriff's office and I'm a bit confused. Is someone else handling the case now?

"How are you today, Janelle?" Agent Mallory sounds like he's usually kind of pissed off and his smile seems stiff.

"Doing okay," I say.

"I'm not a big fan of the rain," he says back.

"Me neither." Even if it was sunny, my parents wouldn't want me outside the house even in the backyard without them looking. Not that the Omaha Strangler would take me. He likes pretty girls like Andrea.

Agent Mallory stands up and starts talking to Mom and Dad again. I listen long enough to know that he doesn't have any new information about Andrea, it's all anonymous leads they're checking on, so I kind of tune out. Maury's on the TV and he's doing that thing where they do DNA tests to see who's the baby daddy. Whenever a guy hears he isn't the dad, he runs around celebrating and whooping it up.

Then I look and notice the one guy who isn't dressed in a suit. He's the kind of guy who looks older than he actually is. And he's short, almost as short as me, but he ain't fat. Even though it's the end of April and kind of warm, the guy has on a brown windbreaker and gloves. He barely has any hair left on the top of his head, which makes him look older. He keeps looking from Agent Mallory to the window like he's making sure someone isn't stealing their car.

He has on a pair of khaki pants but they don't fit him too well. They're too long and it's all bunched up at the bottom of his legs. Then the guy in the windbreaker looks over and he sees me looking at him. He's startled and for a second, he looks frightened like I'm glaring at him.

Maybe I am. We both look away and I'm thinking that maybe I don't know what's really going on inside me. I mean, when I'm at school I'm aware of everything that people notice about me, from the zit that appeared on my nose Thursday morning (I swear it wasn't there when I looked at myself when I went to bed) to how I can't wear my blue pants anymore because they are too tight on my butt and I'm afraid I might split them in the rear if I bend over.

Anyway, I start to listen to Agent Mallory again, mostly because I got nothing better to do (the TV is on commercial). "…the sheriff's office, the Omaha Police, and the FBI are doing everything we can to find your daughter."

"What do you mean, find her? Do you mean her or her body?" Dad sounds muzzy but I can hear the pain in his voice. He's still pretty nice around the police but you can tell that he's getting mad they can't find anything out about where Andrea is.

"I don't have to tell you that the Sheriff's office suspects this case is related to the other disappearances that have happened over the last two months." Agent Mallory looks like he doesn't quite know what to say. "The suspect…"

"The Omaha Strangler," Dad interrupts.

"We don't like to use that nickname but yes. There are reasons to be hopeful. For one thing, we haven't found Andrea yet. In every case so far, the bodies have been found in public bodies of water within a day or two of the girls going missing. Personally, that gives me hope."

Dad looks like he's going to say something but he doesn't for a few seconds. It's what he does when he doesn't know what to say but doesn't want you to talk instead. Finally, "So you think she might have run away?" A spark of hope flares in his eyes for a second.

Agent Mallory looks over at the man in the brown windbreaker, who is glaring at the FBI guys. "It is a possibility," Mallory says in a hesitant tone, "From what information the Sarpy County Criminal Investigation Unit has gathered, Andrea had no reason to run away. She appears to be happy and well-adjusted. But that is definitely a possibility."

The spark in Dad's eyes dies. "So, they send in a new guy to tell me what I already know, that my Andrea is gone and that you don't know anything about where she is." His voice rises up at the end the way it does when someone is getting madder and madder.

"Well, as I said, multiple law enforcement agencies are devoting every available resource at…"

"I heard all that," Dad interrupts him, which isn't what he usually does. "I don't know why they sent three of you guys here to tell me that."

"I am here giving you an update…"

"Then why didn't you just come out and say you got nothing new. Absolutely…" Dad wants to keep speaking but Mom goes and put her arm around him and he shuts up and kind of rocks back and forth on his feet. I think he is going to cry but he doesn't.

"We're tired, that's all. I thought…," Mom says, "…we thought that maybe since it was someone new that you'd have some good news. That maybe… A miracle, perhaps."

Agent Mallory takes his hand and smooths back his hair, not like it was out of place, but like it was something he did but didn't know about, the way Mom sometimes takes off her glasses and puts one end of them into her mouth when she's thinking hard.

After a moment, Mom continues, "I know that… We know that Andrea probably didn't run away. We can accept as God's will whatever happened to Andrea. We just want to know. We want to give her a proper funeral, and we want the man who did this caught."

"I understand. And we are pursuing literally every possibility, every lead, every suspicion. If it is the Omaha Strangler, he has killed at least four girls, and we will find him."

"We appreciate that, Agent Mallory."

There is a pause. Agent Mallory looks over his shoulder and nods his head toward the door. As if on cue, the other FBI agent turns and walk out of the house. I twist my body and see him standing a foot outside the closed door. The only people left in the room is Dad and Mom, me, Agent Mallory, and the man in the brown windbreaker.

"Can we sit down?"

Mom looks puzzled, but she nods and kind of leads Dad to the couch. Agent Mallory sits down on the lazy boy that Dad usually uses because he has a bad back from high school football. The man in the windbreaker doesn't look like he wants to sit down. He makes a motion with his hand to his mouth and I figure he wants to smoke a cigarette. Dad had quit smoking a few months ago, but he took it up again after Andrea disappeared. Mom doesn't even get mad at him for it. Although now Dad goes out back to smoke. Like maybe they think I won't notice that Dad's smoking again because he isn't lighting up indoors anymore.

For a big girl I can be real quiet. So, I kind of step back and lean against the wall next to where Mom has a china hutch filled with her collection of owls. Nobody's paying me any attention.

"As I said before, we are doing everything within our power to find your daughter. We still have hope that she might be alive…"

"There was that girl a few years ago in Florida," Dad says. He's staring into the kitchen but he's not really looking at anything. "Everyone thought she died, but she was alive the whole time."

Mom says that there is always hope, but we all know that the last time she was seen was at the Kum n' Go out by the highway and that she was talking to a guy who looked like what people say is the Omaha Strangler (dark hair and eyes, good looking, but not remarkable in any way).

Agent Mallory doesn't say anything for a second so I guess he figures he doesn't have to say how little a chance there is that Andrea has run away or is in a religious cult. *She's dead*, is what he's thinking but she's never been found. I was the last person to see her alive.

"There is something we might be able to do," Agent Mallory says.

Chapter Six
Wednesday, October 12, 2016

"Happy birthday!" Mark yelled when he opened the door to his mom's small ranch home.

The whole place smelled faintly of dog urine, thanks to Mom's Shih Tzu, Snickers, a toy-sized beast Mom treated with near reverence. He walked in at 5:25, or about five minutes before they expected him.

He heard his mother from the basement yell, probably a greeting of some kind.

The layout of the house: small entry, narrow living room to the left, cramped kitchen to the right, three small bedrooms beyond the living room, were as familiar to Mark as the lines on his hand. He'd grown up in the house. Now his sister and niece lived there with Mom.

"You're late," Stacy said when she looked up from the stove. Mark wondered sometimes how Stacy felt about sleeping in the same bedroom she had when she was a kid. "Please tell me you listened to my message and at least picked up a card."

Mark held up a card tucked into a blue envelope. "Two steps ahead of you."

"Your present is over there," Stacy gestured to the top of the entertainment center, which held three gift bags. "Mom thinks I picked it up for you at your request."

"How much do I owe you?" Mark asked, reaching for his wallet.

She waved him off. "Nothing. Just be normal tonight."

"I'm always normal," Mark replied, wounded. What he wanted to point out was that he made more than his sister and did not have any children. He did not. For one thing, Stacy secretly enjoyed taking care of her brother. Also, if he had spoken of that, the conversation might have gone down a rabbit hole of family history and would have ruined the evening. "What are you cooking? I thought we were having KFC?"

"Broccoli," Stacy said in a you-are-a-dumbass tone of voice. One of the few vegetables the two of them had liked as children, broccoli featured prominently at all their dinners even as adults.

Mom appeared in the kitchen. She stood only a hair over five feet tall, which meant that she could hug her only son in such a way as to not actually touch his bare skin. Mom squeezed him tight while he returned the affection with a leaning-back hug of his own.

He wished her happy birthday, which she pooh-poohed. "Thank you, sweetheart. I've been so… somewhere else lately. I must be getting old," Mom said. She often was "somewhere else" and had been "somewhere else" for many years. Had been since Mark was in middle school. "How are you? You look like you haven't slept in days. Did you do one of your little road trips again?"

Mom did not reference Mark's consultations with the FBI. She never mentioned the FBI, nor did she ever hint that her son had abilities beyond the ken of all other humans. She preferred the illusion of her son spending his weekends traipsing off to far corners of the country in search of fun and excitement.

To be honest, Mark had no idea if his mother even truly understood his ability. He suspected that Mom's subconscious created a map for her awareness to follow, a map filled with blackened areas marked "DANGER" and "STAY AWAY." On this map, the country of her second son, Mark Edward Peter, was a place surrounded by messages that "Here There Be Monsters."

"What's up, loser?" Skylar asked as she walked into the kitsch-filled kitchen. Fifteen years old, a freshman at Eastside High School, Skylar had the awkward coltish build of teenagers whose body parts seemed to grow at different speeds. Once the acne cleared and her body discovered proportionality again, Skylar would be a spitting image of her mom.

"Skylar, be nice," Mom said.

"She is being sarcastic," Stacy said, "which is how she and Mark communicate."

"Where were you?" Mark asks.

Skylar shrugged. "Taking a dump. Reminder, everyone, do not go in there for a few minutes. Grandma has still not fixed the exhaust fan. It's a little dicey in there."

"Skylar!" Mom threw up her hands. "I cannot believe the things you say. Stace, your daughter has a mouth."

Stacy opened the fridge door and rooted around inside for a lemon. "She lives for your reactions, Mom."

"I know what you eat," Mark said to his niece, "and it does not surprise me that the result is so bad. As it comes in, so it goes out." He sat at the same kitchen table he'd sat at as a kid, began to stuff his mouth with potato chips.

"Please, Uncle Mark, like your diet is any better." Skylar patted her stomach to emphasize how hers did not bulge.

She looked an awful lot like her mother: dark hair, somewhat round face that she hid with long straight hair, a thin, shy smile (complete with braces) that peeked out when no one else was looking. Skylar was, Mark guessed, one of the smartest students at Eastside.

"My bathroom has a working exhaust fan," Mark said.

Stacy had brains, but Stacy's high school years were rough and she never quite recovered from it. Mark's sister once worked as a paralegal; she should have gone to law school.

"How's your cat?" Stacy always enquired after Mark's roommate.

"Frodo is well," Mark answered. "I mean, he's a cat; he eats, poops, and goes on long nighttime excursions. It's a nice, quiet, and boringly perfect existence."

"Sounds like you describing your own perfect life," Stacy answered.

"I don't know about crapping in a litter box," Mark said thoughtfully. "And I've tried cat food before. Yes, I really did. But outside of that… I do like boring."

The KFC was sitting in the warmed oven. When the broccoli finished (tender and crisp with a touch of lemon), everyone sat at the small table. He didn't particularly like Kentucky Fried, never felt the need to buy it himself, but he enjoyed the smell immensely. Mark took a breast, three biscuits, a small scoop of mashed potatoes, and an even smaller one of coleslaw.

Conversation drifted along from safe topic to safe topic: Mom's garden, Stacy's workplace drama, Mark's painted figurine hobby, Skylar and her soccer team.

After the meal, Mark sat back in his chair and imagined his stomach as an inflatable beach ball, now nearly twice the size it had been only a half hour ago. Mom, who ate one drumstick and a tablespoonful of mashed potatoes, got up and began to bustle the dishes.

Skylar, perhaps as a birthday present, got up to help, which Mom fiercely protested. "Sit down, sit down. I know how I want my dishwasher filled."

"C'mon Grandma, it's your birthday," Skylar protested. "Anyway, I know how it goes. I mean, we do live here."

"Just let me be. Sit down and talk to your uncle. Tell him about school."

"It's lovely that you got up," Mark said, "but Grandma is old school when it comes to dishes."

"You're lazy," Skylar replied. "Grandma, please. It's your birthday."

"Can I ask you a question," Mark said to his niece. "Do you know Ms. Hapke?"

Skylar's smiled dipped a little. "I have her third period for Freshman Civics."

"What do you think of her?"

His niece pursed her lips, considering her answer. Even though uncle and niece both spent their days at Eastside High School, they occupied different worlds.

"She is very strict," Skylar said judiciously.

"Ms. Hapke?" Stacy said. "I just checked and you have a B in her class. Only grade that isn't an A."

"I know. She's unfair." The dam had broken and Skylar unleashed a torrent of a story about something that had recently happened in Civics. Apparently, Skylar had turned in an assignment a few days late and received a very bad grade upon it. Mark noticed that she did not mention anything about the assignment itself or of the assignment's quality. Skylar's gripe, it seemed, resided in that another student had turned in the assignment on the same day and did not have any points taken off. This kind of unfair treatment, Skylar added in something of a crescendo, was one of the things that sucked about high school and maybe even the whole world.

"Uh-huh," Stacy said when her daughter completed her account.

"You don't believe me?" Skylar's face darkened. Like her mother, Mark's niece had a temper.

"I didn't say that exactly. I happen to know two things that color my perspective of your story."

"Oh really?"

"Girls, be nice to each other," Mom said. "It's my birthday."

"Yes, really," Stacy said. "And, Mom, I am being nice. I merely know that my daughter is incredibly intelligent. However, I also know that in most of her classes, she doesn't have to work too hard. Therefore, when one of her teachers expects a little more from her, Skylar tends to think that teacher is being unfair."

Skylar sniffed. "Wow, all I know is that the other girl who turned in her assignment at the same time is an idiot. And here I am graded on a different scale. How is that fair."

"When you're smart," Stacy said, "good teachers expect more from you. Tell her I'm right, Mark."

Both his sister and niece turned to look at Mark. He cleared his throat for a second and said, "Ms. Hapke strikes me as the kind of teacher that pushes all of her students. In a good way."

Stacy smiled. "Remember Mr. Morrissey from eighth grade? At the beginning of the year, you thought he was awful. By the end of the year, he was your favorite teacher."

Harrumphing, Skylar sat in a moping way. Mark could tell she would consider the matter more later on. Skylar was the kind of fifteen-year-old who would actually mull over what adults had to say.

Eventually.

He loved having her as a niece.

Mom, sensing the end of the argument (and it wasn't that much of an argument), came back in with her cake. Set into a 9x13 pan, the chocolate with chocolate frosting cake held three candles. One for yesterday, one for today, and one for tomorrow. Mom insisted on baking her own cakes, saying that store-bought ones tasted too fake.

Also, as tradition, Mark cut the cake after they sang "Happy Birthday." He got some frosting on his gloves, which meant that he'd have to wash the pair that evening in the laundry room sink. Mark owned about a dozen pairs of driving gloves, so he didn't mind.

Truth be told, Mark felt so comfortable at his former home that he wished he could take his gloves off there. Alas, there were other people at the house, as well as objects that his mom, sister, and niece all felt were special.

Despite the love he felt for his family, Mark did not mind escaping his childhood home an hour later. His own place had fewer people living there. Fewer bad memories.

Also, Mark roomed with a cat, Frodo. Not owned. Roomed with. Frodo took no shit from anyone.

Chapter Seven
Thursday, October 13, 2016

"You know, I sometimes wonder why they make us do these things," Ms. Hapke said to Mark. "It isn't like we don't have anything better to do. You know, like grading or preparing lessons."

The two of them stood outside the cafeteria, a sheet of paper in her hand. Happy shook her head. Every time the building had a staff development day, the principal, Doug Chester, built into the morning meeting some kind of morale-inducing activity. Last year, Chester organized a game of dodge ball (Sue McDermitt from Foreign Language broke her ankle). Two years ago, Chester had a color run/walk, where finishers were doused with colored powder at every station. However, rather than colored cornstarch, Chester had somehow acquired chalk dust. He personally drove three teachers to the Urgent Care inside the Hy-Vee for medical treatment.

This year, it appeared, Chester decided to play it safe. The staff had been paired up and given a sheet of paper. They needed to solve the clues to find certain locations. Then, using a Mystery Hunt app on someone's phone (which one partner needed to download), they would receive a clue. The first team to visit each location and solve the puzzle would receive a gift certificate from Gorat's Steak House.

Mark had drawn Happy as a partner. By sheer coincidence, they had been paired together. Once the staff had been divided into teams, the principal stood on a table and blew into an oversized blue whistle. About a third of the pairs tore off, not unlike greyhounds from a starting gate.

Mark and Happy agreed that they had no interest in winning the prize. "Don't get me wrong," Mark said, "I love gift certificates, but there's only so much I'm willing to do to get one. You know?"

He felt somewhat uncomfortable around her, and kind of hoped that she'd suggest they just go their separate ways. However, she proposed a rather slow walk. "Sooooo," Happy drew out the word, "may I ask you a question that you would be under no compunction to answer?"

Mark felt his shoulders shrink a little bit. Whenever he got to know someone, that person would eventually ask a question about the gloves, or the way he avoided contact with other people. Either way, he dreaded the inevitable conversation.

He decided to tell Happy the standard lie he'd developed over the years. Best to get it out of the way as soon as possible. "I wear the gloves because I have a severe mysophobia, which most people call germaphobia. Wearing gloves is one of the few ways that I am able to hold down a job." He spoke in a quick recital-like tone. "Yes, this is a form of obsessive-compulsive disorder. You should see how organized my house is. Yes, I do go to therapy. Yes, there has been a little improvement. However, all the medications available for mysophobia I've taken have resulted in some undesirable side effects. Therefore, I wear gloves whenever I'm not in my house. I have no doubt certain segments of the student population has noticed my particular eccentricities and are even now mocking me behind my back."

"Like Kyler," she said.

"Exactly."

Happy asked, "Did you memorize that speech? It sounded like you memorized that speech and were waiting for a chance to spring it on me."

"It's a subject that comes up."

"That wasn't even what I was going to ask you about," Happy said as she twisted her blue and blond hair in her fingers.

"Oh, really? What were you…?"

"I wanted to know if you knew that your fly was unzipped."

Mark blushed and checked his pants. His zipper was fine.

"I'm kidding," Happy said, "I wanted to know about the gloves. I don't give a hoot, though, as long as your answer isn't 'I wear gloves so the police won't be able to lift any fingerprints from the murder weapon.' I was just curious. Everybody's a freak somehow."

"You're not a freak."

In an authoritarian voice, she said, "Oh really? Ask me why I want people to call me Happy."

"It's not because you possess a pleasant disposition?" Mark replied. "Okay, then, why do you…"

"Because my first name is Daffodil. Daffodil Freedom Hapke. I have the dumbest name this side of Beverly Hills. It's one of many reasons I don't really like my mom. She drinks milk out of the carton. That's another reason. Also, she's a verbally abusive alcoholic, but this is neither the time nor place for…"

Suddenly, Lawrence and his partner (some health nut named Suzie from science who coached girls' basketball), came bursting out from the north gym at full throttle. She had a phone in her hand and appeared to be engrossed in it.

Lawrence carried the clue sheet, upon which he dripped desperate sweat.

"You okay?" Mark asked.

"Help me!" Lawrence gasped amid gulps of air. "Seriously, I might die."

"Keep the hell up, Wheezy," Suzie said. "What's the next clue? Let's get it at it."

"Ummm…" Lawrence looked at his sheet. He read in a breathy voice, "It's a poem. 'Where Kirkland taught there you will go, in his room…'"

Suzie interrupted him. "That's in the 300 wing. C'mon slowpoke." She grabbed his hand with such force that Lawrence winced. They both began to run toward the 300s.

As they ran off, Lawrence looked over his shoulder and called out, "Mark, tell my husband I love him. Tell him I thought of him at the last…" His voice trailed off as Suzie pulled him up the stairs.

Mark and Happy looked after them for a few moments. "We ain't gonna win this thing."

"I'm guessing not," Happy agreed. "Do you think Suzie's gonna kill your friend?"

"We could watch," Mark said, "I can bring up all the security cameras from my laptop."

"Nah, that would be cruel."

They walked in the opposite direction for a while, and the silence between them felt comfortable and charged.

Mark looked over, "May I ask you a question?"

"Is it of a personal nature that I might not answer?"

"Maybe," Mark answered, "I'm not a good judge of that."

She smiled. "Please ask away."

"Why do you teach? You're smart, you could do a bunch of other stuff. Why deal with moody teenagers all day?"

"It beats working for a living," Happy replied with a smile. She continued seriously, "I like the kids. I like that I'm helping them be less dumb, even if it's only marginally so. I like watching them grow up and change. It works the other way, too. I'm heartbroken whenever I see one of my kids get screwed up and go down the drains. Before I started here, I taught in Council Bluffs. I had this kid named Tommy Sprague and he overdosed last spring. I had him Freshman year. Goofy kid. Nice kid. Fucking dumbass with all the drugs he did. I went to his funeral and cried my eyes out. Asked myself if I could have done anything more. Most people who knew Tommy probably thought the same thing. He was such a goof, but you loved him. And I knew that even though I had to watch this nice kid get buried at the age of 17, it's still worth it. Worth it a hundred times over. Because I know, I know that I'm on the front lines of something important. Something worth fighting over."

Happy paused for a second. "Wow, that came out really sappy."

Mark felt something move inside of him and knew he had fallen at least a little in love with this woman. Not that he would have shown it. "Summers off help as well, right?"

"An olive in the martini," Happy agreed. "What about you? Why are you here?"

"I went to school here," Mark said. "Not that that matters." It did. "They needed an IT guy. I applied, got the job. It's not as noble as your reasoning."

"That's it?" Happy asked.

"The pay is good, too. And I like working with Lawrence. We're both hardcore nerds…"

Happy interrupted him. "How hardcore?"

"I paint miniatures for our D&D campaign."

"Oooh, nerdy and a little artistic. I watch Doctor Who religiously."

"I speak Klingon," Mark said.

She whistled. "Damn. Best I can say is that I own the entire animated Star Trek series on DVD."

"That's impressive."

"Not quite as," Happy said.

"It helps to not have a social life in college. You probably did keg stands," Mark said. "I'm sure you know plenty of good in-jokes."

"Ever you want to reverse the polarity of my neutron flow, just let me know."

"What?" Mark felt his face redden.

"It's an in-joke, silly."

Another team rushed by, arguing about whether the next clue could be found in the media center or the social studies book room.

"If you won this gift certificate," Happy asked, "which we both know we won't. But if you did, who would you take with you to dinner?"

The question sounded full of import, even though Mark couldn't figure out why she would care that much. Maybe she wanted to play D&D.

"I'd probably go by myself," Mark said, "but if I did take someone else, it would probably be my friend Bill. He works for the FBI. Or maybe Lawrence, whom I work with. Or maybe my niece. You have her, actually. Skylar Peter, third period."

Happy snapped her fingers. "That's your niece? Well, that's obvious. It's not like Peter is a common last name. You know, she's smart."

Mark smiled. "Gets it from her uncle. Skylar's mom is dumb as a sack of kittens." Mark stopped and politely asked, "By the way, who would you take?"

Happy looked at the clues for a few seconds. "Anyone who could help me solve this thing. It's only fair."

"Oh," Mark replied. "I thought that each member of the winning team got a separate gift card."

"They do."

"I don't think that you..." Mark's voice trailed off. "Okay..."

"I think your brain needs glasses," Happy said in an offhand manner. She kneeled and took out her pen. "Watch this."

Mark kneeled as well and watched as Happy turned the clue sheet over, marked two large spots on each end of the blank page. She drew a line between them. "Do you see what I'm doing here, Mark?"

"Making a line?" Mark said after a moment.

"These two things are dots. Does that help?"

"Um." Mark concentrated until he finally said, "Hey, I got it. Connecting the dots."

"Yes. That's what I'm asking you to do." Happy looked at him expectantly.

Mark frowned and mumbled to himself. "Who'd I take out to dinner? My friend. Niece. Who she'd take out… oh!" He looked up.

"There it is," Happy smiled.

"We should have dinner together?" Mark asked

"Knew we'd get there in the end. How about we start with coffee? Saturday at six." She wrote her number and address on the sheet and handed it to him. "Here you go."

Mark took it and looked at it. "Hey, on the back it says 'Clue' in big letters."

"Funny that." Happy said, regarded him for a second, "You look like you want to go to your office for a few hours."

It was like she'd read Mark's mind. "Kind of."

"I want to go to my office too. We introverts need our space."

"Not that…"

"Me either…"

They stood looking at each other for a few minutes. "I'm probably going to make a few phone calls as well." Happy agreed, just about tearing out the strand of hair she was playing with.

"Me too. My sister, for one."

"The one who's dumb as a sack of kittens."

Mark shrugged. "She's not. At least, she's not about coffee."

"Saturday then?"

"Saturday."

Mark walked off, suppressing the urge to look back at Happy. He gave in, once, and felt sure she had been looking back at him. He let his mind wander over the past five minutes, confused at exactly what had happened. He began to walk a little faster. He needed to ask his sister exactly what he'd just done.

Chapter Eight
1996

Last year, that was fifth grade, was okay. I had a pair of really good friends: Danny Toblasky and Josh Bognich. But then two things happened. One was that over the summer, Josh's dad got a job in Houston and they moved away. So, then it was Danny and me, and somehow it stopped being cool. Like when it was the three of us, it made it seem like we were a gang, you know? Like there was a group of us going to a movie at the Cinema Center, buying tickets for The Client, sneaking into True Lies like we were breaking some law. Then Josh moved, and it was just me and Danny.

The second was that we all started middle school.

Middle school sucked. Like somebody flipped a switch on all the other boys. First, it was Mike Jennings. One day we were lined up to go to the library and he was in front of me. He turns around and whispers "Hey, Markie, heard you were a fag!" so that everybody in line could hear. Mrs. Mohacek, who was really old (like 50) was nowhere nearby. All the kids began to snicker.

That was, like, the second day of class. Pretty soon, Mike's friends begin to join in. Seth Wendell, Stevie Hruska, Asher Cooper. They were all big kids, too. And here I was a puny kid even by the standards of seventh grade. Dressing for gym with all these kids who have underarm hair is pretty awful, especially when you don't have any extra hair anywhere.

I couldn't talk to Mom about any of this. For one thing, what the hell could she do? She's working two jobs (her regular job at Con-Agra and Friday nights at Romeo's Mexican Food and Pizza) and Stacy apparently spent weekends sleeping with the entire basketball team, based on what she and Mom argued about.

Then the other shoe dropped. On that Friday, Danny didn't show up at the gym before school started. There's a whole table of us that hang out. I mean, neither of us are the center of attention there, but it's good to attach yourself to a crowd. Maybe he got sick, but between first and second period I see him in the hall. He didn't even say hi.

I'm not stupid, so I figure either I pissed him off or he doesn't want to be seen with me. Danny can get pissed sometimes for no reason, so I decided to see if I could find him after school so we could talk. I caught up to Danny, who was walking home from school (we lived a few blocks apart).

"Wait up," I said.

Danny pretended not to hear me, so I ran after him yelling. We happened to be the only two kids in the Greens, a field next to the school. Danny and I crossed this old bridge to get to the side with all the houses that back onto the Greens. In between a couple of the houses – I never knew who lived in them – was a small path that led to 78th Street. Across 78th there was this little church, Christ Redeemer Baptist. The church's parking lot was small, so a lot of cars parked on the street at all hours of the day. Danny had told me this was causing a lot of issues for the neighbors, although I didn't see why.

Danny checked around to make sure we were alone, he stopped. "Listen, Markie," he said. "I can't... I don't want to hang around you anymore. Okay?"

"What?" I asked. I'd heard Danny perfectly well, but I didn't want to hear him, if you know what I mean. Meanwhile, my stomach began dropping out of an elevator.

"We can still be friends," Danny explained, "but we can't hang out anymore."

"At school?"

"Anywhere. I'm hanging out with Ed Carlson and Dustin Lebeda now."

"Dustin?" Dustin was this asthmatic kid who looked like he'd be blown over by a stiff breeze. Ed couldn't think his way out of simple multiplication, but kids like Mike didn't mess with him because Ed was twice as big as any other kid in our grade. "Ed?"

"You've been getting really weird lately." Kids could be mercilessly honest.

"No, I haven't."

"Yeah, you have. I mean, how did you know about Mrs. Mohacek's daughter?"

He was referring to an incident that had happened Thursday in Spanish class. We had all just had lunch and were pretty rowdy. Mrs. Mohacek yelled at everyone and said go to our seats. The path to my seat took me past my teacher's desk. She was an organized woman, and every piece of paper on her desk look tidy. The only thing out of place was a picture frame, which had been knocked down. Always a considerate child, I picked up the frame to set it up right.

When I picked up the frame, I nearly passed out from the stream of images and little home movies that flooded my mind. I saw Mrs. Mohacek, young and wearing a pair of green pants, chasing a little girl across a room, a little girl throwing a tantrum, an older girl wearing a nice dress and holding a candle, and many, many more things besides.

I didn't pass out but I did kind of stumble. Maybe my face did something weird. Either way, it was enough. Seated in the front row as always, Mike let out a whoop of cruel laughter.

"Markie almost fainted!" he announced to the entire class. "He grabbed that frame and he acted like it weighed a thousand pounds."

I dropped the frame on her desk, hard enough that I heard the sound of the glass cracking. I hurried to my seat as quickly as possible.

Mrs. Mohacek came over and looked at the picture frame with sadness in her eyes, but she did not rag on me in front of everybody like some of my other teachers liked to do. To the entire class, instead, my teacher said that she would appreciate it if we would not touch the things on her desk.

As one might expect, I felt like absolute horsepucky. I liked Mrs. Mohacek and didn't want her disappointed in me. When she stopped talking, there was a silence. I felt like I had to say something, something that would make her smile or something.

A look of surprise on her face, Mrs. Mohacek said, "Yes, Markie? What is it?"

"Is the person in the picture your daughter?" I asked.

"It is. Her name is Ashley."

"Is she getting married?" I asked. For some reason, this seemed true. I had seen, had seen her talking to her mom – Mrs. Mohacek – about how she and somebody named Scott were going to get married.

Mrs. Mohacek smiled. "She is. They only got engaged this weekend, in fact." Her smile sagged. "I… I don't recall telling you boys and girls about that. Markie, how did you know that Ashley got engaged? I haven't even told any of the other teachers."

I could feel my face getting red and I tried to make myself small in my seat. "I don't know," I said. Although, I probably mumbled it.

My teacher had looked at me with a puzzled expression on her face, but something about how I looked kept her from following up.

So that had happened in Mrs. Mohacek's class. To Danny, I said, "I don't know. I just knew."

"Or Jenny Waller's parents getting divorced?" Danny asked, referring to a girl I had spoken to in English. "How did you know where Marla could find her necklace?"

"I don't know," I repeated.

"It's weird, that's what it is. You've been acting really weird too. Like, you're doing things with your hands." Danny waved his hands around like a spaz.

"I don't do that."

"Yeah, you do. Everybody sees it. Why do think Mike and his gang call you retard? I don't want them coming after me because they think I'm your friend. We can still be friends, Markie, we can't talk or anything at school or hang out or anything." He said this angrily, but he kinda stopped and said in a nicer way, "Sorry, my man."

Strangely enough, I saw that Danny did mean it. He felt bad. Like so bad that he couldn't even look me in the eye kind of bad. And maybe even stranger, I understood. I was always really good at being able to look at things from someone else's point of view. Mom said I was always like that. She liked to call it a mark of maturity.

"It's okay," I said after a minute of the two of us not looking at each other. "Hey, do you remember that time that we went putt-putt golfing and you hit the ball so hard that it bounced off the tree and whacked that fat guy in the back of the head."

A ghost of a smile crossed Danny's lips. "Yeah, I remember. I about peed my pants trying not to laugh when the fat guy was looking for the guy who hit the golf ball."

Another awkward silence grew after he stopped talking. I think I was trying in some small way to get Danny to remember the fun stuff we did, and therefore not want to stop being my friend. But it was seventh grade, and things were a lot harder that year than fifth grade.

"Bye, then," Danny said to me.

"Okay, bye." And I turned away from him, my only friend. I remember turning away first, mostly because my best friend had told me to get lost and it was the only thing I could do to save a little face.

That was September 16, 1996. I had thought that getting dumped by a friend was the worst thing that could happen to a seventh grader.

Oh boy, was I wrong.

Chapter Nine
Friday, October 14, 2016

Bill checked his watch and hurried along. He eschewed the elevator for the stairwell, humming tunelessly as he climbed the two flights of stairs. His hum did not signal any kind of contentment. In fact, it indicated the opposite.

His cough seemed worse that morning. Damn allergies. The woman in the office checked him in with a minimum of fuss. He presented his insurance card, but the woman at the desk did not seem to remember him. He wondered if this was by design. Perhaps the woman's job entailed her pretending not to notice anyone. After all, most people don't care to advertise, or even acknowledge, that they were going to a psychologist.

The waiting room seemed designed to be as calming and nondescript as humanly possible. From the creamy white walls to the forgettable magazines on the side tables, the décor seemed designed to slide away from one's attention. Even the muzak coming from invisible speakers left no trace on the consciousness.

"Mr. Mallory," the woman called. "Dr. Kucera will see you now. Second door on the right." She gave Bill an empty smile and turned back to her computer screen.

Dr. Kucera stood up when Bill came in the room. "Hi Bill," she said. "How are you're allergies?"

"Right now? Terrible." Bill waved his hand around the room.

"They always seem to be terrible. You might need to go to a doctor. Kucera shut down any appearance of jocularity. "It might also be psychosomatic. Who knows? You have a very difficult job, even if you won't tell me everything about what you do."

"Are you sure you'd want to?"

Dr. Kucera shook her head. She was in her fifties, muddy hair and a kindly, lined face. Bill could see why she excelled as a therapist. "Would you like to get started?"

Bill sat without answering.

"Okay," Dr. Kucera said, "How is Mark?" In a very subtle way, she said the name Mark in quotation marks, as if she did not entirely believe in his existence.

"He's fine," Bill said with emphasis. He bent to his briefcase, opened it, and extracted a thin manila folder. "This is a copy of the report I gave to my boss. As always, this file will leave with me."

"I understand." Dr. Kucera nodded her head. She opened the folder, extracted the report, and began to read.

For seven minutes, the two sat in silence save for his coughing. Bill watched her face register minute changes.

"This mother sounds like a piece of work," she muttered as she read about the death of Quinn Hughes.

He didn't interrupt. Bill had been seeing Dr. Kucera off and on for six months, and he knew her habits by now. Knew, for instance, that she talked to herself when deep in concentration.

"Okay," Kucera said at last, "I think I understand the case. Mark touched the crucifix and went into his trance state for approximately how long?"

"I'd say it took about ten, fifteen minutes. About the average time."

"Do you have the video?"

Bill nodded and took his computer from out of his bag. He turned it on, waited a few minutes for the computer to boot. When it was ready, he pressed play and pivoted the computer back to the therapist.

She hit pause. "You don't like to watch, do you?"

"He's my friend," Bill answered with a hacking cough. "He made us promise not to record him. We use a hidden camera. I'm not fond of breaking my promises. Besides, this... trance state, it's painful for him. I don't like to see him in pain."

"Sorry, I forgot about your past." Kucera hit play again and watched as the hidden camera on Dylan's suit jacket replayed the scene in little Quinn's room.

Mark complaining about having to do this again, Bill prodding his friend, employing every trick he knows to get his friend to perform his special trick once more.

A silence.

The bear saying, "I love you."

Sounds of Dylan's microphone rubbing against fabric as she looks through the closet.

Dylan's voice, sounding so large, asking Mark if there is a way to test his touch. Then Dylan calling out his name.

The next ten minutes of the video are virtually silence, save a few comments, Dylan's heavy breathing and the occasional sounds of paper tearing.

"It's the mother," Bill is saying, his voice deeper on the recording.

Silence. "A throw pillow." Dylan's voice sounds strange, angry, muffled.

Kucera stopped the tape. "You know," she said slowly, measuring each word. "Every time I see Mark go into his trance state and draw all those awful pictures, there is part of me that is filled with wonder. This man offers us a glimpse into a way of looking at the world that I cannot even fathom, let alone explain using our current level of scientific knowledge."

"That is cold comfort indeed, doctor." Bill felt annoyed, as he always did at these biweekly meetings. His stomach felt heavy, suspecting that if he knew, Mark would never forgive Bill for the betrayal. Mark valued loyalty far more than most men he knew. It was one of the reasons Bill could prod him to use his gift to find missing children and solve impossible homicides.

After a pregnant pause, Bill coughed before asking if she had seen anything on the tape that suggested Mark might be heading toward a psychological collapse.

"There is another part of me that feels horror…" Kucera's voice trailed off. "I've been noticing a few more facial contortions this time. The entire episode lasted nine minutes…" Kucera checked her watch, "…and 41 seconds. I noticed seven distinct facial contortions. They appear to be like before."

"You mean with the random facial muscles firing?"

"Exactly," Kucera said. "I hypothesize that the muscle flexes are more or less random. However, I would need all the tapes and a great deal of time to see if there is any connection."

"What kind of connection could there be?" Bill asked.

She shrugged. "Who knows? Maybe there is a secret language in there. Maybe there is a secret code that talks about the location where these drawings are occurring? It's not out of the question, Bill. And there are people a lot smarter than me who could come up with some even more interesting questions."

"Just stop," Bill began.

She talked over him. "I know I've said this before, but I truly believe that Mark Peter needs to be studied. In a clinic, with a research team who could make a proper job of understanding his amazing gift."

"Seriously? Give him over to a bunch of scientists who could very easily spend their time injecting him, forcing him to see the most horrible things. Have you ever been to the Holocaust museum in Washington D.C.? There are collections of glasses, of hair, of all these things that belonged to the Jews they sent to the gas chambers. What if they took Mark and tossed him onto that pile of glasses?"

"They would never do that."

"Maybe they wouldn't, doctor," Bill said, fighting back a cough, "but that's something I thought up just now. There are people a lot smarter than me who could come up with some even more interesting things to do to Mark."

"This is the United States, not Nazi Germany."

"I work for the FBI, doctor, and I know there are parts of our government that never see the light of day." Normally a phlegmatic man, Bill felt his blood boiling. "Has it never occurred to you that Mark may not be the first to exhibit this ability? It's a reasonable assumption. And if not, why hasn't the world ever heard of the ones who came before?"

Kucera, to her credit, reflected on what Bill said for nearly a minute. "That may be true," she said, "but I want you to listen to me as well. This arrangement for Mark has been, by necessity, ad hoc. After all, no one really knows what he is truly capable of. We don't know how his gift works. And, most importantly, we don't know what kind of damage he is doing to himself."

"He is… haunted by many things," Bill admitted. "Things in his past, the visions he has seen. Don't think I feel good about the arrangement. And if Mark ever truly wanted to quit, refused to go to some scene of tragedy and to make his drawings, I would let him go. We'd protect him."

Kucera nodded. "You love him. He's like a son to you."

"Something like that. It's what makes this…" Bill gestured to the room, trying to put his thoughts into words.

"I know," Kucera replied, "and when I want something more systematic, I'm not suggesting we turn Mark into a weapon. I want to help him live a long, happy life."

"Mark?" Bill said in an incredulous tone. "A happy life flew the coop long ago."

"Maybe we can find your friend a more peaceful one."

Chapter Ten
Friday, October 14, 2016

"**B**ullshit!" Skylar screamed at the referee. Or, rather, she mumbled in an aggressive manner toward the referee in such a way that the referee would not actually hear her. "I was so not offsides."

The crowd which gathered to watch the Panthers (the club team of Eastside) take on the Thunderbolts Bellevue West on a cold, crisp October morning greeted the referee's call of offside with a smattering of applause and general indifference. Most of the crowd consisted of family members, so the numbers were not large.

And Skylar had clearly been offside. By at least two yards.

Mark hurried down to the soccer field. He was technically late, but he didn't mind. He wasn't there to watch the game anyway.

On each side of the field stood a thin strand of bleachers that ran about twenty yards both ways from the center line. Mark saw Stacy at the end of the front row, her thick hair flapping in the wind like a dark flag.

She saw him back and waved a hand in greeting.

"You're late. Where were you, my date-having little brother?" Stacy asked when Mark sat.

Mark raised his eyebrows. "And here my sister goes, ragging on me before I've even got settled. I think I should get bonus points for attending my niece's soccer game."

"Your bonus is the opportunity to keep me company while I try not to fall asleep," Stacy said. Mark knew his sister loved Skylar from one end of the earth to the other, but…

"I think it's nice that you go to these games when you clearly hate watching any sport."

Stacy, growing up, was very much not an athlete. She did yearbook and debate. Even now, Stacy preferred to not sweat whenever possible. She did yoga a few times a week to keep in shape, and she liked to go on walks in nice weather. Stacy once claimed that the only balls she wanted to touch were those of a divorcee who moved in down the street, a man Stacy referred to as "a complete DILF."

"What can I say?" Stacy sighed. "She's my daughter. I don't know where she gets her love of running around. From her dad, I imagine."

Stacy rarely brought up Skylar's dad, and Mark knew better than to pursue that line of conversation. It rarely ended well. Stacy had gotten pregnant at the age of twenty to a man whose career ambition was to smoke a lot of pot. Surprisingly, he turned out to be real shitty at child support.

Mark's reply got swallowed up by a thread of excitement that ran through the crowd. A long pass from one of the full backs had resulted in a breakaway by Skylar. She poured on speed as she chased the ball. The keeper saw the danger and went out to cover the ball before Skylar got to it. Mark and Stacy both got up as Skylar and goalkeeper ran toward each other.

Skylar got there first, popping the ball into the air and leaping to the side to avoid the sprawling keeper. The ball arced lazily into the air, chased by the Bellevue West defenders. Both sides screamed as the ball bounced into the net.

Teammates swarming over her, Skylar looked for a second not like a teenaged girl trying to look cool but a little girl with a ponytail thrilled to feel the wind whipping her face.

Mark had been like that once, had felt free. In the midst of his joy for his niece, he felt a pang of sadness at that part of him that kept him from experiencing such simple joy.

"What was that look on your face?" Stacy asked when the game had restarted.

"Happiness?"

"For someone who has a date tomorrow, you have a funny way of showing it."

"It's just…"

Stacy held up her hand. "I know, little brother. You don't have to go if you don't want to."

"It's not just the girl. Bill told me about some murder that…"

His sister's face darkened. She really did not like Bill. "I don't want to know the details."

Mark nodded. "It reminded him of an old case, a really bad one. But the guy who did the old ones died."

"So, he thinks it's what? A copycat."

"I don't know. Bill wasn't telling me the whole truth. I don't know."

"I assume it's one of the cases you helped the FBI with," Stacy said.

Mark nodded.

"Even though I've been telling you for years to go tell Bill to go piss on himself."

"It's not like that. He's not using me."

"Yeah, he is." Stacy did not like Bill, obviously. "He is, and this shit he makes you do is walking you to an early grave. I don't want to see you drop dead of a heart attack at age 50."

"What I do helps solve crimes. I help save children."

"You know what, Mark?" Stacy's voice filled with passion. "The FBI is actually pretty good at solving crimes on their own. It's what they're trained to do. And does Bill know what helping them is doing to you?"

"I've told him about the dreams," Mark said.

"Uh huh." Stacy gave him a look.

"I am an adult, Stace. And I've chosen the way I'm living my adult life. I know that makes you mad, that I get to make my own choices, but that's how it is."

Mark felt the words come out of his mouth, and they felt wrong. His sister winced. The crowd roared briefly at a long strike attempt by the Thunderbolts, but the ball sailed over the crossbar.

"And your choices affect... I don't feel..." Stacy searched for words, "That is, I don't want to control your life. You think I do, but I don't. I just don't want. I want you to be okay, brother. That's it. Let's not do this right now. The whole argument thing. We'll be mad at each other for days."

"That's a good idea. A good idea."

For a few long minutes, they watched the game, even though Skylar knelt on the sideline with a paper cup of water in her hand.

"I didn't mean what I said," Mark said at last.

"I know, I didn't either."

More silence.

"So, you're not bummed out about seeing a girl in a romantic situation?"

"It's just coffee."

"Forget that. You were cagey over the phone. You owe me details. Now, Markie."

Slowly, over the next five minutes, Mark found himself explaining how he and Happy met, how they worked together on the scavenger hunt, how Happy had asked him out. Stacy may not have ever gone to law school, but she asked so many detailed questions that Mark felt like a prosecutor was questioning him. "I don't know what she was wearing, Stace." "She sounded friendly." "What does seductive-sounding sound like? Please do not show me, Stacy." "No, I don't remember exactly how she phrased it… Why are you looking so weird?"

"I'm not even sure I'm going." Mark ended with. Despite the cool morning, he felt sweat popping out on his forehead.

"Oh, yes you will. I will personally drive you there myself." Stacy looked downright wicked. "You like this girl."

Mark looked up, away from the soccer field toward the tall hill. He pointed. "Who's that, do you think?"

"That is a weak attempt at deflecting this conversation and it won't work," Stacy replied.

"No, I'm serious," Mark said. "Who is that guy? He's leaning against a tree. I swear to god he's staring at us."

Stacy took a microsecond-long glance. "Probably some deadbeat, pothead dad looking at his little girl all grown up and regretting his life choices. Now, what does your girlfriend teach?"

"Not my girlfriend," Mark choked, "and I'm not even sure…"

"We've already decided that you're going. If you don't promise, I'll tell Mom you have a date."

Mark's eyes widened in shock. "You wouldn't dare."

"I fight dirty, little brother," Stacy said. "Details or I take out my cell phone and make a phone call." She widened her eyes in faux-innocence, "She'd be so excited to hear this information."

Mark looked up again. The man with the binoculars had disappeared. He had existed, right? Stacy had seen him, she said she had. Had she even looked up? "Fine, you win."

Chapter Eleven
1996

Like I said, seventh grade was sucking the big one, as far as I was considered. And it was only October. Danny had stopped wanting to be my friend a few weeks ago. Things had only gone downhill since.

Some background info: Mom and Stacy had begun to really fight. It started with Stacy dating some guy Mom didn't like. Stacy was sixteen, four years older than me. Her boyfriend was nineteen, I think. He wasn't in high school. Either way, Stace had become this complete wasteoid. As in smoking cigarettes and pot, skipping classes at Eastside, breaking curfew. Every few days they had a little screaming match in the living room. And that was really weird because Mom wasn't a yeller.

So yesterday I came home after a long day at school. Looong day. I'll explain why in a second. I walked in the door and Stace and her boyfriend were on the couch, making out while Smashing Pumpkins blares on the stereo. They didn't even notice me come in. He had his hand up her shirt and I said, "Come on." All I wanted was to come home and sit on my bed and stare at the ceiling. That was it, and now I had to listen to the Smashing Pumpkins at ear-splitting levels while I had to think about Steve sticking his hand up my sister's shirt.

Steve pulled his tongue away from my sister's mouth long enough to tell me to fuck off.

"Hey, come on," Stacy said softly. She sounded stoned.

"No, forget this kid." Steve gave me the finger. "Let's go to your room." He stood up, half pulling my sister to her feet, which she did with stoned reluctance.

So, Steve was a winner, my sister had gone all in on tanking her GPA, and I was the biggest loser in the seventh grade.

As for what happens at school… Let's say that most of the seventh graders ignore me. Except it wasn't ignoring exactly. Is there a word that means how they never seem to look at you but out of the corner of your eye, one of them points at you and does something to make his friends laugh? The first time it happens, maybe you turn to look at them and they're looking at you while they're laughing. Every time after that, I concentrate on something else and hope my face isn't turning red.

I can't ask them what they are laughing about, because they'll say "nothing" or "some freakazoid, you wouldn't know him." Then they'll laugh some more. I can't fight them either. Who am I going to beat up? Little Markie Peter hasn't grown an inch in two years while some of the kids have got underarm hair.

Basically, not having friends in the seventh grade sucked the big one.

Of course, if all the other kids sat around and laughed at me when my back was turned, life wouldn't be that bad. Not great, not even fun. More like a D on a quiz. At least it's passing.

But what would middle school be if it weren't for kids like Seth Wendell, Steve Hruska, Asher Cooper, and, worst of all,

Mike Jennings. For a while, too, I could deal with it. I mean, all they really did was call me names.

That's it, that's the sum total of number of things that they said about me. I know what the words mean, and it brought my daily grade down to a D-, but I could live with it. Still passing. Still able to go home and tell Mom about the things I did in class and act like it was okay.

Then a week ago, while we were sitting in social studies class, Mike decided to up the ante. The teacher was Mr. Butterfield, who used to play in the minor leagues for the Yankees. If it's possible to play for the Yankees in the minor leagues. I don't really know the sport, but Mr. Butterfield likes to talk about baseball a lot. And in October, that means he didn't really teach so much as talk baseball.

Now, a week ago, one of the kids got him started on how to get some player out between first and second… something, something, something baseball. Mr. Butterfield gets all excited and starts drawing a diamond on the board and he starts moving little X's after some poor O who had to stay on the white line of the chalkboard. I'm thinking about me being a knight standing outside a rocky outcrop, a trail of smoke coming from the entrance. I'm on my knees, long spear in hand, staring at the…

WHAM! My right ear about exploded.

My head whipped forward and to the side without me even thinking about it. I about fell out of the chair. Behind me, I could hear snickering. Right behind me sat Mike Jennings and Steve Hruska.

"What's wrong?" Steve asked in a baby voice. "Did Markie hurt his ear?"

One of those two had gone and flicked my ear, hard. Maybe not a bruise, but I felt it. Of course, Mr. Butterfield did not see a damn thing. When he got going on baseball, a freaking marching band could rumble down the center of the classroom and he would not have noticed.

The other kids sure did. Every eye in the entire classroom shifted in our direction. Their sidelong gazes burned a hole into the side of my head.

Should I have made a scene? Should I have hit Steve Hruska back? Yeah, I should have. I would have gotten suspended, and probably would have gotten the shit beaten out of me on the Greens after school sometime later, but the ear flicking would have stopped. Bullies don't like it when their victims hit back. That's what I should have done.

Now, most of the teachers always go on about how kids need to talk to an adult when they're being bullied. Those teachers mean well, but they forget that a kid in the middle school is a different species than an adult. Kids got their own rules. About sixth grade, it became uncool to talk to adults about stuff. About the time a kid hits thirteen, there ain't nothing more important than being cool.

I was the least cool kid at Eastside Middle School.

Chapter Twelve
Saturday, October 15, 2016

Mark did not generally like to have conversations with himself. His sanity, if his sanity were a sailboat, already suffered from small leaks in the hull and tattered sails. Talking to himself might be a sign, nautically speaking, that he had lost his keel.

Happy had suggested a place not too far from his house; the Dundee neighborhood had a great many coffee houses, few better than Caffeine Dreams.

"It's just coffee," Mark said aloud as he walked. The cooling wind caught up the dead leaves and the leaves' rattle mixed with the sounds of cars. With cars and people walking on Underwood Avenue, travelling to and from the Dundee Dell (for the convivial atmosphere), Dario's (for the food), Mark's (for food and expensive drinks), the Cork and Bottle (because they had the best outside seating in the neighborhood), and the Underwood Bar (for those who wanted to get drunk).

He crossed Dodge Street at 49th Street, giving a quiet middle finger down the street to the CVS Pharmacy. Stupid mass-produced business – the pharmacy had replaced one of the few bars he didn't mind going to (the 49'r – at least on the nights it didn't have live music).

"This is not a date. This is just coffee," he repeated to himself.

He walked south on 49th to Farnam, taking a left at a darkened lot which had been turned into a community garden. One of the things he loved about Omaha was the Dundee neighborhood. Grand, old houses, walkable restaurants to get take out (he missed Trovato's, which had closed a few years before), one or two places where Mark could get a beer on a weekday night that didn't have overly loud music.

The night even smelled wonderful. Someone in the neighborhood had been baking bread and left their windows open. The sound of the traffic, the sheen of small puddles on the sidewalk from an afternoon shower.

"It is not a date," Mark repeated again. "If it was a date, I would not be going. I would be walking the opposite direction. I would be shooting myself with a tranquilizer gun."

He could not, for some reason, quite remember exactly what Happy looked like. Mark remembered wavy blond hair with purple and blue streaks (they reminded him of lightning), blue eyes that lit up like electric bug zappers on summer nights, and a smile that promised something funny was on the horizon. The next sentence, perhaps, or the next turn of the road.

"The reason it cannot be a date is because I do not physically touch other human beings. When I touch other human beings, bad things happen. For one thing, they get to know all of the bad things I've ever seen. And I have seen some very, very bad things. Not just my stuff, but I've been tracking some of the sickest criminals of all time. Most girls would rather hold hands and feel all tingly. They would rather not experience, say, getting raped and strangled by a next-door-neighbor who smells like Old Spice aftershave and keeps saying keep calm, sugar. That kind of experience, I have learned, leads to women screaming incoherently and slapping their ears to try to get the visions out of their heads."

Caffeine Dreams, at the corner of 46th and Farnam, resided in one of those brick buildings that probably began life as an office for lawyers or architects. It had been converted to a large, open space filled with small tables and couches. You could get an expresso, yerba mate, or even a banana-chocolate smoothie.

"Hey, you're here early," Mark said when he saw his date… his potential friend who wanted to have coffee with him, already there.

"I wanted to make sure to pick a seat that backed against a wall," Happy replied, her voice serious, "that way, I don't let anyone get behind me with a gun. I'm ninja like that."

Mark looked and saw several tables that had such seats. However, Happy had chosen one that afforded a view to the entire coffee shop. He said as much to her. She looked around as well. "Well, one never knows if one should have to fight one's way out of a coffee house. Of course, maybe I got here early because I'm always on time and I'm slightly nervous tonight? Or maybe you should get some coffee."

"I don't drink coffee."

"It's good that we met here at a coffee house," Happy said.

Mark smiled. "I do drink tea, though."

"He drinks tea. Hallelujah!" When he came back holding a cup of tea, she gave him an up and down examination. "Do you wear the same clothes every day?"

He swallowed a sarcastic answer. Mark adhered to a very utilitarian philosophy regarding clothing. For one thing, he rather liked plain clothes. He wore khaki pants nearly every day, although he would switch to black pants on occasion. For shirts, except for a few polos, Mark wore nothing but button-down shirts in colors guaranteed to match any of his pants (i.e. blue, green, white). He owned a pair of black work shoes and nine pairs of black socks.

"Everything I wear fits with everything else," Mark answered, "at least when it comes to non-workout clothes. That way, I can pretty much grab anything in the morning with the expectation that I will match."

"At least you rhyme," she said in her sing-song voice.

"Usually, when I explain how I organize my life, people always listen with slightly amused expressions on their faces. For instance, I have a modular approach to personal fashion. I see how you…" Mark gestured at Happy's clothes. "It's like you're wearing layers of clothes that shouldn't go together, but they do. I cannot understand how it works. I'm like that with everything. I use either castile soap, vinegar, or baking soda on literally every cleanable surface in my house, for instance. See, you're smiling." Mark's voice dropped in slight disappointment.

"I'm not trying to make fun of you," Happy said passionately. "Never. I guess I smiled because the way you go about your life is so radically different from mine."

"No modular clothing system?" Mark asked.

Happy shrugged. "My apartment? It's complete chaos. It took me over an hour and a half to get ready tonight. My bed is covered in rejected outfits."

"Jesus." Mark felt compelled to add, "an hour and a half to have coffee?" Immediately, he felt like a complete asshat. Happy looked amazing, just amazing.

She raised her eyebrows, causing him to begin sweating. Mark continued with the reckless voice of someone losing control of his narrative, "I mean, it's not like you don't look great. Still, it's an hour and a half. I mean, it takes me ten minutes to shower at the most. Drying, using a squeegee on the shower door, putting on deodorant, dressing. That's gotta be twenty, max." Mark felt his mouth beginning to ramble on, knew he was messing up in some indefinable way, but could not help but wonder what getting-ready-routine took four and a half times longer than his own.

Happy asked, "Would you like me to break down my routine in minute-by-minute blocks?"

Mark paused. "I… would? I'm curious about your routine? I have a feeling I'm not supposed to ask questions about your personal hygiene. Sorry. I'm not very good at this."

In the corner of the room, a young woman with hair the shade of strawberry Kool-Aid began to tune a guitar.

"I'm not either, to be honest," Happy said. "Let's talk about something else, such as the likelihood of enjoying the musical stylings of a girl who has both a 'This Machine Kills Fascists' and 'I Heart Taylor Swift' stickers on her guitar case. Personally, I'm intrigued."

"Crap," Mark said, spinning toward the young woman, who was bent over her guitar, tuning the strings. "She's going to do covers. I can tell. And not deep cuts either, but Bob Dylan's greatest hits."

"There's nothing wrong with Bob Dylan, greatest hits or otherwise," said Happy.

Mark said, "Sure, when they're sung by Bob Dylan."

"You do realize that Dylan has a terrible voice. He's a genius, but not a great singer. Anyway, there's something spiritual about listening to someone live baring their soul. Even though Dylan wrote the songs, they still connect."

"Yeah, yeah," Mark conceded. "I'm cynical."

"And you're looking to score comedy points," Happy added.

Satisfied that at the sound of her guitar, the young woman straightened in her chair and introduced herself with, "Hi, I'm Monique." She then said, "I first heard this song when it was done by Miley Cyrus." Mark turned and gave Happy a triumphant glance.

Monique launched into a cover of "Look What They Done to My Song, Ma," which was about as cool a cover song as one could do.

They listened quietly for a while. Happy shifted her chair so she could get a better look at Monique, and so happened to scoot right next to Mark in the process.

"So, can I ask you a question about the gloves thing?" she asked in a quiet voice.

"It's a hygiene phobia thing."

"No, I mean… is this like for all time? The not-touching-other-people-thing? Because I think I like you and I know you like me." Happy looked down and touched her crazy wavy hair. "I want to know what to expect going forward."

For several long seconds, Mark looked down at the table. "I misled you. I shouldn't even be here."

"Okay, so this is pretty much a permanent feature." Happy began to nod her head, as if talking herself into something. "Okay, okay."

"You deserve someone who…"

"Please stop with the moping crap," Happy interrupted him. "You know what I need? Since we are being completely honest? I need someone who makes schedules and routines, who has an organized closet and always shows up on time. Does that sound like anyone you know?"

"Lots of guys are organized."

"I also need someone who makes me laugh, which you do. I need someone who is kind of nuts like me," Happy said.

"You are many things, Daffodil Hapke, but you don't have lots of issues." Mark felt his voice grow hoarse.

"Bull," she replied, "I'm just better at hiding them. You're a freak of nature who cannot help but let other people know it. Look at me. I love my job, but I'm not really good at it. I am terrible at relationships. I have all kinds of weird health issues."

"Like what?"

"Are we sharing weirdo health notes?" Happy smiled but she had tears in her eyes. "Okay, I am allergic to an entire array of dyes and perfumes. If we date, you'll probably have to change every personal grooming product you use."

"What about animals?"

"Dogs. And pretty much all of spring."

"Well, I have a cat named Frodo." Mark asked.

"I love cats," Happy said.

"I am mildly allergic to chocolate. Break out in hives. Used to make Halloween a real suck."

"Chocolate allergy? That's nothing. I have a genetic condition known as situs inversus. It means that all of my organs are flip-flopped. My heart is on the right side of my body, my spleen's on the left. Luckily, it doesn't really affect my health at all. But if I ever get a new doctor, it freaks them the fuck out when listening for my heartbeat. Beat that." Happy's smile resembled that of an athlete in the midst of a game.

"Nice, nice. How about I had cryptorchidism."

"What's that?" Happy asked.

"Undescended testicle." Mark made a boom sound with his hand.

She waved him off. "Please, that got taken care of by the time you were one."

"Okay," he said, "I developed cataracts in my left eye when I was a teenager."

"As a teen?"

"They don't just happen to old people."

"Cataracts. Not bad." Happy stroked her chin. "When I was a teenager, I was a cutter. I would steal one of my dad's box cutters and go to town whenever things got really bad at school. Girls can be so shitty to each other. Most kids cut their arms. Not me. I used to cut myself on the insides of my thighs. That way, no one could see the marks. And I thought that no boy would ever want to see that area either. I was a real bundle of fuck-my-life in high school. To be honest, I wish I were farther away from that fat high school kid."

"I was bullied in school too. Mostly middle school."

"I'm shocked," Happy deadpanned. "You?"

"It was pretty bad. And I have the no touching thing," Mark finished.

Happy conceded the point, stating that "you kind of have the trump card in this game of Who's More Screwed Up."

Mark did a little dance in his seat, forgetting that he wasn't the kind of person who danced in his seat. For a short time, the two of them listened to the young woman with purple hair begin to pluck at her guitar. For her second song, she began to play Nick Drake's "Black Eyed Dog." To their even greater surprise, they both knew the song from the first few notes, and rushed to see who could tell the other the name of the song first (Happy won).

"So, what would happen if I did touch you?" Happy asked quietly, barely audible under the music.

"A black-eyed dog he knew my name," Monique sang in a thin voice.

"Bad stuff. Bad." Mark shook his head, like he needed to be reminded.

"It can't be too bad," Happy said and leaned forward with her finger.

Mark reacted as if he'd been electrocuted, falling out of his chair, which also fell and banged on the ground. The young woman stopped the song and the attention of every person in the coffee house focused on the two of them, to Mark's great joy.

Before anyone could reach out to him, Mark leaped to his feet and mumbled some kind of goodbye to Happy. He rushed out the door. Vaguely, he heard her say something but his face felt full and red from self-directed anger. *I should have known*, he mumbled to himself, and repeated the phrase.

Happy caught up before he made it across the parking lot. He stopped amidst the dark cars and turned toward her. "Please, just stop. Please."

"I'm so, so sorry," Happy said. She looked miserable, about to cry. "I had this impulse to. It won't happen again. I thought that maybe it wasn't that big a deal…"

"I wear gloves everywhere I go," Mark said, letting some of that anger poke out toward her. "I am seriously broken, and I should have not been here tonight."

"No, please. I thought that maybe if you trusted me, it wouldn't be a big deal."

"It's not about trust."

"What is it, then? Please," Happy begged, "I want to understand."

Mark opened his mouth, closed it again. He looked around to see if they were alone. They weren't, although he didn't know that. "You're not going to believe me."

"Try me."

"When I touch something, or someone, I get visions. Or something. I don't know what exactly, but I'm able to draw memories. I think they're memories."

"That sounds like a gift," Happy said.

"Well, I almost never get the happy memories. If I were to touch you, I'd probably sit here and draw a picture of you in high school cutting your thighs."

Happy attempted a smile. "I don't think I would mind if you could share that."

"And I would be able to feel that pain you felt. It would come to me in dreams, while I'm driving, whenever. The memories come back to me." Happy opened her mouth to speak but Mark continued, "That's not the worst. It's a two-way street. You would feel my pain."

"Again, I don't think I would mind."

Thinking for a second, Mark dug out his phone and scrolled through the pictures. After a minute, he found what he was looking for. He handed it to Happy.

"What's this?" she asked, confused.

"Her name was Quinn McFee. She was seven years old. She disappeared a few weeks ago. Her case is one of at least sixty that I've helped the FBI with. I touch things that have an emotional connection to the crime, then I fall into a trance and I draw.

"That drawing is of Quinn's mother smothering her with a pillow. I felt Quinn die. I have felt other kids die – get shot, disemboweled, burned, and drown. The drowning one was really bad. I wake up screaming twice a week, at least. If you touch me, Happy, you'll get a taste of what I've touched. Do you want that?"

Happy looked at the image, recoiled. "You always win at the 'Who's More Screwed Up' game, don't you?"

"Undefeated." He reached out and took the phone back.

"I'm so, so sorry."

"It's awful," Mark said, "but sometimes I help find them alive. Sometimes I help their murderers go to jail. I need to go. Just don't say anything about this. To anyone. Please."

"I won't," Happy promised, but Mark was already stepping away.

Chapter Thirteen
Sunday, October 16, 2016

In every city, there were unloved commercial areas. Places without attractive buildings or restaurants with shaded windows where the customers inside look like specters. Places with no bars and no last call explosion of noise as men and women pour out into the cold air.

Businesses line those unbusy streets, small businesses of the kind which need no street traffic. Places that people seek out because they need something specific. Places which rent forklifts or specialize in commercial air conditioning units.

At night, no cars run down those streets, no people take their pets down them for a stroll. The lights seem dimmer on those streets at night. Every city has them.

One such place that existed in Omaha sat off the I-80 interchange at 60th Street. Years ago, some enterprising spirit had built the Stop Inn a few blocks south and east of the interchange. They must have looked at the cheap land at 57th and F and thought that people would come. People would come to a strip motel, 15 rooms around a kidney-shaped pool three minutes from the interstate. People would turn down F Street, see the Stop Inn sign (a neon affair in the shape of a red octagon), and want the clean rooms for significantly less than what the Howard Johnson or Holiday Inn off of 72nd were charging.

The owners of the Stop Inn were wrong; sometime in the 1980s, the Stop Inn became the F Street Apartments (although they kept the same red octagon sign). The motel rooms became efficiency apartments, except for the former front desk, which had been converted to a two-bedroom. Over the years, the F Street Apartments attracted a certain kind of resident. Poor and quiet always. And if they had a nasty habit (drinking, drugs, etc.), they kept their broken bits behind thick closed doors.

For some reason, however, the swimming pool remained open, despite the fact that few of the residents used it. A few every summer would totter out on white stick legs to rest on the dirty yellow plastic chairs which surrounded the pool. The pool water seemed dimmer somehow, although young men in red polos tended to the water every spring. Every now and then a few grandchildren splashed around in the pool, kids brought in to Grandma's and dropped off for "just a few fucking hours so I can get some cleaning done."

On Sunday, October 16, several people got up and left without looking over at the small kidney-shaped pool. They did not see, in the fall morning sun's shadows, something bobbing there near the metal ladder. In fact, the pool service was scheduled the next day to come drain the water for winter.

One person, Imelda Jones, finally, did see something odd out her window. She squinted and put on her glasses and still saw something there in the pool. Imelda threw a robe over her flowery pajamas and lime green crocs on her feet and went outside, shivering at the chill. She walked to the rusty fence surrounding the pool and looked at the shape in the pool. To her surprise, the old woman did not scream. Imelda staggered a step but said nothing. Instead, her unsteady hand reached into the robe's pocket and pulled out a cell phone. After the call, Imelda turned away from the shape in the pool, no longer feeling the chill in the air.

Men and women in uniform soon surrounded the pool. One or two helped to set up a perimeter of yellow tape which closed off the entrance of the F Street Apartments, a few others clumped together to talk, the rest stared off in the distance. In these situations, the uniformed officers spread out, spider-like, to gather information. Witnesses, physical details, more witnesses. Cars sped along I-80, humming to the police as they worked.

Bill arrived and parked it a few doors down in the lot of a taxidermist. He recognized Dylan's Jeep. She appeared as he got out, coming back from the crime scene.

"It's a bad one. No one knows anything yet, but it sounds like this is our guy."

"How do you know?"

"She's in a pool of water. It looks like she was strangled. She's pretty and young," said Dylan. "The press is here, too. All four stations sent vans. If they aren't making the Vandergeest connection now, they will be soon."

"Parmero here yet?" Bill asked, referring to the special agent in charge of the Omaha field office.

"On his way." Dylan shook her head. "When do we call Mark?"

"We don't," Bill said. "He's retired."

"This is Eric Vandergeest. We have to." Dylan did not much care for Mark, but she had worked with the two of them long enough to have garnered respect for the man's ability. "We both know that Vandergeest is…" She searched for the words. "… that he has abilities like Mark's. I've read the letters."

During Vandergeest's first set of murders, he sent a series of letters to the FBI. Once Vandergeest had thrown himself off the bridge, the FBI had released them. Only a handful of people, including Dylan and Bill, had read the original letters.

The ones in the official file were forgeries. "We do not know if this is Vandergeest," Bill said. "If it were, where has he been for the last five years? People die from violence all the time. Let's not jump to conclusions."

"The girl was strangled," Dylan persisted. "White zip ties around her wrists. The police aren't stupid. They're already talking amongst themselves. Somebody is going to leak this soon and that's it. Omaha will be the lead story for the nightly news."

A Toyota Odyssey pulled into the taxidermist's parking lot. Parmero, a short man who ran marathons in his spare time, got out.

"When did you get a minivan?" Bill asked.

"My car's in the shop. This is my wife's." Paremero clearly wanted to skip the small talk. Dylan filled him in on the basic information of the victim.

"I think it's Vandergeest. So does the OPD. Bill's not so sure."

"We haven't heard from him, have we?" Parmero asked. "If Vandergeest is back, he'll contact us. Maybe the OPD. He loves taunting the cops. Until then, these cases are everyday murders."

"I think we should call Mark. Get him in here."

Parmero looked at Bill questioningly. Bill felt a tickle in his chest, but shook his head in return. "Mark's retired. Every time he uses his gift, it costs him."

Dylan cursed, something she did like a sailor. "Mark, he's a… I know he's your friend, Bill, but the next time he spends more than three minutes in my presence without whining about something will be the first time. A few bad dreams aren't uncommon when you deal with the shit we deal with. Tell him to suck it up and fight crime." She pushed her short hair back; a gesture Bill had noticed she did whenever she dug her heels in.

"You know, you only see him when he's working for us. Speaking as his friend, I can tell you that he is scarred by the things he draws. It isn't a case of sucking it up. You didn't know him when he first started helping us. He used to laugh a lot more. I mean, he's never been…"

"Normal?" Dylan ventured.

At that moment, Bill wanted desperately to punch his fellow agent in her face. "Dylan, some other time, some time when we've both had a few drinks, remind me to tell you about Mark's life story. Not now. Later. Because it takes a while to tell. Then, after we have had a discussion about my friend's past, I'll ask you if you feel whether his complaints had any justification. But for now, remember that Mark, who is only 34 even though he looks older, has helped us find lost children, children kidnapped by family members, child abductees, people lost in the woods, murder weapons, murder victims, murderers, three very expensive paintings, and one pregnant llama."

"A llama?" Dylan asked.

Parmero cleared his throat. "Before your time. And it was giving birth when we found it. Time's wasting. I'm going to miss church as is. I'd like to be home in time for at least one football game." Without looking back, he walked toward the hive of police cars.

Dylan looked over at Bill. "If it is Vandergeest, you'll have to ask him. Have to make him come back."

"He's retired," Bill insisted before giving in to the spasm in his chest.

After he finished, Dylan pressed on, "If it's Vandergeest, we won't be able to catch him on our own. Vandergeest is… gifted, too. We'll need Mark."

Chapter Fourteen

Date: 9:17 a.m., Tuesday, October 18, 2016
       From: BillMallory@yahoo.com
       To: mpeter@eastside.edu
RE: Update
Mark,
Someone at the World-Herald put two and two together (they probably had a source in the OPD) and I'm sure you saw the effing headlines. We have a meeting in ten minutes. Every agent is being pulled in. I got home last night at midnight and left my house at 5 a.m. Right now, we are reacquainting ourselves with the details from Vandergeest's initial crimes.

I know that you remember Vandergeest's letters as well as I do, and you might feel in danger. If you'd like, Dylan would be happy to take you to a gun range. If I recall, you bought a revolver a few years ago.

To reiterate, you are not in danger.

However, Dylan figured you might feel better if you had a little experience with using your firearm. She may try to get you to come out of retirement. Just letting you know.

Reminder: Do not e-mail me at my official e-mail. Use this one. We can't have you linked to this case.

Bill

PS: How did the date go?

Date: 10:18 a.m., Tuesday, October 18, 2016

From: dhapke@eastside.edu

To: mpeter@eastside.edu

RE: About Saturday

Hey

Things ended a little bit weird on Saturday. Maybe we should talk?

Happy

Date: 10:01 a.m., Tuesday, October 18, 2016

From: lchang@eastside.edu

To: mpeter@eastside.edu

RE: Date Night

You are sitting three feet away and are basically non-verbal. What happened?

L

Date: 10:19 a.m., Tuesday, October 18, 2016

From: dhapke@eastside.edu

To: mpeter@eastside.edu

RE: RE: About Saturday

Not weird in a bad way, not in a way that I would have expected when I left my place to go to the coffee house. Maybe we can have lunch?

Happy

Date: 10:36 a.m., Tuesday, October 18, 2016

From: dhapke@eastside.edu

To: mpeter@eastside.edu

RE: Forgetting about it

If you don't mind me saying something, you are full of crap. You have a bunch of issues, I get that. I have some issues too.

Date: 10:41 a.m., Tuesday, October 18, 2016
From: dhapke@eastside.edu
To: mpeter@eastside.edu
RE: Your issues?

How about my uncle touching me inappropriately when I was five years old? How about that we haven't spoken to anyone on that side of the family for seventeen years? I fully acknowledge that you have a lot of crap to deal with. I do too.

Date: 10:48 a.m., Tuesday, October 18, 2016
From: dhapke@eastside.edu
To: mpeter@eastside.edu
RE: Stuff

Mark,

Apology accepted. Just for the record, you actually wrote a complete apology, not one of those "sorry you were offended" passive aggressive things. I appreciate that.

Happy

Date: 10:50 a.m., Tuesday, October 18, 2016
From: dhapke@eastside.edu
To: mpeter@eastside.edu
RE: Stuff

That you expressed interest in the uncle thing but did not want to pry… Thank you.

Regarding the whole Shit the Principal thing… Ha!

Now, to business. We have already established you are completely wild about me; let's talk about our plans for the weekend. Don't worry, I'm not planning on touching your face or anything. Relationships are built on trust, and I promise not to invade your space without your permission.

Date: 10:52 a.m., Tuesday, October 18, 2016
From: dhapke@eastside.edu
To: mpeter@eastside.edu
RE: Stuff
Yes, you are wild about me. I know it. You know it. We don't even have to discuss it. It is known.

Date: 11:01 a.m., Tuesday, October 18, 2016
From: lchang@eastside.edu
To: mpeter@eastside.edu
RE: Date Night
Now you are laughing quietly. Are you suffering from a mental illness?
L

Date: 10:54 a.m., Tuesday, October 18, 2016
From: dhapke@eastside.edu
To: mpeter@eastside.edu
RE: Stuff
I literally can hear you sputtering in your e-mail. It's a good thing you make me laugh, or else I might reconsider you going with me to the movies on Friday. And dinner. I like Indian food.

Date: 10:55 a.m., Tuesday, October 18, 2016
From: dhapke@eastside.edu
To: mpeter@eastside.edu
RE: Stuff

I'm going to have to end this conversation. My students are looking at me because I just laughed out loud.

Friday. Movie. Dinner. Indian.

Happy

Date: 11:01 a.m., Tuesday, October 18, 2016

From: sconstantino@eastside.edu

To: mpeter@eastside.edu

Mr. Peters,

I'm having some issues with my computer. Sometimes I'm online and I get sucked into this vortex / spam website.

Could I bring it to you to have you remaster it or something?

Sam

PS: You don't go overboard when something like this happens, do you? It's not like I want the browser to take me to any weird websites. I mean, this happens all the time I'd imagine.

Date: 11:31 a.m., Tuesday, October 18, 2016

From: shamrickthompson@eastside.edu

To: mpeter@eastside.edu

RE: ICW Presentations

Still waiting on the timeline for the ICW makeup presentations. I need those ASAP. That is, by tomorrow at the very latest.

Also, I want you to mark a few days on your calendar after the start of second semester. You will help code in all the class requests.

Susan Hamrick-Thompson

Date: 11:50 a.m., Tuesday, October 18, 2016

From: shamrickthompson@eastside.edu
To: mpeter@eastside.edu
RE: ICW Presentations
Everybody is busy, Mark. You and Lawrence will have to find the time.
Susan Hamrick-Thompson

Date: 12:21 p.m., Tuesday, October 18, 2016
From: lacystacy22@icloud.com
To: mpeter@eastside.edu
RE: Bill
Mark,
You're not helping Bill with this thing on TV, right? Right?
Stacy

Date: 12:30 p.m., Tuesday, October 18, 2016
From: dcarlson@eastside.edu
To: mpeter@eastside.edu
RE: Security Cameras
Their messed up again. Can you come down ASAP?
Dave

Date: 12:55 p.m., Tuesday, October 18, 2016
From: lacystacy22@icloud.com
To: mpeter@eastside.edu
RE: Bill
Mark,
I'm only trying to look out for you. Just be careful, okay? How did the date go? I've not called because I'm a good sister who doesn't pry. But you WILL tell me. Soon.
Stacy

Date: 2:01 p.m., Tuesday, October 18, 2016

From: sconstantino@eastside.edu
To: mpeter@eastside.edu
Mark,
You are my hero.
Sam
PS: Thanks for being cool. By the way, I have some extra Husker tickets for Saturday's game. I'm not going. You want them?

Date: 2:09 p.m., Tuesday, October 18, 2016
From: lacystacy22@icloud.com
To: mpeter@eastside.edu
RE: Call Me ASAP
Look, Mister "I'd rather not talk about it," you will be talking about it. One phone call to mom, am I right?

Date: 2:30 p.m., Tuesday, October 18, 2016
From: dhapke@eastside.edu
To: mpeter@eastside.edu
RE: Last Period
It's going soooooo slow. I swear, half the kids are asleep. Ever have one of those days when you are thinking of about six thousand things other than your actual job? Today is that day. Of course, one of the things I'm thinking about is you, so that's not so bad.

Date: 2:30 p.m., Tuesday, October 18, 2016
From: dhapke@eastside.edu
To: mpeter@eastside.edu
RE: RE: Last Period
Awww… Maybe eat lunch tomorrow?

Date: 3:08 p.m., Tuesday, October 18, 2016
From: shamrickthompson@eastside.edu
To: mpeter@eastside.edu
RE: ICW Presentations
Tick Tock, Tick Tock

Date: 6:49 p.m., Tuesday, October 18, 2016
From: TrickyDick@gmail.com
To: mpeter@eastside.edu
RE:
Are you my pal?

Chapter Fifteen
April 23, 2012

I was the last person who saw her alive. It was March 6th, I didn't feel like going outside because I'd had such a bad day. I mean it was worse than my usual bad day.

It started off with my normal routine – I had to pick which of the three sweatshirts and which of the three pairs of pants to wear (one pair of sweatpants, two pairs of jeans that don't make me look too hideous). I had to think about wearing makeup and decided only to wear enough to make my pimples go away. I walked to school. Dad could've driven me because he doesn't work or anything, but he had stopped driving me. It was his way of telling me that I was fat, and I think he was kind of hoping that it would get me to lose weight.

So, I walked to school. Andrea couldn't drive me neither because she had dance squad before school. Not that I would have gone with her anyway. Since the school year started and she started dance squad and got real popular, Andrea had gotten to be a total bitch.

She didn't even tell me I was fat. It was like that part was too easy to be a bitch with me about. We're sisters, so she knew all of the things that could set me off. I knew stuff about her too, so it was about even at home. Not at school.

So, I picked the red Nebraska sweatshirt and a pair of blue jeans that didn't smell because I only wore them on Monday and managed not to spill anything on them. And it was kind of warm, so I didn't have to wear that stupid coat that Mom got at the Goodwill near where she works in Omaha. Andrea wore that dance squad jacket like it was made of gold, but all I got was a big puffy coat that made me look even bigger.

I got two ways of walking to school. The first is that I walk a few blocks to where the highway runs through town and turn left, walk about a mile and there I am. But that means walking down the highway and a lot of people from Springfield High School drive down there and I don't want them looking at me. So, I went the other way, which is by the railroad tracks past where our street ends. So, I followed that way for a while until I got to the dog food mill. I turned right and followed Cedar Street until it turned into 4th. I turned left and thought about getting a donut at the Daybreak Donuts, but Ryan Cobb was in there and he always makes pig noises at me in the hall, so I kept walking.

Like I said, March 6th was kind of normal. I went to classes and tried to sit real small so that no one picked on me and the teachers didn't call on me either. I saw Andrea a couple of times between classes, but we have an understanding. She didn't say hi to me and I didn't say hi to her. Like I said, she was working hard at getting popular and she didn't need people knowing that we were related even though Springfield is a small town and everybody knew already.

The only thing interesting that happened that day was in algebra class when I got an A on a surprise quiz Mrs. Loudermilk gave us the day before. I about dropped my jaw when I saw it. I folded it up real nice so that I could show Mom later. I figured she might even put it on the fridge next to the pictures of Andrea in that Ann's Fashions advertisement in the Springfield Shopper.

When I got out of school, I thought about walking back my usual route, except it had rained and I didn't want to get my jeans wet because I thought maybe I'd have to wear them Friday. My other jeans had spaghetti sauce on them and I didn't want to wear the sweatpants.

I was walking along the highway on the sidewalk about halfway when I hear a car slowing down behind me. The music's going loud and I figured some of the kids were about to say something to me so I kind of hunched up a little bit and I felt something hit my back. It was a freezee from the Kum n Go and it hit me between my shoulders.

One of the kids, I never found out which, laughed and they drove off. I looked away from them when they drove off because I didn't want them to see my face and how red it gets when I get ashamed.

There were other people on the sidewalk walking home, and I heard them laughing. So, I cut through the grass and climbed the fence. I didn't even care about dogs or anything, that's how bad I felt.

When I got home, I was all out of breath but Andrea was home before me. She was in her room, but I could hear her talking on the phone real loud. She's a loud girl – always talking loud and even walking loud and everything. Even though by then I was crying, I could hear her talking about some teacher who had pissed her off.

"Like, I want to take his class anyway," is what I heard before I slammed the door to my room. I take off my sweatshirt and look and of course it was a blue freezee they threw on my red sweatshirt. I was sitting there crying a little bit and Andrea knocked on my door.

"You okay?"

"I'm fine! I want to be alone!" I yelled back at her, but I shouldn't have done that. Andrea was usually a bitch, but sometimes she could be real nice. Unfortunately, I didn't feel much like having anybody be nice to me. Sometimes, when you're down, it feels better to feel like everyone in the world hates you.

She goes away. I sit in my big bra and big panties and try to blot the slurpee with some Kleenex. Some of it got on my jeans too, but it wasn't near as noticeable. I hear a noise from my closet and I open it to see Andrea wiggling through the hole.

Andrea and me got rooms next to one another and each of us has a closet that is half the length of the wall between us. All that was between the two closets was a thin board. So, without Mom and Dad knowing we put a hole through that little wall so that we had a secret passage between the two rooms. Back before Andrea turned into a bitch, and before I grew like a balloon, we used to sneak into each other's rooms at night and we'd try to scare each other. We also used it when Mom grounded one of us. We'd sneak through the hole and play quiet with one another.

So, Andrea crawls through the hole and looks at me in my bra and panties and I'm crying.

"Janelle," she said, "what's wrong?"

She's not being a bitch for once. She doesn't even look at me like I'm gross even though I'm almost naked. I don't know how, but I tell her about the freezee and about how all the kids call me Jawhale and Jafatass. Then I talk about how I don't have any friends anymore, but by that time I'm crying too hard and Andrea probably didn't understand hardly anything of what was coming out my mouth.

She sat kind of on my desk while I talked and blubbered on. Andrea went and did the most amazing thing, she actually hugged me which was weird because since the beginning of the year she'd been acting like I smelled like dog poop. Instead of telling me that I need to lose weight or smile more like Mom does, she says that she got some extra money and she was feeling hungry so maybe she'd go down to the Kum n

Go where they got a Goodrich in there and get us some ice cream.

Now, if I wasn't such a pig, I wouldn't have needed Andrea to be nice to me. Or if I hadn't been a pig, maybe I would have said no I'm going on a diet right now or something. But I kind of nodded and Andrea smiled at me and she gave me another hug and said she'll be right back. I picked up my sweatshirt and jeans and I was walking toward the kitchen where the washer and dryer are in the back by the back door. I saw Andrea get into her car and that's the last I seen her.

Chapter Sixteen
Wednesday, October 19, 2016

As he couldn't whistle, Mark would do something he called air whistling. His mouth pursed as if to whistle and he blew through his lips. He could control the sound enough to air whistle whatever song he wanted.

As he pulled into his driveway, Mark air whistled Harry Belafonte's "Angelina" and drummed his fingers on the steering wheel in time with the music. His hand reached up and hit the garage door remote without even looking at it. The garage was detached from the house, connected only by a thin paved path that took a surprising circuitous route to the front porch.

He pulled his little Toyota into the small garage, stopping when his windshield touched the hanging ping-pong ball.

Still air whistling, Mark leaned over and grabbed his computer bag, the bag of groceries that would soon become a hearty and bland meatball soup, and his coffee thermos.

He did all this in that thoughtless way of those who follow the same schedule every day. Mark rather liked schedules and air whistled his contentment in routine (which is not at all the same as happiness), all the way from the detached garage to the front porch.

"Hi Mark, you didn't even see me wave, did you?" Bill asked from the porch swing.

Mark dropped the thermos, which bounced harmlessly onto the grass.

"Tonight? Are you kidding me?" Mark asked. "I can't do it. I have plans." A note of desperation hid in the words. "I'm retired, anyway," he added.

"Not here on FBI business," Bill said, holding his hands up in a don't-get-yourself-in-a-tizzy gesture. "This is a purely personal visit. With a small bit of business at the end. I wanted… Did you say you had plans for tonight? What is it? A date?"

Mollified that he wouldn't have to help catch a murderer, Mark picked up his thermos and brushed past Bill. He felt kind of angry but a little relieved as well. "Not a date," he said as he opened the door. "Not tonight, at least."

When the door opened, Frodo the Cat streaked out and rubbed against Mark's legs in feline giddiness. Mark bent down to pet his cat.

Bill's thin face morphed into surprise. "Not tonight?" When Bill spoke, Frodo looked at the agent with suspicion.

"Maybe this weekend. It's complicated."

"So, last weekend went well?" Bill shook his head, the look of surprise now a sly grin. "I'm happy for you. Genuinely happy. Go to dinner, make small talk, eat. That's not so hard."

Mark gave his friend a sardonic smile. "Big advice from the divorced FBI agent who lives in a one-bedroom apartment."

"Separated. Anyway, life is about nuance, Markie," Bill used the nickname he'd given his friend many years ago, "and this is one we should discuss over dinner. I bet you're making soup tonight. Or frozen pizza. Probably something Italian."

"Meatball soup." Mark smiled ruefully. "Jesus, am I predictable."

"You make it sound like a bad thing." Bill pointed under the swing. "I made some of that cheesy garlic bread you like." Apparently deciding that he'd had enough petting, Frodo gave one last reproachful look at Bill and slinked down the steps of the front porch. "That cat has never liked me," Bill muttered.

"Cheese bread? That is the first decent thing you've said tonight," said Mark, who felt bad about bringing up the divorce. "You should have started with the bread. Always lead with bread."

"Looks like you might be leading with a French loaf this weekend," Bill suggested.

Mark laughed, "You forget the no-touching-rule. Anyways, it's more like a breadstick."

"Shit, I'm a matchstick, and I'm still getting dates," Bill roared. "Anyways, there's somebody for everybody. Maybe you'll find a way around the no-touching rule. What's she like?"

Instead of answering, Mark said it wouldn't take long to get the soup going. He'd already rolled the miniature meatballs that morning. He'd fry them with onion and garlic in his large pan. When browned, he put it all in the cast iron pot. He'd add beef stock, spices, tomato paste, whatever vegetables he could find in the freezer, and a box of macaroni. Add heat, wait 15-20 minutes or until the macaroni was cooked. Serve. With cheese bread.

"So, what is it you want me to do?" Mark asked from the kitchen.

Bill could hear the alertness in his friend's tone. Not for the first time, a wave of guilt washed over the FBI agent. Forcing that feeling down, he replied, "I'd like you to help me with my parent's 50th wedding anniversary present."

Mark poked his head out. "Aren't you literally 49 years old?"

"I am," Bill said.

"Cutting it a bit close to the right side of wedlock, weren't they?"

Bill pretended indignation, "They were very much in love, in case you're wondering."

"Hmm." Mark returned to the cooking. Soon Bill could hear the sound of meat frying. Mark spoke up, "I don't mean to rain on your parade, but are you sure I can help? I'm crap at buying presents for people. I'm glad to help, don't get me wrong, but don't you know anyone else to help."

"I don't need help choosing a present. I'd like to use your gift. Actually, I'd like to pay you as an artist."

For several seconds, Mark did not reply. Bill walked into the kitchen.

"You want me to touch something?" Mark said without looking over his shoulder. "I dunno, dude."

Bill reached into his pocket and pulled out a plastic baggie. "It's a locket. It has pictures of both my parents. Dad gave it to Mom the first Christmas they were together. She's worn it every day since, even when she went into the hospital for the hip replacement."

"I'd forgotten about her hip. That's not something I'd like to see again." Mark had gone with Bill to the hospital after his mom had the accident.

"Look, Mark. You don't have to do it. God knows I owe you so much."

Mark shook his head. "You don't owe me anything."

Bill grumbled in his low voice, "Anyway, if you don't want to do it, let me know. It's no pressure. I know that when you're in that fugue state, your drawings are incredible…"

"Isn't it funny I can't draw anything beyond stick figures in real life?"

"… and I thought it might be nice if you could use your gift for something kind and beautiful, not some kid getting lost in the woods…"

"… or smothered by her own mother."

"Exactly."

Mark used a plastic spoon to move the meatballs around the frying pan. The looked almost ready. "For you, I'll do it. And for Ron and Judy; those are good people."

They let the subject drop and instead talked about Bill's kids, which was a nice, safe subject. They did not talk about the murder investigations or the possibility that Eric Vandergeest was back and killing again.

Between the two of them, the cheese bread disappeared like a fart in the wind. After they'd eaten pushed back from the table, Mark's expression clouded over. "I don't get to control what I draw, Bill."

"I know."

"Maybe I'll draw your dad hitting your mom."

Bill replied evenly, "He never hit her."

"I might draw them having kinky sex. You sure you want to see that? There might be all kinds of weirdo sex toys. Like to see the look on their faces when they open that present."

"I can always look away."

"Oh, no, no; you're looking too," Mark said, "I don't want to be the only one who has to remember seeing your dad wearing leather chaps."

Bill laughed so hard he had to wipe away a tear. "Seriously, now," he said, "I'd like to pay you for doing this."

Mark interrupted, "Don't need the money." Years ago, the city had quietly given Mark part of the proceeds from the estate of the man who'd damaged him. "I'm reminding you that you never know what you're going to get. What if all I draw is your parents fighting? Or your mom having an affair? Your dad accidentally running over someone with their car and driving away?"

"No way my folks ever cheated or anything else," Bill said, citing the framework upon which his life and career had been built.

"Do you ever really know anyone, Bill?"

Bill snorted. "C'mon, what is that, narration to some cheap TV show? 'Do you ever really know anyone?' I know you, Mark. You know me. I know my parents."

"I'm just saying," Mark said.

Bill folded his arms. "I'll take that risk."

Mark knew his friend could be stubborn as sin and knew better than to push it further. "Fine. Set it up."

Mark's living room was not terribly large but it was spare. All he had was a couch, a side table, a chair, an entertainment center, and a rack of paired dumbbells that ranged from 10 to 30 pounds. It took Bill about ten minutes to set up the easel. He used expensive stock paper and clipped the stack of pages to the easel to make sure Mark didn't accidentally jar the paper loose.

Instead of slightly ill-fitting khaki pants and a button-down shirt, Mark came back from his bedroom wearing baggy sweatpants and an oversized sweatshirt.

Bill wondered if Mark even tried on his clothes at the store. *Probably not*, he thought, as his friend cared so little for how he appeared to the world. Mark had once mentioned that he washed all his newly bought clothes before he ever wore him. He never shopped for clothes at the Goodwill, never set foot inside a Goodwill, never came within a hundred yards of any thrift store or garage sale.

"Did you ever do anything like this before?" Bill asked.

"What? Use my power for non-nasty stuff?" Mark asked. "When I was in high school, I took this art class. Mrs. Barry. Everyone called her Mrs. Deb. She was from the South. Anyway, I thought she was pretty nice. So, for the last portfolio, I thought it would be interesting to see what I could do. So, I went to a bunch of garage sales and bought up whatever was cheap and looked like it held sentimental value. I grabbed a… what did I get… a tennis racquet, a worn stuffed animal, a broken watch, and an old tie.

"I took all this stuff home and I get everything ready. After my Mom went to bed, I got up, put the four things together, took off my gloves, and grabbed all four items at once."

"What happened?" Bill asked. Mark had never talked about this before.

"I drew some of the strangest, most surreal things I've ever seen. And I woke up with a headache."

"What did you draw?"

Mark looked at the ceiling for a second. "Imagine taking a couple of short stories. Four of them. Imagine taking all the words in the four short stories and jumble them together. It's kind of like that except for memories. I remember drawing a little girl with snakes instead of arms, a rooster floating over a waterfall, stuff like that. Drawn in photographic detail."

"You sound either like an artist or a man who's insane."

"It's awful," Mark said, "either way. I have the drawings somewhere in the basement. I'll show you some day. Okay, let's do this before I lose my nerve."

When Mark grabbed the locket, his eyes did that rolling in the back of his head thing that always looked so Hollywood. Bill sat back on the worn couch and watched images unfold.

The first image was of a young woman sitting behind a desk. She was beautiful. Her dark hair roiled from her face like curving water. Her eyes crinkled from her smile as she looked upward at a man with much darker skin, Ron Mallory, looking so very young.

"Wow, she was a looker," Bill whispered. Then, louder, as if narrating, he continued, "They met in a library. I wonder if this was the first time they ever talked to each other. I can't see what book it is…"

After a few minutes, Mark made his waving motion and Bill took the first sheet away. Mark's face began to contort, his expressions unrelated to any emotional state. The pencil dashed across the page, and for several minutes Bill could not make sense of the image.

His mother's face, still young, began to appear. He could see his father's arm around her. They were in bed, naked. "Oh, shit," Bill said, "I think I see my mom's nipples." But, true to his word, Bill refused to look away. "I'm going to have to burn that picture."

Mark continued to draw. The next image was that of his dad looking into a mirror, still young but not quite so young. His mom's arms wrapped around his dad. She was pregnant.

Then a drawing of his mom in a hospital gown holding Bill.

A drawing of Bill holding his mom's hand as they walk on a bridge.

A drawing of his mom, no longer young but somehow still young. Bill could not explain it, He wondered if this was how his dad saw his mom, as eternally young.

A drawing of his mom while eating dinner at some fancy restaurant.

His mother, now middle-aged, hugging a teenage Bill in a football jersey with the word "Vikings" across it. His thin, smiling face still looked a little annoyed.

A drawing of Bill walking away.

A motel room, some trees visible out the window. He had no idea where the room was.

His mom, still youthful in her sixties, eating an ice cream cone.

When Mark dropped the pencil, he staggered. Bill grabbed his friend's shoulders and guided him to the easy chair.

"How long?" Mark asked after drinking some water. "How long was I under?"

Bill checked his watch. "Twenty-seven minutes. That's a record."

"Are the drawings okay? I won't see them for a while. It's like they need time to load into my head."

"They're beautiful, Mark. Beautiful."

Mark smiled wanly. "Oh, hey, I forgot something."

"What's that?" Bill asked.

"My art teacher, Mrs. Deb. She gave me a D for my project."

"She gave you a D? Wow, that's cold."

"On it, she told me to stop doing drugs."

"If she only knew what you did to get those drawings," Bill chuckled.

"No shit. I'm happy the drawings turned out okay. I think I'm going to regret doing it, though, when I start seeing the images."

"There is one, a nude of my mom…"

"It's not that," Mark said, "it's that your parents have had a full, happy life. Right?"

Bill nodded. "I'd agree with that."

There was a pause.

"It's that I'm wondering," Mark said quietly, "if it's easier to deal with nightmares every night than it would be to see all the wonderful things I can never have."

That night, hours after Bill Mallory had gone home to a lonely one-bedroom apartment, a shadowy figure emerged from the darkness of a neighbor's tree. The figure took a few hesitant steps towards Mark's house. In the figure's hand was a dead cat, its gray head twisted to an unnatural angle. Vandergeest laid the still warm Frodo on the welcome mat in front of the door. He arranged the corpse just so, in an almost loving manner the way a parent might place a fussy child sleeping into the crib. Vandergeest withdrew into the shadows of the trees again, perhaps imagining Mark's face the next morning when the front door opened. He turned and Vandergeest was gone into the night.

Chapter Seventeen
Thursday, October 20, 2016

The next morning, Mark wandered into Suzy's, a little retro café near school, and saw his friend Lawrence already seated. Lawrence raised a hand in greeting but did not wave it about in some mockery of joy.

Winding through the morning customers, Mark nodded at his friend and slumped into the seat, his backpack thumping to the ground.

"Frodo," Lawrence said, "was the best cat. And I hate cats."

Mark nodded again.

"He was there? On the front porch?"

Mark said, "Yeah. Frodo's neck looked funny. I am having the vet look at him."

"Do you think…" Lawrence trailed off.

Mark looked out the window. He still couldn't decide what to tell his friend. They'd been working together for years and Mark had never said a word. Mark was a regular guest at Lawrence and Micah's house to play Settlers of Catan and

Star Frontiers. Mark had brought some things to show Lawrence but was afraid to tell him everything.

To be honest, Mark was afraid Lawrence would be angry at him. Mark would be, were Lawrence to keep such a secret for so long.

"… would want to hurt you," Lawrence was saying, "you're probably the most non-confrontational person I've ever met."

It took all of Mark's will to say, "I have an enemy, actually."

Lawrence's eyes widened. "No way. Who?"

"It's kind of complicated. I need to explain," responded Mark, "You know that I'm always wearing gloves of some kind, even during the hottest days of summer."

Lawrence said, "You wearing gloves is one of the first things people tend to notice. If you are going to tell me that you have OCD, I should tell you that I figured that out a long time ago."

"I don't wear gloves because I have OCD. I wear them because…" Mark inhaled and exhaled, "because when I touch people or certain objects, I know all about their history."

"You're joking, right? Are you telling me you're psychic?"

"Don't use that term. That makes me look weird. I get images in my head and I can draw them. I mean, it looks like an artist did it. You've seen me draw before, right?"

Lawrence nodded, mentioning that they'd played Pictionary together.

"I can barely do stick figures, right?" Another nod. "This is a photocopy of a drawing I did three years ago." He held out a sheet of paper to Lawrence. "It's shrunk from the original."

Lawrence took the facedown sheet and looked at it. "It's a dude with a knife coming toward the, I dunno, camera lens? It's creepy. This is happening in a house, maybe an old lady's house. Look at that couch. You did this?"

Nodding, Mark said, "It's the first of four drawings I did after I touched an antique watch that belonged to a woman named Dorothy Gross, whom the police found murdered in her home after Dorothy's daughter hadn't been able to contact her mom for a week." Mark drew a second piece of paper out. "This is the second image."

After taking the drawing and looking at it for several seconds, Lawrence gave Mark a troubled glance. "You really did these? This one, it looks like this guy is about to rape Dorothy."

"Eric Vandergeest did. Then he did this." Mark offered the last two drawings from his backpack.

Looked at them for only a moment. He took them all and turned them face down. "You really, really did that?" he asked. "You can touch anything? And you have to draw it?"

"Not just anything." Mark took off his right glove and touched the fork. "This silverware or napkin or table, I can touch them no problem. I think it's because there's no personal history there. I don't even want to think about how many lips have caressed this here fork."

"You know," Lawrence answered, "I'm not sure I do either."

"That's why I'm a little OCD. Just a little. But if I went to your house, I'd have to wear gloves. There's no telling what objects would set me off. It could be your couch or a book or a pair of handcuffs that you and your husband like to use on the weekends. Then, boom, I'd be drawing all kinds of intimate moments."

"How did you know about the handcuffs?" Lawrence asked sharply. "Oh, you were guessing…" He reddened.

A young woman who looked eerily like Dorothy Gross from the photos, brought plates of food (Lawrence knew what Mark liked). They began to eat in silence, but Lawrence clearly was thinking through the information.

"Sooooo, do you, like, work for the police?" he asked.

"The FBI, actually. And it's completely unofficial. My name does not appear on any server, computer, or whiteboard of any person at the Bureau. Only a handful of people know who I am, and the information I provide never sees the inside of a courtroom."

"Why do they use you then?"

"I am often able to tell them exactly how a person died, where their body is, and who did it. It saves the investigators a lot of time. I've also helped find a few kidnapping victims. Alive. Obviously, that's meaningful to me. As you know."

"Yeah, I know, Mark."

They ate for a little while. The French toast was fine, Mark thought, but found eating the sausage patties (as opposed to links, alas) analogous to chomping on a meat-flavored eraser. As for the fruit cup… He found two usable grapes and one chunk of honeydew. The remaining pieces of fruit only made Mark sad, contemplative of the fact that all human beings would one day die. He mentioned this to Lawrence, who nodded.

"I'm thinking that these pancakes were prepared by an alien who had been shown pictures of pancakes before but received no actual information as to how to correctly prepare them." He lay down his fork. "They could use those pancakes to serve as a heat shield for space-bound rockets. You know, you're kind of a superhero. By day, you are mild-mannered and slightly asthmatic Mark Peter. At night, you are still mild and wheeze if you run for a city block, but you solve crimes. It's kind of cool."

"Not so much. I get a lot of nightmares. Sometimes when I'm awake." Lawrence made a noise. "Yeah, once while I was driving. I get headaches, too. I'm not helping the FBI anymore. But now there's this guy. Vandergeest. The guy who killed Dorothy?" Mark pointed at the picture.

"From five years ago? Yeah, I remember he died."

"He might not have. I think he killed Frodo. No one's connected the dots yet, but…"

"Wait, you think Vandergeest is after you."

"Yeah. He is after me."

Looking off into the distance, Lawrence sorted through this. "Mark, you are my friend. I have to ask: is there any chance that Vandergeest is after me too?"

"No," Mark said softly, then more loudly, "Absolutely not. No chance in the world."

Despite the rise in volume, Mark did not sound certain.

Chapter Seventeen
Friday, October 21, 2016

"So," Dylan said, "tell me about this case. I wasn't here when Vandergeest did his original murders."

Mark stared straight ahead, not answering.

"Hey, I'm sorry about your cat."

"Let's not talk about that," Mark interrupted.

When Mark woke up, Frodo had not been there. That was not unusual. When Frodo didn't pop out to rub against Mark's legs when he went downstairs to make breakfast that was unusual. Mark called out to his cat. Nothing. He'd jingled this feathery cat toy to get Frodo to come out. Nothing. He looked downstairs to see if the cat entrance had been blocked. Nothing.

Mark walked outside, and almost tripped over Frodo's body.

"I'm a dog person myself."

"That makes all the difference in the world, Dylan." Mark did not look over. "I'm all better now. Thank you for that."

"Fuck off. I'm trying to be nice."

"You're probably one of those people who think men who have cats are weak, right?" Mark asked. Dylan sputtered, confirming what Mark had long thought. "So, if you don't mind I'd like to not talk about Frodo."

Mark had learned several things over the past 24 hours. He learned that Bill got very concerned over Frodo's death, insisting that the cat be given an autopsy (officially, an autopsy performed on an animal is a necropsy, but Frodo was smarter than most people Mark knew, and necropsy sounded so very cold). He'd subsequently learned that Frodo's neck had been broken and that the kitty hadn't suffered. Mark asked this several times of the veterinarian to make sure. As to what happened, Bill could not say. But the question of who killed Mark's cat sat unasked like a bomb.

"Let's talk about something else," Dylan said finally.

How about not talking? Mark wanted to ask. But then he realized that he did want to change the subject. "What about?"

"The murders. The original ones." Dylan had something of a one-track mind.

"Fine," Mark sighed, "What do you want to know?"

"Everything."

"You know there are case files. There's even a book devoted to him. The Heartland Hunter, I think it's called."

"I've read the case file. I've even read Toby Kocher's book. It's called The Hunter in the Heartland, by the way. But you know things that weren't in the files or the book." Dylan looked over. For a second, Mark actually saw that she was curious.

"Jesus, I don't know," Mark said. "Where are we going, anyway?" They had taken Dodge out past 180th Street, past the suburbs to an exit which led to a roughly paved road. The government-issue sedan took the transition from rough pavement to gravel without protest. She was taking him shooting. Bill's idea.

"I know this guy. He has some land out here. Thirty acres. He doesn't mind a little target practice. We're kind of dating, actually."

"He's not going to be there, is he?" Mark asked, memories of gym class crowding into his mind.

When Dylan said no, Mark relaxed a slight bit. "What do you want to know? He murdered nine people that we know of."

"There were more."

Shaking his head, Mark agreed. "Probably. I don't know how many." Privately, Mark thought at least 15, but he didn't want Dylan to know that.

"What was he like? Vandergeest. Betcha he was a fucking nutjob." Dylan pulled from the gravel road onto what might have been a driveway. Really just a pair of tire ruts, dug deep into the ground. "It gets a little bumpy," she said.

Of course, Mark thought as he bounced in his seat as if he were riding a bull, *it would be less bumpy if you didn't drive so fast.* "He wasn't a nutjob," Mark said. "He was someone who expressed his sexual fantasies by killing young women. There was nothing insane about him. Just evil.

Dylan didn't respond, didn't even seem to hear. After a few more minutes, she slowed the car and they came to a copse of trees. "Here we go." They got out of the car and Mark retrieved a case from the trunk and handed it to Mark.

"I bought this," Mark said, "during the first wave of Vandergeest's murders. I got paranoid. You read the letters, so you know why. Never shot it, though." Mark took the .38 revolver out of the case, looked at it.

"Hey, watch it." Dylan reached out and redirected the barrel of the gun so that it wasn't aimed at his chest. "You never heard of the cardinal rule of guns? Don't point the motherfucker at someone unless you plan on firing."

"Sorry." Mark felt embarrassed in a way he wouldn't have if he'd been with Bill. "He wasn't a nutjob, you know."

"Vandergeest was a serial killer. He might have been rational, legally sane, but he was a nutjob. Anyone who did what he did has to be."

Part of the problem with Dylan lay in the fact that she saw the world as either one way or the other. "Well, I've known killers who suffered from madness," Mark said, "Their minds feel like those fun house mirrors that distort everything. Vandergeest wasn't like that. His mind worked."

"What, was he like that Hannibal Lecter guy from Silence of the Lambs?" Dylan had taken Mark's weapon and began to load it for him. "This is some old ass ammo."

"Well, it's what I got," Mark responded. "Hannibal Lecter is some kind of superhero. I'm serious. He never makes a mental error in any of the books. Real life serial killers are not uber-geniuses. Some are smart, most aren't. Vandergeest was normal in a lot of ways. He had a job and girlfriends. He went out with his co-workers on Friday nights. What was different about him was that what he really cared about was acting out his murderous sexual fantasies. If he saw a girl walking down the street in front of his house, he imagined following her home and bull- rushing her as she unlocked her door. He got hard thinking about tying the girl up, raping her, and choking her to death. What kept him active for so long was the fact that he could suppress his urges long enough to find the ideal circumstances for subduing his victim."

"He got lucky, too," Dylan said.

"You read the letters. It wasn't luck." He tried to change the subject. "It's cold outside."

"Well," Dylan said, flipping back to condescending, "gunfights don't just happen in climate-controlled conditions. They happen in the real world. They happen quickly, even though it doesn't feel like it when you're in the action. And they usually end pretty quickly too. Man up, little dude."

I could shoot her. The thought burst through Mark's mind in an instant. Hide the body. God knows I've seen it done in my head often enough. "So, where do I shoot?"

Dylan made an oh-yeah-I-forgot gesture and went back to the trunk. She emerged with some cardboard squares, a marker, and a staple gun. On one of the squares, she wrote "HEAD" in big letters and surrounded the word with a face-shaped oval. The second one received a "CHEST" designation and a third became "GUTS."

After spending a second looking at the trees, Dylan selected one and walked over to it. She stapled the first square at about the correct height, looked at her own chest and stapled the other two. "There," Dylan said, a little pleased with herself.

"Wow, hope you didn't have to sell blood for those targets."

"Don't worry. You probably won't hit them anyway." Dylan walked back. "Now, show me your shooting stance."

Mark looked at his feet. "There's a stance?"

"There are several. Okay, here's what you need to do…"

"No touching, okay?" Mark interrupted.

Dylan gave him a look. "Do I look stupid? Or do I look like someone who's worked with you for four months? Give me a break. Stupid babysitting duty." Mark hadn't thought about that, that Dylan wanted to be in the action and resented this task. "Just do what I do. You're right- handed?"

"Yeah."

Dylan shrugged. "Whatever. Stand with your feet a little more than shoulder-width apart. No, move your right foot back about six inches. Bend your knees a little bit." She sounded professional, quiet. "Hold the gun in your right hand. Do you have to wear the gloves?"

"I bought this gun secondhand," Mark replied, not bothering to say what would happen if he touched it without the glove.

For a second, Dylan looked like she wanted to say something, but instead did a small eye roll. "Whatever. Hold the gun and cover your left hand with your right like this. Bend forward a little bit, like you're about to fire a gun with some recoil, not that weak-ass .38."

When Mark managed to position himself correctly, Dylan gave a kind of approving nod. "I don't think I look like they do in the movies," Mark said.

"Well, you don't look like most cops." The agent seemed to realize she'd been insulting and softened her voice, "I don't give a crap how they look in the movies. What I care about is that you put a bullet in the bad guy, not in the wall three feet to the side.

The first five bullets managed to miss the targets, even though Dylan had placed Mark only ten yards away. "Are you even aiming?" Dylan asked in frustration.

"It's harder than it looks."

"Here," Dylan said, taking the gun. She examined it, pointed it at the tree, and fired four times. Four holes appeared, one in "HEAD" and three in "CHEST." If that tree had been a human, it would be an ex-human after Dylan finished shooting. Mark felt his face reddening. As if he needed yet another example of how he faltered in the trials of modern manhood.

For the next half hour, Mark inhaled lungful after lungful of gun smoke as he peppered surrounding trees with stray bullets. Dylan kept up with tips for improved marksmanship, "Don't pull the trigger, squeeze it," and, "look down the sights so that it looks like one bump of equal height and perfectly between the other two bumps."

After what seemed about two weeks of pumping rounds of lead into the thin air and beyond, Dylan's frustration won out, and she told Mark to take off his noise-cancelling headphones.

"You are the worst shot I've ever seen. If you ever have to use that thing," she gestured at the revolver Mark was putting back into the case, "please pray to God that you are no farther than a foot away from your target. Even then, who knows?"

Although he tried his best not to feel like an utter fool, Mark felt like an utter fool. He nodded his reply and hoped she would not try to make conversation. They got into the car and Dylan took the uneven dirt track with the same fervor as before.

Before they reached the gravel road, she spoke. "I don't see why everyone is so surprised," Dylan said, staring off at the trees.

"That I can't shoot a gun?"

"No, I assumed that. That Vandergeest is back. I mean, when he jumped off the bridge, did you guys look for a body?"

Mark nodded. "Bill said that they've never sent so many people out into the river. And he didn't quite jump."

"What happened?"

"Have you ever seen an entire city in a panic?" Mark asked.

Dylan shook his head.

"It's spooky. They called him the Bike Path Strangler at first, mostly because a lot of the bike paths in Omaha are next to little creeks. But Vandergeest got pissed off about that. He thought that 'Bike Path Strangler' sounded pretty weak. So, he sent a video of him murdering Mandy Irby to the news channels and put it on YouTube."

"Shit," Dylan whistled. "I've seen that video. Forced myself to watch it."

"I haven't seen the video, Dylan, I've seen the murder itself. I can tell you Vandergeest put the camera on top of a bookshelf in order to film it. I can tell you that I smelled urine because Mandy was so scared."

"You lived that shit?"

"I was there at the beginning, with Megann Artis. That didn't ding anybody's radar. Megann was a troubled girl and had run away from home a few times before. Megann's mom told everyone she could that something was wrong but… you know."

"She was a troubled girl."

"Even after they found the body in Papio Creek right off of Giles Road, strangled. The police suspected that it was some kind of drug thing.

"But Bill asked me to see if I could help. So, I said I would."

"I've seen the drawings."

"What happened was that I went to the apartment where Megann lived. Her mom answered the door, you could smell the alcohol rolling off of her. You could see why it was that the police didn't believe the mom. She was white trash, you know? It was pretty easy to look at the mom, at how Megann didn't do so well in school, how she was starting stuff with other kids…"

"Like fights?"

"High school stuff. Not hard to look at a kid like that from the outside and think that she got messed up in some kind of drug deal or got the wrong boyfriend. But that mom, I think her name was Jenny, you could tell she loved her kid. The alcohol was the only way that Jenny knew how to get through the day. I think she died a couple of years later. Some kind of disease, but she really died the day they found her daughter in the creek.

"Anyway," Mark continued, "Bill does his whole spiel about how maybe I could help, that it was unofficial and the FBI would deny any involvement of outside parties. And, yes, she asked if I was some kind of psychic."

Dylan gave a little smile. "You hate that."

"Yeah, I do. So, Bill gives his spiel and Jenny says sure but she'd like to watch. I didn't care much for that but I was already there."

"Did you complain as much as you usually do?"

Mark gave her a glare. "You ever been raped and murdered? No? Well, I have been in people's heads as they have died some thirty or forty times. You get to feel everything they feel. Everything. I felt every knot in the ropes Vandergeest used to tie Megann up, I felt her fear as he raped her, I felt my lungs beg for air as Vandergeest choked the life out of her while he watched. He was wearing a ski mask, but I had to look into Vandergeest's dead, heavy-lidded eyes as he did it. So, yeah, maybe I bitch and moan a little bit before I do my drawing thing. You know what? I still do it. Every single little time."

Holding up her hands in a defensive motion, as if she were warding off a knife attack, Dylan said, "Whoa. Jesus, sorry."

"You've had a lot of fun with me since you came on," Mark said, his anger showing in his cheeks, "and I haven't said shit. How about I take off my glove here and we shake."

Dylan shied away from Mark a few steps. "I said I'm sorry."

After a moment, Mark looked away. "I shouldn't have said that. My cat died yesterday. It's very… I don't know. I'm under a lot of pressure right now, so I got this huge headache too. A migraine."

They sat silently for a few minutes, each lost to their thoughts. Finally, Dylan spoke, "So what happened after Megann?"

Mark took a deep breath. He did not like thinking about the murders but he'd rather do that than think about his cat. "He kept killing. The FBI let the Omaha Police know that there was a serial killer on the loose. Then Becca Northrup got taken. She wasn't white trash. She lived with her parents in Regency, was a 4.0 student at Westside, and played varsity volleyball. She was good looking, blond-haired, and had parents who were friends with the mayor. Two days after Vandergeest took her, I was snuck into Becca's room, disguised as a lab tech, and…" Mark waved his hand in a 'you know the rest' kind of gesture.

"I've seen those pictures. Do you often…"

Mark kept talking as if he hadn't stopped. "They found Becca floating in Standing Bear Lake. After the third victim… I can't remember her name."

"Chelsea Ossman," Dylan prompted.

"Yeah, they found her at the Candlewood Lake, people started thinking that maybe dumping them in water was part of his ritual, his, I don't know, M.O. or something."

Dylan chimed in, "Actually, there's a difference. The M.O., the mode of operation, is the practical part of the crime. What kind of tools a guy might use to break into the house, for instance? But what you call his ritual, we call it a signature. It's what a guy like Vandergeest has to do to get off. Vandergeest's signature was strangulation. He had to strangle the women. M.O. was what he used to do it. He used his hands, a rope, a belt. That means of strangling the victims didn't matter. What mattered was that he had to strangle them. It turns out that dumping the bodies in the river was part of the M.O. He did it because it erased a lot of the DNA. After Ashley Chong, victim number four, he stopped putting them in the water. The report never said why."

"It's because he sensed me looking for him."

"Excuse me," Dylan goggled.

"I can't explain it, but I think that Vandergeest was kind of like me. He wrote some letters asking if they had… 'eyes in his head' is how Vandergeest put it. That letter he sounded puzzled."

"I wondered if he was referring to you," Dylan replied. "It's a bit unclear." Mark didn't respond for a second, prompting Dylan to ask if he were okay.

"Frodo was a great cat. Loved that cat," Mark said to himself. "Anyway, Vandergeest changed his M.O. with Andrea Hawkins. He left the Omaha metro area and he buried her in a field. When we found her, his letters got paranoid. He started to get sloppy."

"Didn't he dump his next victim in some woods out in the country?"

"Mandy Irby. And don't use the word dump." Mark rubbed his eyes with the palms of hands. "I saw her death. She wasn't a piece of garbage."

"Sorry," Dylan said. "We just use that word. It's what people like Vandergeest think about their victims, that they're garbage."

"With Mandy, the FBI got DNA evidence."

"Didn't the press start to wonder how you found all these bodies?"

"It came up, but no one had any idea about me, so everyone chalked it down to good fortune."

"Probably Vandergeest's good fortune to not get caught."

Mark shook his head. "It wasn't luck. I said that Vandergeest was like me; I think he could sense when he could get away with kidnapping the girls, when no one else happened to be looking his way. Again, and again, people nearby when the kidnapping occurred talked about how they looked away for a second and the girls were gone. Just gone.

"So, we get the DNA and even a partial fingerprint. By this time, Vandergeest's breaking down. His letters sound wild. He takes Kayla Poole and Samantha Whitaker only a few days apart. He doesn't even rape – Vandergeest liked to write that he 'experienced' them – Kayla. Then, a license plate. He grabs Abbie Kessler in broad daylight. She's the one with him…"

"On the bridge. I've seen the video."

"The one from far away?" Mark asks. When Dylan nods, "There's a closer one. He mentions me by name. It wasn't released. Anyway, you know the rest. Vandergeest jumps, takes Abbie with him. We find Abbie's body a few days later, but not Vandergeest."

"Now we know why." Dylan says appreciatively.

"Now we know why."

Chapter Eighteen
1996

By mid-October, the ear flicking thing had spread from Mr. Butterfield's class to just about every one of my classes. I don't know how it happened, but it seemed like I had one of my four "best friends" in every class. What is more, either Steve Hruska, Seth Wardell, Asher Cooper, or Mike Jennings managed to get within flicking range in each one.

My schedule from hell looked a little like this:

Period 1 – English – Asher to my left and back – Not so bad because Asher was big and fat and had trouble getting to me while the teacher's back was turned. But he did like to call me "faggot" a lot in a nasty undertone.

Period 2 – Math – Mike Jennings to my left – This class sucked. The teacher, Mrs. DePrima, was one year away from retiring. Her favorite teaching method was to pass out worksheets, tell everybody to be quiet, and stare out the window at the oak trees until the bell rang. As long as everyone was quiet, you didn't have to do anything. Ear flicking, as it turned out, could be conducted in near silence. Once or twice, Mike actually drew blood.

Period 3 – Wood Shop / Art (depending on the day) – My one class without any of my four buddies. I didn't really enjoy shop class that much, and Mr. Eastlack did not seem to trust me around the really dangerous machines. However, I did look forward to art class. Miss Chambers made the period semi-enjoyable.

Period 4 – Social Studies – Mike to the back, Steve to the right – Almost as bad as math.

Period 5 – Study Hall – Because Asher and Seth could not sit still to save their lives, they both sat at the front of the room. As I was as quiet as a fart around a pretty girl, I sat in the back row. Easy 40 minutes.

Period 6 – Music / PE (depending on the day) – Given the chaotic nature of these two classes, I could have an ear flick-free period or one of absolute horror.

Period 7 – Spanish – Seth sat right behind me – Fortunately, Ms. Cuadrados ruled the class with an iron fist. Even though he sat behind me, Seth never once tried to flick my ears. Ms. Cuadrados would have eaten him for almuerzo.

Period 8 – Science – Mike to the front – During note taking, it wasn't so bad. When we had to do some experiment, Mike would find a way to my ear. While Mr. Arent explained the lab, I could see him eying the lab tables, coming up with a plan of action to get near enough for his favorite move. Worse, I could see a bunch of other kids looking from one of us to the other, trying to figure out the same thing.

That Tuesday was a bad day, a really bad day. Asher managed to tag me a few times during English, Mike about ripped off my ear in Math and Science, and Seth got to me during Spanish because the sub spent the entire time getting all the other students to behave.

During Social Studies, Mr. Butterfield actually noticed that I had taken to sitting with my head between my hands (the only method I knew to keep the ear flickers at bay, one that caused them to flick the backs of my hands instead – it helped).

"You okay, Mr. Peter?" he asked in a puzzled, helpful tone.

Now, if he had taken me aside after class, I might have told him what was happening. Might. But, given how he'd asked me in front of God and the entire seventh grade, I told him I was fine.

"Are you sure you don't have an ear infection?" he asked. Several students snickered, which he ignored.

"No, Mr. Butterfield," I replied meekly.

"Well, if they start to ache, make sure to tell your mom to take you to the doctor. You don't want to mess around with an ear ache."

I could hear them snickering from behind. If Mike and company felt any gratitude toward me for not ratting them out, they expressed it with a renewed bout of ear flicks, each one resounded like a fleshy pop.

Needless to say, about the time the last bell sounded at 3 p.m., I was done with school. The one thing I could say about my life was that even though my days at school descended regularly into hell, once the final bell sounded, things got better. Mike and his buddies usually forgot about me once school ended.

As usual, I dawdled until everyone else had filed out of class. Best not take chances with Mike. Out of sight, out of mind.

I walked to my locker, looking around to make sure none of my "friends" followed. At the locker, I exchanged a few books and stared at the back of my nearly empty locker for a few seconds. Another day done. I looked to my right, nobody. School had cleared out quickly.

Looked to my left to find Seth, Steve, Asher, and Mike all waiting for me to see them.

"How's your ears?" Seth asked in his little, whining voice. I didn't respond.

"Maybe you'll hear better in your locker," Mike said.

I have to say that Mike's response to Seth made absolutely no sense. How would one hear better in a locker? Mike and his friends were idiots. Not quite at the drooling level, but not too far from it (although Steve probably did drool on occasion).

So, with little fanfare, the four of them managed to stuff me into my locker. Steve tried to jam my backpack in after me, but after three attempts Mike told him to quit and they closed the door. The second the door closed; I could hear the four of the them begin to make nervous noises.

"Hey, retard," Mike whispered through the thin sheet of locker door metal, "if you make a peep and get us in trouble, I'll kill you."

I heard the voice of Mr. Haffey, the vice principal, boom, "Hey, you, what are you still doing here?"

Everyone knew that Mr. Haffey hated kids. Rumor had it that he'd once beat up a seventh grader who was marking up the bathroom with one of those sharpies. Apparently, the kid who got the snot kicked out of him was so scared of the vice principal that the kid had never said a word to his parents.

"We're leaving," Mike's voice sounded vaguely resentful, but not pissy. Mr. Haffey didn't take any shit from students.

I didn't hear anything for a second. "Well, go on." Mr. Haffey said impatiently. The four of them walked quickly away. All I had to do was say something, anything. The adult was that close. Yet I remained silent, fighting to keep my crying from giving me away. When Mr. Haffey left, I wondered if Mike and his friends would come back for me and let me out. Maybe they would drag me to the bathroom for a swirlie.

The minutes dragged by, each slower by turn. One or two other people, adults, came walking down the hall. I began to need to use the bathroom. I couldn't think of what to do.

When I really had to go, I began to explore the locker. I didn't have much room to maneuver, but I got my right hand up to the part where the lock was. I felt a flat piece of metal, a little hinge, which I pulled up. That, to my great surprise, unlocked the dang thing. I fell out onto the tile, able to get my hands up.

My bladder screamed at me to get up, which I obeyed. When I got back to my locker, I discovered that Mike had taken my backpack with them.

Shit.

Chapter Nineteen
Saturday, October 22, 2016

Happy and Mark stood in the dark parking lot off the side of the Big Lake Road. The sun had just set and Big Lake Park looked tinted a cool blue. The remnants of the day's sun still hung orange and red in the air. It had been a hot day for October, still nearly 60 degrees at after 7 p.m. Mark's Prius was the only car in the lot.

They got out of the car and Mark led her down the path to where a creaky dock jutted into the lake. He pointed and said, "That's where they found her. Natalia Chavez."

"I thought you were joking when you told me that you wanted to take me to a crime scene," Happy said.

Mark looked puzzled. "What exactly did you think I meant when I said I wanted to show you where a young woman had been murdered?"

"I thought you were being euphemistic," Happy explained.

"Euphemistic?" Mark looked confused more than annoyed. "Isn't a euphemism when you use a nice word for something bad, like 'passed away' for dead. What's worse than murdered that I would have used the word murdered?"

"Really murdered?" Happy asked. "I don't know. We had Indian food, and now, boom, guess what happened here?"

"Murdered. Jesus, is that some kind of slang that the kids use nowadays for sex or something?"

"No," Happy said, "although it could be by now. I guess I thought maybe you meant a movie or something. Some scary movie, not a real-life murder scene."

"I kind of say what I mean," Mark said. "Not so good with the euphemisms."

"It's one of your nicest attributes," Happy said, "Where some men might escort me to a Thai restaurant or the museum, Mark Peter takes me to the place where a young woman was murdered." Oddly, she did not sound too terribly unhappy, incongruous with the scene thought it might be. Instead, Happy's voice buzzed with bemusement.

"Technically," Mark murmured, "Bill said that this was only the dump site. She was killed somewhere else."

"The dump site and not the actual scene of the murder?" Happy said. "Well, that makes all the difference."

"I wasn't trying to be romantic…"

Happy chimed in, "This isn't even a date? Not a holy-shit-I'm-with-a-man-at-a-murder-site kind of date?"

"Dump site," Mark corrected and wanted to smack his forehead. "I mean, this is a date, or at least I wanted to be with you. I wanted to show you something about me."

"Are you trying to tell me something?" Happy asked, unfazed.

"No, oh no. I mean, this is really impacting my life right now. So, if I'm weird, weirder than usual, I wanted you to know why. Also, uh, I told you stuff about me that no one except the FBI and my sister knows."

"And your cat, too."

"And my cat, too. And Lawrence, now."

Over Tikka Marsala, Mark had told Happy about his cat. How he'd found Frodo in a storm drain when he was still a kitten. How Frodo liked the smell of bleach and rubbed his
146

face against Mark's hands whenever he cleaned the bathroom. How Frodo would sometimes wake Mark up with his impossibly loud purrs in the middle of the night. How Frodo did not seem to mind getting wet.

Happy had asked him if he was going to have a remembrance service or something. "Like a funeral for my cat?" Mark had asked. Happy said people did that, it was a thing. But Mark had shook his head. Frodo was his cat, his friend. He did not need a remembrance service. He needed his cat back.

They walked a little farther out on the slick dock. Because of her foot, Happy grabbed Mark's (long-sleeve covered) arm for support. She rather liked that he was far more concerned about skin contact than that she needed help at all.

"You feel proud," she prodded, "of being able to help find the murderers?"

Mark nodded. He added after a second. "It's a gift like that, but it's getting harder. I don't even think I can do it anymore."

"Have you," Happy gestured at the lake, "used your gifts on this case?"

"No," Mark said, "but Bill wants me to. He hasn't said so, but I know. The thing is: whenever I touch a victim or one of their personal effects, I get images in my head. Forever."

"Drawing doesn't get rid of them." Happy knew enough to phrase it as a statement.

"Yeah. And it's so frustrating. Can't draw for shit in real life, but when I get those visions, I turn into El Greco or something."

Happy squatted and ran her hand through the grass. "It doesn't feel sad here." She looked back at Mark. "You didn't say Picasso."

"What?"

"Most people, when they talk about drawing skills, mention Picasso." Happy pulled a few blades of grass, her head cocked so that her ear faced him. "They say, 'You paint like Picasso, draw like Picasso, sculpt like Picasso.' That sort of thing. Like most people don't know another artist except for Picasso."

Mark said, "Well, there's Picasso's cubist period, for one thing. For another, in El Greco's paintings, everyone looks agonized. I don't draw happy pictures."

"How did she die?" Happy asked suddenly, gesturing toward the lake again, as if Natalia still floated there, bumping up against the dock pier with every lapping wave.

Mark shuddered. "Killers put the bodies in water to get rid of DNA evidence. He strangled her. Vandergeest always strangled his victims. Sometimes he used his hands, sometimes he didn't. With Natalia, Vandergeest tied a piece of rope around her neck, and probably straddled her while he choked the life out of her. He likely did it slow, because…" Mark shook his head, as if flinging away a ghostly memory. "…because he liked the feeling of control. I've been inside his head. He liked, likes to look into his victims' eyes when they die. He did it slow and, when he finished, he dumped Natalia out here like she was a piece of trash, some empty bottle of water."

Neither of them spoke in the silence, instead they listened to the water. When Happy reached up a hand to touch his shoulder, Mark did not jerk away. She had been ready to say that she wasn't going to touch his skin but then didn't.

"I have the power to do something about it, too." Mark lifted up his small, gloved hands. "I could make one phone call and be ready to do it in an hour."

After a moment, Happy seemed to realize she was supposed to speak. "But you haven't yet," she said.

"I'm scared. Every time I do this, it gets harder. Every time. I'm such a wimp."

"Hey." Happy's hand squeezed against his shoulder. "Hey."

"You don't know." Mark sounded like a child and far away.

"I know what painful thoughts in your head feel like. Look like. Remember I told you I used to cut myself?

"When I told you, I made it seem like that was because of Nikki West. There's a story there. Nikki was a complete bitch to me, no lie. But I had other shit too. Like my dad calling me Chub Girl, calling me that even in middle school and I knew he was making fun of me. Like the fights he would have with my mom about whether I was really his. Like him sitting me down when I'm thirteen and telling me that he's not going to pay one red fucking cent for college because I was not related to him. Like my mom screaming, and I mean screaming, at me after Dad finally left, telling me that I was the reason Mom and Dad got divorced.

"So, yeah, I get shitty memories. I totally get why you don't want to do it again. I can't believe I'm telling you about my parents. I'm never going out to Kearney to visit either one of them. Not if I'm really sick. Not even if I ever get married to some wonderful guy who never says mean things to me. Not even if I wanted to rub the fact that I've turned out normal in their faces. Never."

Mark nodded his head. When Happy had finished, he said, "Damn."

"Exactly," Happy laughed. "Damn."

Something had settled between them, not unlike a large and shaggy dog that loved nights spent watching TV on the couch. "So, I guess we're both buggered up," Mark said.

"Looks like it," Happy agreed. "You okay with that?"

"I think so. This is kind of virgin territory for me."

Happy burst out in laughter, a dam burst of laughter.

"What are you laughing at?" Mark said, "Oh." When Happy quieted, he furrowed his brow and began again, "Speaking of that kind of territory. There are probably certain things that couples do…"

"You can say the word sex." Happy started to say more but looked away. "I'm not very big into the constant touching thing anyway. I'm a little bit like a cat. So that's something. Maybe we could touch now, and get it out of the way. Does it work like that? Like ripping off a Band-Aid? Touch each other once and it's all good?"

Mark wistfully shook his head. "You get the firehose every time, or at least the first two or three times. Even Mom couldn't handle it. Always assumed no one else would want to try…"

Mark's voice dropped away, felt it melt into the sounds of the stream. Happy's hand dropped and found Mark's glove. Her fingers, long and thin, entwined themselves into the warm fabric of his fingers. He stole a glance at her, at Happy staring out into the stream where a girl's body had been found. He knew that she was aware of his gaze, yet still she wore a smile on her face. A sad smile, perhaps, he couldn't tell.

"Would you like to come to my mom's house for dinner tomorrow?" Mark asked, surprised at the words coming from his mouth.

If Happy found the request unusual, she did not say anything at first. "I'd love to," she replied.

He leaned into her, felt her thin arm through the layers of clothing which separated him. He felt, or at least he imagined he felt, her body heat tearing through the fabric toward him; felt Happy leaned back into him; felt a happy warmth radiating from somewhere deep inside him all around, all the way to the tips of his fingers; and could feel the heat flying toward this strange girl holding his hand and leaning against him.

"It's really screwed up," Mark said.

"There's always something," she replied in a thick voice. "If it was easy, maybe it wouldn't be worth it."

Mark murmured his agreement and pulled up his hand so he could brush her hand up against his chest. Where his heart beat wildly against his ribs.

Chapter Twenty
Sunday, October 23, 2016

Stacy cooked with a vengeance, as usual, wearing an apron that said "Kiss the Chef". She cut the onions like they had tried to kidnap her dog. As she did, Mark's sister muttered a torrent of curse words, a stream of invective that swam under the chopping sounds to fill the entire house in a miasma of stink.

From the kitchen doorway, Mark watched his sister pensively. One arm crossed around his waist, the other by his chin, his finger rubbing his lips. "Would you prefer I call Bill and tell him not to come?" he asked.

The onion massacre held for brief ceasefire, and Stacy turned around. Waving the knife in the air, she said, "No. I actually want to see your 'friend'. We have a few things to discuss." Stacy used air quotes around the last word. "I'd like to ask him a few questions. Number one, is that lunatic Vandergeest alive and killing again? Number two, what is the FBI doing to stop him? Number three, does Vandergeest know about you?"

"Hey, sis," Mark began.

But Stacy waved the knife in front of her. "Don't 'Hey, sis' me. Two girls are murdered in the manner of Eric Vandergeest. Then Frodo gets killed. Pardon me for thinking it seems like more than coincidence. Man, that was an amazing cat. Also, and I'm wondering this, is Bill going to drag your ass out to the murder sites to help the FBI find Vandergeest? Again? You said you were done, Mark."

"I am." Mark gave a half-shrug. "Bill is my friend, Stacy. And never, not once, has he ever forced me to do anything. I've always volunteered."

Stacy made a 'hmm' kind of noise and dumped the onions, garlic, and peppers into the hot pan. The food whistled, fizzed, and popped. "Yeah, and holding the objects of murder victims, seeing all the shit that you've seen. No effect on you at all, right?"

At the counter, buttering the bread, Skylar shot Mark a glance of some kind.

Rather than answering, Mark took a second to sniff the air. He loved the smell of onions, peppers, and garlic frying. Their combined odors melted with that of the meatballs in the oven. He heard his mom's step, the familiar creek from the living room floor, and felt his mom's hand rest for a second on his upper arm, which caused him to jump almost imperceptibly.

"You two fighting?" Mom asked. She'd been in the bathroom, again. The second time in the half-hour Mark had been there. Mom looked at him, a swirl of emotions crossing her face. Foremost among them was concern.

"Your daughter is not very happy with me at the moment," Mark said. In childhood, Mark and Stacy developed a habit of saying "your child" whenever the other kid had done something bad. "Your child ate all the Oreos," your child didn't wash his hands after he used the bathroom."

"She does seem a bit upset." Mom did not sound particularly displeased; in fact, she sounded as distracted as she usually did. "Any idea why?"

For many years now, ever since Mom went on her anxiety medicine, Stacy and Mark (and now Skylar as well) had made it a point to keep upsetting information amongst themselves. Mom did not react well to upsetting news.

So, Mark shook his head. "Just general disagreeableness," he said.

Mom nodded, added that Stace could get like that, and hugged his shoulder in her most genuine show of affection. When she released Mark's shoulder, she walked into the kitchen. "Need any help with cooking?"

"No, Mom," Stacy started in a shout but modulated her voice, "everything's under control here. Maybe you could get some spaghetti from the shelves downstairs?"

"I can do it," Skylar started, but Mom pooh-poohed her back and said she was more than capable of getting a few boxes of pasta from the basement.

When Mom disappeared down the stairs, Stacy's eyes flashed warning. "If your friend says anything that sets her off," she said, gesturing to where Mom had gone, "I will not be holding back."

"Bill isn't the only one coming over tonight." Mark said. He hadn't mentioned anything before, mostly because he didn't quite know how to broach the idea.

"Is one of your old gamer friends in town?" Stacy asked, a note of hope in her voice. She'd occasionally bring up Mark's friends who had all drifted away over the years.

"Err, no… Just that Happy and I were talking. I mentioned dinner and now she's coming over."

In an ideal world, Stacy and Skylar would have given Mark a pleased smile. Perhaps they would have added a "that's nice" or an "oh, I've heard good things about her." Then neither of them would ever say another word about Mark bringing home a girl for dinner.

Sadly, Mark did not live in that ideal world. What instead happened is that Mark's revelation of Happy coming over acted as a grenade. First Stacy and Skylar's eyes widened. Second, the two women looked at each other and their mouths dropped open. Finally, Stacy's anger, which had begun to fade in the steam of cooking vegetables, became incandescent rage. "You invited your girlfriend over and didn't tell us?" Stacy yelled.

"You have a girlfriend?" Skylar asked. Her brow darkened. "The civics teacher from school? Her?"

Mark lifted up his hands in an "I can explain gesture," but Stacy all but threw the metal spoon at his hand. "Take over," she hissed. "I need to change."

She had been wearing an UNO Mavericks sweatshirt and jeans, which seemed perfectly adequate to Mark, but he knew better than to say anything. He stepped aside to let her pass, and Stacy gave his own clothes a once-over. "This is what you're wearing?" she asked and turned away before he could answer.

Philosophically, Mark went to the stove to keep cooking. "Aren't you going to change?" he asked Skylar.

"Uh, no," his niece responded, sounding very much like the 15-year-old she was.

Mark stirred the peppers and onions around the bottom of the Dutch oven and reflected on how unevenly Stacy had sliced the vegetables.

Forty-three minutes later, at 6 p.m. precisely, Mark went out to the driveway where Happy was pulling in. Stacy, now dressed as if she were going to the Flatiron Grill instead of at home, had suggested that Mark escort his young lady into the house rather than wait for her.

"It's called good manners, you little shit," Stacy had added. She may have still been angry.

Ten minutes before, Bill had arrived. Stacy nodded a greeting from the kitchen, Mom acted as if Bill were someone she'd met before but could not remember when, and Stacy gave him a big hug. He and Bill bumped fists as per usual. He coughed extravagantly, blamed the dog for his allergies.

"You told me not to bring anything," Happy said as she got out of the car. She leaned back in. "So, I baked a peach cobbler."

After the various greetings, Stacy took Happy by the arm and steered her toward the sofa. Mom followed, although she looked puzzled at exactly who Happy was.

Skyler remained with Bill and Mark, looking sourly in the direction of the couch. "What's the deal with you? You don't seem very pleased." Mark said.

"I am very happy you are dating someone," Skylar said. Then, because she inherited Stacy's habit of saying whatever came to mind, added, "but did it have to be Ms. Hapke?"

Bill asked, "What's wrong with her?" Since learning Happy was coming to dinner, he had been wearing a little shit-eating smile. "She seems nice."

"As a person, maybe, but she's a really unfair teacher. She doesn't like me or my friends."

Not ten feet away, Happy sat on the couch explaining how she came to Eastside High School. "After college, I got my master's at Lincoln," she explained. "Originally, I wanted to get my doctorate but life kind of got in the way."

"What happened?"

"I realized that I hated writing academic papers. The thesis, which was called 'Cowardly Lion: The Historical Genius of William Jennings Bryan,' just about cost me my sanity."

"I had this college professor," Stacy said, "for the history of the Soviet Union. I loved that class."

"Where did you graduate from?" Happy asked.

Stacy replied, "Well, I didn't."

"Which is too bad," Mom said in a soothing voice. "I don't understand why. You are so smart."

"Skylar is why," Stacy said, "and she is not going to make the same mistakes I made. Well, considering I made every single mistake possible during my teenage years, Skylar won't be able to help but repeat a few of them."

Happy couldn't think of a thing to say to that, so she asked about the Soviet history class.

"It really was fun, but literally the only thing I remember about that class is a joke the professor told near the end of the semester. Not even sure I remember why it's supposed to be funny. Okay, here it is: Stalin, Khrushchev, and Brezhnev are on the train to communism. The Glorious Train to Communism! It's rolling along fine, then it slows down, and soon stops. Stalin stands up and says, Comrades, I will take care of this. He goes to the front of the train, shoots the conductor, and goes back to the passenger car. He says the train will begin moving momentarily. It does not move. Khrushchev stands up and says he will take care of this. He goes to the front of the train, jumps off, finds the body of the conductor, brushes him off and puts the conductor back in the driver's seat. Then he goes back and assured the others that the train will begin moving momentarily. Nothing happens. Then Brezhnev stands up, says he will take care of this. He goes to the windows of the passenger car and lowers the shades. In complete darkness, he sits and tells Stalin and Khrushchev to close their eyes and pretend the train is moving."

Stacy widened her arms in a ta-da gesture. Happy laughed a little but Mom shook her head. "You should have finished college," Mom said. "Who's finishing dinner?"

The cheese bread came to the table a little too browned, but everything else turned out fine. The six people tucked into the food with gusto, albeit uneasily.

Skylar broke the bubble of small talk by asking Bill about how work was lately. "You know, with the Vandergeest case?" Stacy shot her daughter a very hard look.

"Oh, what's that?" Mom asked.

"It's, uh, an embezzlement case," Mark said, "at the school."

"We're in an advisory role," Bill explained, "this is the jurisdiction of the police."

Stacy leaned over to Happy, who looked confused, and said, "Certain things we don't talk about in front of my mother. Like murder. She's a bit sensitive to dead bodies and what not." Then, a bit louder, "which my daughter should keep in mind."

Skylar ignored her mother's warning and continued, "Yeah, three women have been embezzled already by this Vandergeest guy. This time."

"His name sounds very familiar," Mom mused. "Is it on the news? I never watch the news. Too much evil in the world that I'd rather not know about. I have my magazines and my books, that's enough for me."

"Three victims?" Stacy asked. "I thought there were just two. Did they discover another embezzlement victim?"

"Yes." Bill said. "This morning. Another damned embezzlement. A young woman, again."

"And this Vandergeest person stole all of their money? Why don't they arrest him?" Mom seemed concerned at this, rubbed at her head as if a headache were coming on.

"He's in hiding. We think he's in the Omaha area."

"Do you think Uncle Mark would be able to help?" Skylar asked. She'd never seen Mark use his gifts and had never touched him.

Stacy, who had, answered, "Bill knows that Mark is far too busy to help with an FBI investigation."

"We have not formally asked Mark to help us," Bill admitted with a burping cough.

"And you never will." Stacy's voice was icy.

Mark tried to jump into the conversation, said, "Stace, maybe I might know something."

"They can do this on their own. They don't need you," she replied.

Happy and Skylar had both unconsciously leaned back away from the discussion. Bill sat quietly, watching. Mom seemed confused, as if she'd turned the television to a sport she'd never seen before and could not understand the rules.

"Sometimes you have to forego your own happiness in order to help others," Mark said. "After all, it's a lot of money that's being stolen right now. I'm already feeling guilty that I haven't used my computer skills to help find Vandergeest."

Stacy stabbed at her salad, causing a tomato to burst open at one end and spray Happy with juice. "You already have enough work to do, and the FBI has computer experts of their own." She looked over at Happy. "Sorry about that."

Mom stood up and announced that the conversation was over. She stood and went to the counter. After pulling off a few paper towels, she went over to dab at the smeared tomatoes.

"Enough of this. You two," Mom said dabbing while looking at Stacy and Mark. "I swear, sometimes I wonder if you have ever left your teens the way you carry on. Getting angry over nothing." Mom turned to Happy and said, "They really do love each other, but you know how family is."

"Oh, I know," Happy agreed. "Mark can be quite stubborn, I've found." She smiled at him fondly.

"Stacy too," Mom agreed. "Let's find a different subject, shall we? Mark, how is that cat of yours?"

Chapter Twenty-One
1996

How would I explain losing my backpack? When I left school, it was nearly 4:30. My mom got off work at five. That meant I had to get a move on. I could say that I left it at school. Mom knew I was forgetful. It would buy me a day at most. She would be all over my ass tomorrow to get my homework done.

Okay, that's an option. Maybe tomorrow I could get Mike to give me back my backpack. There wasn't much in there, right? Books, notebooks with notes from my classes, pencils, erasers. No way he wouldn't give them back to me. Maybe he would draw all over the notebooks, write down nasty words about me. I… I could deal with that.

This would be okay. I bet he wouldn't even care. I could make him give my backpack back to me. He couldn't keep that.

I had reached the greens by then. The day had grown windy and I pulled my windbreaker tight against my body. A thought stopped me in my tracks.

The journal. Mike had my journal. No, no, no, no, no, no.

Okay, to back up. Mrs. Newkirk, my English teacher, had asked each of us to keep a dream journal for the past few weeks. When she gave us the assignment, you could hear everybody groan. I did, too.

I mean, I like Mrs. Newkirk and everything. She's kind of trippy, going on about how beautiful the sunset she saw last night was and everything, but a dream journal? C'mon, that is so stupid.

Most of the kids planned on making up a bunch of stuff. At least, that's what they were telling each other when class got out. But I'm the kind of kid that does his homework. So, I grabbed an old notebook, a small one, from this crate downstairs that had all of Mom's old college stuff. It didn't have anything in it.

So, before I went to sleep that night, I put the notebook and a pencil next to the lamp on the table. Mrs. Newkirk said we needed to tell ourselves to remember our dreams before we went to sleep, and that way we would better be able to recollect and write the dang things down.

I said my prayers, asking God to protect Mom, Stacy, and our cat Mittens. Mom kind of peeked in and said goodnight (she'd begun knocking, which was good; she also didn't really tuck me in, which was both good and a little bad at the same time). I tossed and turned for a little while, thinking about how little I wanted to go back to school.

When things got bad, I liked to imagine myself as someone completely different than me. I would imagine that I was a good basketball player and that NBA scouts came to my games. I imagined that I was an Air Force pilot. That night, the first night of the dream journal, I dreamed that Jenny Walker and Kori Carter had been taken by a dragon and held in a dungeon deep in the bowels of the earth. I was the knight, there to save them.

The next morning, I woke up and looked at the notebook, its red cover dim in the light coming through the blinds. And I could not remember any of my dreams. "Damn," I said out loud. "I'll make something up for today."

Throughout breakfast and getting ready for school, I didn't think anything more about the dream journal, except for a passing thought that the whole enterprise was stupid. It's not like the dreams I remembered having were that interesting. Who cares about me playing basketball or going skating with Jenny Walker? I mean, sometimes I had some odd dreams. Like a few nights ago I dreamed that I was in a room with a bunch of my sister's friends, some room I didn't know. My eyes kept closing and half opening, and the whole room was filled with some hazy smoke.

Class that day started with the normal ear flicking routine during first period. Mike made second period a solid 40 minutes of stomach acid. After a fourth period spent getting my ear lobes lengthened, I needed a break. Luckily, study hall afforded me a small measure of peace and quiet.

I sat with the red covered, small notebook in front of me. After several minutes of thought, I decided to make up a dream about being in the Olympics. That seemed safe enough. Maybe gymnastics.

The study hall teacher, Mr. Grummand, harrumphed a warning about everyone keeping their voices down. I opened the notebook to find pictures covering the first few pages (at least the first nine), front and back. Given my current grade of a D in art, I was no future artist. The pictures were too good for me to have drawn. They also told a story, one I could follow as I looked at the pictures.

In the first picture, someone who looked very much like me (same glasses, same flat hair, same nose) stared down at a wide cave, entrance shrouded in black. Instinctively, I grabbed a second notebook, one seldom used for Spanish (Ms. Cuadrados preferred that we take guided notes on worksheets, so she could grade our efforts each day – she was a good teacher).

I began to write a story about me at the mouth of a cave. On the back of the first page, I stood in darkness holding a torch in my left hand, a sword in my right. Chunks of sweat adorn my forehead. While I was getting a D in art class (how I came to be drawing this stuff I had no idea), Mrs. Newkirk thought I was a creative writer and encouraged me to write stories.

I began to weave a story about creeping down a long cave. With each picture (I did not look ahead), the narrative grew in suspense. One image showed me battling a trio of hobgoblins, servants to the dragon. The next showed me victorious, three slain bodies around me in various degrees of hacked-up death.

On page 4, I escaped a booby trap, a poisoned dart missing my contorted body by inches. The night Mark, the one who drew these pictures, was one pretty A-OK dude. On page six, I came upon the dragon. Three pages, front and back, depicted the battle between us. Gouts of flame breaking upon my magic shield, dodging swipes of massive claws.

Finally, I managed to plunge my sword into the dragon's neck; the fountains of blood lovingly detailed in its own picture. I finished writing, my hand screaming in pain from the unexpected burst of writing. The story of the dragon hunt covering three notebook pages in my small, cramped cursive.

Nearly the entire period had passed as I wrote. Luckily, no one sitting near me seemed to notice my feverish efforts. Being a social outcast had a few perks. Wondering if the pictures had finished, I turned the page.

Oh crap.

A full-sized image of Jenny Walker in her seventh-grade cheerleading outfit, which had been half torn off, greeted me on the next page. I closed the notebook and breathed heavily for several moments. Only five minutes left until the bell. Looking around again, I opened the notebook and turned the page.

Oh my, part two. I did not need to see the next page, which caused me to shift uncomfortably in my seat. In the seventh grade, I found that nearly everything caused me to pop a boner. The image I drew (I must have drawn it) of Jenny without any clothes on caused another. Parts of her were covered in shadow, which I assume was because I didn't exactly see too many naked girls.

Curious, I hunched over the notebook and turned the page again. Jenny and I were… doing stuff. I'd seen a few R rated movies, so I knew what we were doing. It's that I'd drawn myself doing them.

Just then, the bell rang. Like every other seventh grader (as it turned out), I'd gotten quite good at covering my boners with a pile of books. Trusting that the walk, and the prospect of getting my ears flicked again, would take care of the discomfort below, I began to walk to the next period's class.

Every night for the past few weeks, I'd been keeping my journal next to my bed. Every morning, I woke up and took a look at the journal to find new stories from whatever fevered part of my mind knew how to use a pencil.

I usually didn't bring the notebook with me, but that morning I'd had a nightmarish thought, *What if Mom found the notebook?* She worked two jobs, but usually she had a few hours off in the afternoon. It would not be inconceivable for her to go clean my room, find the red-covered notebook, and decide to have a look.

Of course, that morning, the worst scenario I could imagine was my mother finding those pictures. If Mike saw them… I mean, the drawings were really good, so that the subjects of the pictures (not just Jenny Walker but every pretty seventh grader in the school plus Miss Matson, the school counselor) would easily recognize herself.

"He could make copies of every page; put them up over the whole school. He could utterly ruin me for the rest of my life," I moaned aloud. "This is really, really bad."

I had crossed the small stream and sat at this bench that was less bench and more cigarette butts ground into the plastic.

While I'm pretty stupid as a rule, I did check to make sure that no one was coming. When assured of solitude, I began to talk through my options.

"Option one," I said. "Get Mom to take me straight over to the Jenkins house. This is the nuclear option. She's gonna have questions and I'm gonna have to answer them. Let's put option one aside."

I quickly talked my way through the other options:

2. Wait and See – If this one was to succeed, I needed to convince Mike to give me back the backpack on the grounds of my school books. Pretend all else is inconsequential. This would require me to both stay cool and act. Since neither of these skills were ones I had ever shown even the slightest aptitude for, this one was out.

3. Break and Enter – Steal the backpack from Mike. Also, get out, mostly because Mike's father was a cop.

4. Ask Stacy – She had her own shit going on, and made it clear she didn't have the headspace for any of mine. However, if I ever made a list of what music to listen to, this would be option #1.

5. Commit Suicide – I considered this one for some time. If the photos ever became public, this would become option #1.

While I was talking through my options, saying out loud, "Six," a man appeared at my left shoulder. "Maybe I can help," he said.

Chapter Twenty-Two
Monday, October 31, 2016

Mark and Lawrence came back from lunch to find a student holding a cardboard box. "This came from the office," the boy, bored as it was possible to be, said. "Are you Mr. Peter?"

"Why didn't you leave it in the mailroom?" Lawrence asked.

The boy shrugged, packing the gesture with an ocean of indifference. Then, apparently realizing he wasn't needed, the boy handed Mark the box and left.

Curious, Mark rolled the small box in his hands, examining it from every angle.

"Aren't they sending a new camera to replace the one in the 100 wing?" Lawrence asked.

"It's not a camera, it's a trombone."

"Har-de-har-har," Lawrence yukked. "It's funny because package is too small," he added in a Russian accent.

"You must get that a lot."

Lawrence's eyes widened. "I appreciate the attempt at genital-related humor. It's better than your usual stabs at jokes. That's odd. It's not from the mailroom."

"You sure it's not inter-office?" Mark asked.

Lawrence pointed at the label, which had Mark's name and room number. "Whenever a package is routed through the district mailing system, they put a little sticker on it that says 'Inter-office mail.' They started that a few years ago. I know someone in media services at central admin who bitched about it for, I mean this literally, months. So, no sticker, no district."

"Yeah, but the student who gave this to me said it just came for me."

"Did you look at said student?" Lawrence smirked, "he was probably high as a kite. He was kind of old. Anyway, it could have come from in the building. But then why wouldn't they walk up here and give it to you? Or they'd leave it by your box in the copy room. Okay, I'm stumped."

Some small part of Mark's brain said that he shouldn't open the box, that it would lead… somewhere. Down a path, through a door. "Maybe it's a bomb," Mark joked as he took a box cutter to the brown tape.

Lawrence gave the half-laugh of someone who knew that he wasn't being told a joke but had to fill in the space with something. "So why are you opening it?"

"Curiosity killed the computer science major." Mark lifted the flaps of the box. "Boom."

Inside, crumpled newspaper pages served as packing. He removed them to see a small device resting on yet more sheets of crumpled newspaper.

"Dude, what is that?" Lawrence peeked over Mark's shoulder. "Is that a walkie-talkie?"

"It appears to be." Mark looked at the yellow Motorola device, "but there's only one. Don't they come in pairs? Aren't they supposed to?"

"Yeah, there's that. Also, who would send you a walkie-talkie? Happy?" Lawrence asked.

I really, really hope so, Mark thought. He took the walkie-talkie out of the box and placed it gingerly on the desk, sweeping aside a vintage issue of Dragon Magazine and a printed e-mail from the district director of technology about how to interact more pleasantly with the students (there'd been complaints).

He'd be a fool not to understand that the walkie-talkie could be from someone else. *Not going to say the name*, Mark told himself, *but I'm an idiot, not a fool.* It could be a practical joke from someone, it could be from Happy (although sending a single walkie-talkie in a box without a very obvious puzzle would not be like her).

"This is kind of creepy," Lawrence said. "It's like I'm living in an Alfred Hitchcock movie. Maybe you have to deliver the ransom to the kidnappers or something?"

"Dude," Mark began.

"No, no. Maybe there's someone out there who is part of a terrorist cell, and you're the only person who can hack in to their communications." Lawrence waved that away. "Nah, why would terrorists attack Omaha, Nebraska? This is the most boring city in the United States. I barely notice Omaha, and I live here. Turn it on."

Mark picked up the Motorola and looked at the back, thankful for once that his particular difficulties required him to wear gloves all the time. "This looks new," he muttered. "I could probably touch it."

"Are you going to?" Lawrence asked.

"Shit no."

"Does this have to do with all those murders?"

Mark considered his responses. At the end, he merely said, "it's possible. But I'm still going to look at what's in here."

Lawrence poked at the box. "You should at least wear gloves."

"It's just newspaper, dude, not a bloody knife. See? Omaha World-Herald. Anyway, I will go ahead and text my FBI friend. He's probably going to send a whole team of agents over here. This is going to suck." Mark pronounced the last word as three syllables. "The students are going to flip their shit." He typed in the words: "Don't make a scene, but" into the phone. Lawrence yelped and Mark stopped.

"Mark, there's a message. Oh, mother puss bucket. At the bottom."

Mark looked. Written on the bottom of the box, in black marker, was the following: "Markie – Let's talk. Turn to channel 18. I'll be waiting but not for long."

Mark looked over at Lawrence, who blew out air through pursed lips. "Mark, dude, this is probably when you should be calling your friend, not texting him."

"I'm going to talk to this guy." Mark picked up the walkie-talkie.

Holding up his hands in a whoa gesture, Lawrence said, "Hey, listen, between what happened with that ICW meeting stuff and you getting a sorta-girlfriend, your Hero level has like quadrupled in the last week, but this is seven kinds of creepy right now. This could be a really bad guy."

"You read the note, Vandergeest's not going to wait around."

"Vandergeest? You mean, like Eric Vandergeest, the serial killer?" Lawrence seemed ready to pee his pants.

Mark nodded. "Anyway, I'm talking to him. I'm not in danger and you'll be a witness. Maybe you can, I don't know, write down what we talk about?"

He seemed to consider it for a second, nods and reaches for a yellow notepad and a half-gone pencil. "My objection to this is on the record, Mark."

"Duly noted." Mark turned the walkie-talkie on and, taking a guess, pushed on the "+" button until the display showed 18.

Unhappily holding his pencil, Lawrence saw his friend's eyes close in something like prayer or concentration. When they opened up again, Mark's expression changed to gravely serious.

"Hello?" Mark said, pressing the speaker button at the side.

For several seconds, the walkie-talkie remained silent. Lawrence heard Mark's phone buzz with an incoming message but he couldn't take his eyes off of the walkie-talkie in Mark's hand.

Finally, a reply. "Hello, Markie. About time we talked." The voice sounded like a computer.

"He's using a voice changer," Lawrence whispered (although there was little need to do so). "I use one when gaming online. It's a thing."

Mark did not acknowledge Lawrence's voice, as if the walkie-talkie was the only thing in the world. "What do you want? I mean, who is this?" He sounded panicked.

"Don't worry about yourself, Mark. If I wanted you dead, you'd have died already. I want to get to know you, my friend. I've spent a lot of time trying to figure you out. Years, Markie, years. We have a connection. I can sense you, and I think you can sense me as well. Do you know when I've killed someone, Markie?"

"No"

"Years ago, I knew when you're looking for me. Those times when you're transported away from this world. I could feel your mind's eyes searching. When I killed that beautiful girl in the little slum town and buried her next to a silo. You saw me."

Mark's face had grown white. "I drew you. I can touch things and I can draw memories. I drew you killing her. Strangling her."

"So, I did," Vandergeest's artificially high voice exhaled through the walkie talkie. "I can feel her clawing at my arms as I strangled her, even now."

"So can I."

Lawrence stood without moving, his mouth partway open. "This is unreal," he murmured. Not that Mark would have heard. Lawrence took his phone from his pocket and began to record the scene.

"You haven't tried looking for me this time around." Vandergeest sounded puzzled.

"No. I haven't."

"Why not? You're the reason they found me before."

"It hurts. To be inside their heads, in yours."

"I see. That explains things, to be honest. I'd been wondering why you weren't in the game. This was such a good idea to finally talk to you. Is your friend there? That scared little Asian fellow? Is he listening to us have a chat? Is he calling the police right now? Because these walkie-talkies have a maximum range in the city of about one mile. I'm ripe for the plucking, aren't I?"

"Damn," Lawrence said and began tapping at the phone screen.

"It doesn't matter. He can call all he wants. The police won't come close to catching me. Of course, I might just have a chat with him. Lawrence Chang, 2926 South 114th. Little cream-colored ranch. Nice house with a nice pine tree in the backyard. Maybe one evening I'll find a spot-on top of that office building across the street and wait for him to come home…"

It took three tries for Lawrence to begin talking to the police. He stuttered out that he needed help.

"Don't you, don't you hurt him," Mark said, his voice flat.

"I probably won't. I wouldn't mind getting to know your other friend a little better. The girl. I've seen you out with her. Melted my heart."

This seemed to wake Mark up. "You touch her and I'll kill you. I swear to God."

"You already tried, my friend."

Mark asked, "What do you want?"

"I want you to do something for me. Two things, actually."

The dispatcher told Lawrence that the police were on the way.

"What is it?"

"One, I want the world to know I'm back. Two, and this is for you, let your friend Agent Mallory know that another body will be coming soon. I'll let them know the details."

"I'll tell him." Mark's face was a grimace.

"One more thing, I'd like to meet face to face. Think about how that might happen. I'll be in touch."

Somewhere, far in the distance, Mark could hear the wail of sirens.

Chapter Twenty-Three
1996

"I've got a great plan," The Angry Man said.

My body froze up. For one thing, the dude was far too close to me. For another, I knew he hadn't come down from either path. Not from school and not from the little gate that led to my neighborhood.

He wasn't a very large man, but I could see that his arms were muscular. He had a short haircut that covered up his balding head. He gave me a smile that he must have thought looked normal. However, his eyes didn't smile, and he held himself like he was ready to run a race.

I licked my lips and looked past him, hoping that someone would suddenly appear on the path. Nope. So, I tried to change the subject. "My mom is expecting me home any minute. I'd, I'd better get going."

The Angry man didn't move, but he did lower himself a fraction of an inch. I shifted my body to the right, wondering if I should try to edge away slowly or make a mad dash.

"Hold on, Markie, I really do have a plan."

As I began to nod, a thought came to me. *How did this guy know my name?* The thought began to permeate my body as a wave of cold fear. I felt my body freeze up. Maybe it lasted only a few seconds, but it was long enough for him to take a step toward me, his hand reaching for something behind him at his waist.

I broke like a rabbit, sprinting to my left. I should have screamed. I should have screamed my lungs out through my throat so loud. He caught me within a few steps. So fast. Arms like iron. Pinning my arms with one of his. Pulling me to the ground. A Rambo knife to my throat. Duct tape around my wrists. Around my ankles. Over my mouth.

"Get over here. Don't you make a sound."

I looked at the ground, at the roots of the tree I lay up against. At the gnarled root of the tree, bulging and strange.

The Angry Man who taped me turned me over. Injected something. Darkness.

I get to two-hundred-eleven Mississippi before The Angry Man stops.

Every part of my body hurts. My wrists hurt because they have been in handcuffs for… days, I think. My shoulders hurt because I can never get comfortable. My back hurts because sometimes he likes to cut me with this little pocket knife that he has set on a nightstand next to the mattress. Just cuts, though, and The Angry Man likes to kiss me where he's cut me.

My bottom hurts too.

The only part of me that doesn't hurt is my face. The Angry Man tells me that he doesn't want to ruin my face.

I try not to breathe too loud because The Angry Man is still there behind me. And I will not, cannot look back at him. He doesn't really like it when I look at him. He has something wrong with part of his face; like part of it sloops and makes him talk funny. I hadn't noticed that at first.

But I can hear him breathing. A ragged sound that becomes more regular with each breath.

We are in the basement of his house, I think. It's lit by large fluorescent lights and the walls are painted bright white, while the tile on the floor is some kind of faded green tile. I am on a plastic covered mattress in the middle of the room. The only other thing in the room is the nightstand. On it is his pocketknife, a revolver he points into my face when he's especially angry, and

"There's something wrong with you," he says, although he says it quietly as if I'm not supposed to hear what he's saying.

I know all sorts of things about him, although I know them only as images. I've seen an older woman, his mom, forcing him to wear a dog collar and sleep in the doghouse outside. I've seen him looking at a bunch of high school kids in old-fashioned clothes (like the 1970s or something). One of them throws a can at him. I've seen him doing his job.

I've seen him with other boys. A lot of boys.

The Angry Man is going to kill me with a thin rope cord he hangs on the wall next to the bed. I'd seen it there before, but didn't really see it. Now I can't help but see it. He's been looking at it too.

"It shouldn't be like this. I don't understand." His words sound slurred. I hear nothing for so long that I think maybe he's gone away and I somehow didn't hear him.

He speaks, out loud this time, to me, "Do they call you mouse at home?" His voice sounds curious.

He doesn't like to be talked to, so I don't say anything. The Angry Man repeats the question.

"Y-yes," I say.

"How do I know that?" The Angry Man whispers to himself. I think I know why but something tells me that it would be a bad idea to speak when not spoken to. I have learned that.

He leaves the room. I don't relax exactly, when he leaves, but after he's gone not every muscle in my body is clenched. If I really relaxed, I would think about how much I hurt. So, I look at the mattress I am on, covered in sticky white plastic. It smells like pee.

I have discovered that the chains on the handcuffs are long enough that I can turn myself onto my side, facing away from the door. In this position, I can maneuver my arms so that they don't feel like they're trapped by handcuffs which run through a steel circle imbedded into the concrete wall. The steel circle does not budge, so I am trapped. Trapped. Trapped.

For the 500th time, I imagine my mom or Stacy or some police officer bursting through the door, imagine it fiercely. I can hear Mom saying kind things to me. I can hear Stacy saying mean things like "What do you mean you couldn't escape? Poor showing, my little brother."

Stacy always says things like that, things that sound mean. She never means any of it, of course. *How did I not realize that?* I think to myself. She's always joking at being mad at me, even when I break her stuff. The thought of that (along with the very real thought that I'll never see her, Mom, or anyone else ever again) makes me cry silent tears.

While I am crying, The Angry Man comes back in again. I do not turn around because he does not like it when I look at him. I can feel his breath on my neck. He flicks my left ear with his finger. Really hard.

"I know about that. The other boys," he says viciously. "There is something wrong with you." A pause. "I'm going upstairs to take a shower and then." He stands up and leaves without finishing his sentence, closing the heavy door behind him.

Even though he didn't finish his sentence, I don't think he had to. He's going to kill me when he's done with his shower. He told me he likes to be clean when he kills the boys he experiences.

He's going to kill me.

Chapter Twenty-Four
Saturday, November 5, 2016

"So, you've got a demented psychopathic killer, who everyone thought was dead, coming after you?" Happy asked. Her voice sounded distant over the phone.

Mark frowned into the speaker. "That's a decent one-sentence summary of my life at this moment. And I have a headache."

"I think I remember that case. All of Vandergeest's victims were pretty young girls, right?"

"Yeah. Eleven that we know of. Nine then, two now."

"Well, I should be safe, at least," Happy said.

"Shut up. You're beautiful." The words seemed to escape slowly from Mark's mouth. He hadn't really meant to say that. "Oh, uh." Mark sputtered.

Happy laughed, "Why yes, I was fishing for a compliment, Mark Edward Peter. Thank you. You're not so bad looking yourself."

"Please," Mark demurred, "I'm pudgy, awkward, and balding."

"Well, I think you're hot."

Mark rubbed his eyes. "You need to stop saying… There are so many…" He stopped, trying to find the words to break up with Happy. If they were even dating, that is. "We can't see each other anymore, Happy. Not on a personal kind of level. This Vandergeest, he's coming after me, I think. He could come after my family, my friends. If he knew that I had a girlfriend, I guarantee you that you would be a target."

"Let me see," Happy said, a touch of testiness in her voice, "you want to protect me from this serial killer?"

"Yes."

"And the only way to protect me is to cut off all contact."

"Of a personal nature, yes," Mark said.

"Then if Eric Vandergeest were caught tomorrow, we could be boyfriend and girlfriend, huh?" Happy's voice sounded cold and crisp.

Mark stuttered, "You make it seem like my reasoning is illogical, the way you're talking."

"It is illogical, you dumbass. Do you know who Joseph Bau and Rebecca Tennenbaum were?"

Mark replied the he did not.

Happy rushed on. "They were prisoners at Krakow-Plaszow Labor Camp in World War II Poland. They got married in the barracks of the freaking camp. While the Holocaust was going on. Their wedding bands were made from spoons. Think about that for a second."

"But Vandergeest might kill you," Mark said doggedly.

"Then I'll die. I might die in a car accident tomorrow. A wheel might fall off a plane and hit me as I leave the grocery store. Living in fear of what might happen is a good way to not live at all."

"You're terribly cavalier about this."

Happy laughed, "Maybe, but this is serious. I mean, if you want to break up with me because you don't like me or you don't think we're a good fit together, fine. That's a normal reason why couples break up."

"Are we a couple? I mean," Mark began.

"You are an idiot," Happy interrupted, "and sometimes I wonder about you. I mean, it's not like I couldn't find a relationship somewhere. But you're funny, you're considerate when not being clueless, and I think you're cute."

Happy stopped speaking and the silence between them grew enormous in a few seconds. Finally, Mark said, "I think you're bold and smart and pretty." He found that he wanted very badly to say those words.

"I am, aren't I?" Happy replied, a smile playing in her voice, "which is why you breaking up with me is a really bad idea. I'm close to 30 years old. You're, what, 35?"

"34."

"Neither one of us is getting any younger. I'm not going to beat around the bush here. I'd like to get married. Someday, maybe, even have a baby."

"A baby?" Mark asked. He may have sounded panicked, but, really, a baby? He could not touch other human beings. How could they have a baby? How could he raise a child?

"Yes. Don't freak out. People have them all the time. I know that we both have our limitations. This is the kind of thing that people in a relationship hash out. Should we live in the city or a small town? Should we have a joint checking account? How could you be close to a child without touching him or her skin-to-skin? We are smart people, Mark. We can figure this out."

"I can honestly say I've never honestly thought about having a kid of my own before," Mark said slowly, feeling each word out and trying the thoughts on like a new tuxedo. "I've always thought about how to avoid kids. I bought this spandex bodysuit for when my niece was little. Maybe I could do something like that…" His voice trailed off.

Sounding like a purring cat, Happy said, "See? There's always a solution."

"A kid? Wow." The idea still seemed ludicrous, and probably it was, but Mark found he rather liked the idea.

"About that," Happy said, her tone changing, "we need to figure out some way that we can interact more personally."

"I don't think I understand," Mark said.

"You should come over to my place." Happy made him write down her address. "Do you still have that spandex suit?"

"Yeah, I do, actually."

"Does it still fit?" she asked.

"It should. Not exactly flattering, but…"

"Bring it," Happy interrupted. "I have scissors and… everything else."

She hung up on him. Mark looked at the phone for a second before Happy's meaning became clear. "Oh, shit," Mark said. "Shit, shit, shit." He spat out a few more epithets before becoming quiet. He stood up and went to his bedroom closet.

Fortunately, Dylan happened to be stationed outside Mark's house that evening, sitting in an unmarked van on the street next to his driveway. Anyone with half a brain would look at the van and think "law enforcement vehicle." Which, according to Bill, was kind of the point. He wanted the house to be Mark's safe zone, so he wanted the protection to be obvious and constant. "I'm not going to make you be bait inside your own home," Bill had told Mark a day earlier.

Mark walked out his door wondering if he should call Happy and have her come over. Then he thought about how he wasn't entirely ready to have her in his room, in his bed. Better over there, and I have the option to leave whenever I want.

Another bit of luck found Dylan standing outside the van, an e-cig in her hand. "Caught me," she said as he walked over to her. Since Vandergeest had been proven to have definitively returned, Dylan had been positively not an asshole toward Mark. Sometimes even pleasant.

"I need to go," Mark said.

"Okay," she said seriously. "Is it a number one or number two? Can you get to the bathroom in time?" She laughed at her own joke. "Fine, where are we going? What's in the bag?"

"Just me. You stay here."

Dylan shook her head. "Um, no. We're here to make sure you stay alive. I don't care about your crappy house."

"Please," Mark said, "I need you to do me a solid here."

Dylan rolled her eyes. "First, you need to update your slang. 'Do me a solid.' Come on. Second, where are you going?"

After hemming and hawing for a second, Mark said that he was going to Happy's place.

"To, to Happy's? A…" Dylan's eyes widened. "Shit, Mark, are you telling me this is a booty call?"

Mark looked at the trees in the neighbor's house and said nothing.

"Oh my, you're going over there to do… How are you… I don't really want to imagine that, to be honest. What's in the bag?" Dylan made to peek into it then pulled back. "Again, it's best I don't know. You know what, just go. If something happens, if you die, I'll tell Bill that it was for the most noble cause in the world." Dylan looked to be having trouble not laughing. "Good luck, my friend. God's speed to you." She saluted him with a chuckle.

"Shithead," Mark muttered as he got into the car.

He didn't drive fast on his way to Happy's. Mark did not drive fast, but he did take the turns with more aggressiveness than usual. He had trouble swallowing again, a trouble he'd been having more and more often as of late. Just his luck that he'd finally gotten a girlfriend and then develop esophageal cancer or some dumb thing.

More than anything, Mark tried not to think about what was in the bag or what was going to happen when he got to Happy's. If he thought about it, really doing that. Instead,

Mark turned on the radio. He fiddled from station to station for a minute before he found a U2 song he liked. "And you give yourself away," Mark sang in his warbly voice. "And you give."

Singing was better than thinking.

Chapter Twenty-Five
Saturday, November 5, 2016

As it turned out, Happy lived in in tiny house a few blocks off of Grover Street in a decent, starter-home kind of way. He pulled in front of the house, checking the clock in the car and saw it was 10:45 p.m.

"Okay," he said to himself after turning off the engine, "I need a good line when she opens the door. Maybe something, you know, suave. Yeah, I don't really know any suave lines. Maybe a line from a movie. Shit, uh, Luca Brasi sleeps with the fishes."

Inside the lit house, the drapes moved and Mark saw Happy looking outside. "She's probably wondering what I'm doing, just talking to myself. Okay, let's go. Go, get out of the car."

He got out, holding the bag against his body like it were filled with top secret documents. He walked toward the door, past neatly trimmed bushes. The doormat, lit by the light next to the front door, read, "Go Away."

Happy opened the door before Mark had a chance to knock or ring the doorbell.

"Hey," she said. Happy looked, as she somehow managed to always do, like she could open a vintage clothing store from her own closet. Tonight, she wore a long polka dot skirt with some kind of denim shirt.

"You look, uh, wow," Mark said before stopping to examine his feet.

"I tried on five different things," Happy said, "and I stuffed everything I didn't like back into my closet. Actually, I'm not fond of this outfit either, but you arrived so here we are."

She stepped aside and let him walk in. Mark looked around and tried to take in the sheer riot of Happy's living room. For his own living space, Mark favored quiet, sparseness, and utility. Even the pictures on his walls – large photos of the horsehead nebula, an old-time mill in the winter, a drawing Mark had done once when he'd touched his niece's pacifier (he'd given Stacy the other drawing for Stacy's 30th birthday) – were designed to promote a sense of serenity.

The walls of Happy's living room, on the other hand, seemed designed less as a way to clear the mind from a long, difficult day than as a way to unfold every nook and cranny of Happy's consciousness.

Over there a dreamcatcher, next to dreamcatcher a picture of Aubrey Hepburn wearing a white button-down shirt with the collar up. There a cover of Howard Zinn's A People's History of the United States with a man standing at an anvil, here an amateurish painting of a vase of yellow flowers (Mark suspected that she'd done them herself).

The total effect was that of drinking from a waterfall. You could walk into Mark's house, spend ten minutes looking at the furniture and still not know exactly who Mark was. Happy was the opposite. He saw a love of reading and culture, a love of vintage fashion (plus a lot of old French advertisements for booze). Very few photos of Happy herself, and Mark saw none that had her family.

He stared at the walls in wonder.

"What do you think?" Happy asked nervously.

"It's very filled in. You don't like blank walls very much."

"What fun is a blank wall? That's like saying your favorite color is off-white."

Mark looked at his maybe girlfriend. "It's not uncomfortable. If you went to my place, there's not a lot on the walls. A few photos of nature and stuff."

"What about your family?"

"I keep all of those photos in books on a shelf next to my bed."

She smiled. "Everything in their place, huh?"

"It's the only way I stay sane, by keeping everything separate," Mark replied. "I'm like that school lunch tray where all the food is in their own space."

"So that makes me what? Throw everything into a bucket?"

Mark shook his head. "No. You're more like a stew."

"Happy," she said in a voice, "you're like a stew. Your house doesn't make me feel uncomfortable. Those are the most romantic lines I ever have heard."

"Sorry. I'm not very good at this," Mark said. "I'm really nervous."

"I'm not mad. I mean, you don't seem like the candlelight and red wine kind of guy, but you're honest. That's important to me. I've had previous relationships, actually just two, but both guys were liars and cheats." Happy looked up at the ceiling and smiled again. "I'm old enough to know I prefer honesty, even if it's not graceful."

"You're graceful enough for both of us."

Happy's smile turned into a wince. "Tell me that after you've seen my foot. She limped toward the kitchen. "Would you like anything to drink? I'm on my third glass of wine. I'm nervous."

Mark preferred water and they found themselves at her kitchen table a minute late. Like her living room, the décor in Happy's kitchen could best be described as unruly vintage.

"So, how do we get from here," Mark pointed at the table, "to there." He pointed in the direction of Happy's bedroom.

She raised her eyebrows and a tiny grin creased Happy's face. "Well, I find that walking is the best method. However, if you have an alternate transportation system you'd like to try, I'm game."

"No, I mean…" Mark began.

"How about we hold hands," Happy took Mark's gloved hand in hers, "and drink our wine-slash-water, then we get up and see what happens."

"Okay." He took a shaking sip of water. "I think I'm going to feel like an idiot, wearing that stupid spandex suit."

"Isn't that what relationships are about?" Happy asked. "You know, being exposed in front of someone else?"

"Well, you are you and I'll be looking like a Smurf."

Happy eyed Mark levelly for a second. "Don't be grossed out, okay?" She hesitated a moment more before taking off her shoe. "It's a birth defect." She took off her sock. "It's called symbrachydactyly. It happens, apparently." The second and last toes seemed normal, but the ones in the middle looked like they belonged on a child's foot. "Sometimes I walk a little bit odd but it's a very mild case of it. Between this is the situs inversus and everything else, I'm not exactly a genetic wonder woman."

"It's quite a memento," Mark said, looking back up to meet her green eyes.

"Memento? Memento?" Happy asked in mock anger. "I show you the most sensitive thing about me, a birth defect that caused me vast amounts of internal anguish in high school, and you're making a pun?" She wore a smile, as if no one had ever cared so little about the things she put so much fear into.

"I wanted to make a pun, but I drew a blank. I didn't have much time to prepare."

"Lordy," Happy said, "a 'Little Piggy' joke never popped up?"

Mark slapped his forehead. "Knew there was one."

"Put on your blue spandex suit," Happy said, "I want to kiss you… Wow, that is a really strange thing to say out loud."

He stepped into the bathroom with the paper bag gripped in a sweaty hand. It felt so heavy to hold. A film reel began to play in Mark's mind.

A blond-haired girl, standing outside a Kum n' Go gas station, talking on her phone. She had on a cheerleader's outfit, red and white with the word "Hawks" printed across the front. The girl had that impossibly healthy youthful look, her hair in a ponytail. No one was looking. The attendant helping some angry old man. The camera had gone on the fritz, he could feel it. Mark got out of his car, his hand tight against his side. The girl, feeling so safe, did not even spare him a look. He strolled behind her, he had at least a minute. He watched his hand raise, holding a weighted sap.

"No," said Mark aloud. "Not now. Stay out of my head." He sat on the rim of the bathtub, his hand still gripping the bag. "No. Stay away," he whispered to the air, at the stiffness in his pants, in his mind. "No."

"Are you okay in there?" Happy asked from her bedroom.

"Just fine. Lost my balance."

"The bathroom is kinda small."

Mark said no worries and, with his eyes clinched at thinking about anything, fished through the bag for the spandex suit. The fit was, he thought, a little tight but not uncomfortable.

He emerged from the bedroom, wearing only blue spandex and a nervous grimace. Happy sat on the bed in a nightshirt and, so far as Mark could see, nothing else.

"Well," Happy said, equally nervous, "I have a pair of scissors and a condom."

"Best we not mix those up." Mark walked over to the bed. "I look ridiculous."

She handed him the scissors. "Best you handle this part."

He did, and for several seconds neither of them spoke.

"Oh, hello there," Happy said.

"It's happy to meet you."

"How about if we…"

"Here, let me…"

"Is that comfortable?"

"Yeah, yeah. You?"

"Oh. Oh. Yes."

"Okay. Okay. Is this okay?"

"Mmmm. Harder. Yes."

"Oh God, okay, okay. Oh shit."

"What's… Oh, oh fuck, shit."

"…"

"Oh God. Oh my God."

"That was fascinating."

Chapter Twenty-Six
April 23, 2012

I must have blanked for a second and when I come back Agent Mallory is sitting with his hands out in front of him and he's fumbling with his words.

"Well, it's like this, Mr. and Mrs. Hawkins," he says, "that man over there by the window works for the agency sometimes. He can… I don't know quite how to put… We think he can help find your daughter."

"What, is he some psychic or something?"

The man in the brown windbreaker looks over and talks finally, "Oh Christ, don't call me that." He talks in a really high voice. He also said the Lord's name in vain and I look over and see Mom wince but she doesn't say anything. Then the man in the brown windbreaker keeps going, "I'm not some guy you see on TV telling you about your dead grandma. I'm not some fu…" he looks like he wants to cuss but he chokes it back. "…I'm not some hack or something." When the man in the windbreaker talks, he sounds a little bit like he's choking on something.

Agent Mallory says, "We don't really have a name for what he does. He doesn't really work for us, you see. Not officially."

"I work with computers," windbreaker man says. He adds, as though he doesn't want us to get the wrong impression, "It's easy because I don't have to deal with people."

"Sometimes he helps us with cases like this," Agent Mallory says. "It's not a thing we talk about much, and we expect that you will do the same. If anyone asks, we talk about anonymous sources and people out hiking instead of him.

"Now, as for now, what happens is that we go into Andrea's room and he handles certain objects that Andrea handled. With luck, he'll be able to give us information that might lead to finding your daughter."

"What's his name?" Dad asks. He seems to be aware again, looking around.

"What's that?"

"His name. I want to know his name if he's going to be in Andrea's room, messing stuff around."

"Mark," the guy says.

"What about his last name?" I'm thinking he's mad because he probably figures if the FBI is bringing out psychics, we won't never find Andrea. I'm kind of curious myself. I mean, Mark doesn't seem like anything special. You don't really notice him at first because he's small and he stands really quiet like, but his face is kind of jumpy.

"Actually," says Agent Mallory, "it's better if you don't know that information. Mark, and the bureau, are very concerned that word about Mark's abilities could become well-known. If people knew he could do what he does, imagine how many people would try to call him, stop him on the street."

"It would be awful," Mark says.

"You'd be rich," Dad says. "Plenty of people would pay you lots of money."

"I'd rather be unknown. Besides, I do get paid. It's a thousand, even if it doesn't work."

"Well we don't have that kind of money," Mom says. She looks a little angry and a little frightened.

"It's being taken care of, Mr. and Mrs. Hawkins."

"Are you saying the FBI's paying me?"

"We're taking care of it, Mark." When Agent Mallory speaks, tiny lines appear above the insides of his eyebrows but it's gone in an instant.

"Oh shit, you guys are paying me? Way to make a man feel guilty, Bill."

The FBI agent coughed. "Hey, let's talk about this later."

"You're my friend, I don't like taking money from my friends."

"Well, sometimes…"

Mark interrupts him by waving his hands around as if he's batting away flies, "Listen, forget it, let's just do this. Hey, listen…" he looks at Mom and Dad. "I gotta be in her room, I gotta do this and you can't be there. It's too tough. I don't know if it will work, either. Sometimes it doesn't and I don't know why. But, I won't BS you. If it works, it works, if it doesn't, it doesn't. But you can't be in the room with me. It's too tough and I already got an ulcer."

"We… We understand," Mom says, but the way she says it makes it seem like she doesn't. But Dad isn't saying anything, he's looking at Mark like maybe he wants to beat him up but isn't sure yet.

"Maybe she shouldn't be here," Agent Mallory gestures at me and all of a sudden everybody's looking at me. Like I wasn't here before.

"Janelle, go to your room and stay there until Mom or I come to get you," Dad says.

"But I got a right to hear."

"Janelle, you will go right now," he says in that quiet way that means business. Dad's got this really quiet thing he does before he goes nuclear, so I walk down the hallway and open my door. I keep it slightly open and I hear Agent Mallory talking, but it's in a really low voice and I can't make out what he's saying. Mom is saying stuff too. Also, the agents have come back inside and it looks like they didn't get wet at all.

Before I close the door, I look and notice Mark. He's back at the window but he's looking down the hallway. He looks tired and you can tell he really wants a cigarette. He sees me looking and he kind of nods his head real quick. It's like he's saying hi or something, but I guess I kind of don't mind it.

Anyways, I hear Mom and Dad getting up from the couch and I close the door real softly. I had been thinking about going under the bed cause I got some food under there – a pack of Little Debbies from the store and some brownies in a Tupperware.

I remember the hole in the closet, and I wonder if I can still fit through the hole even though I'm a biggie. I really want to see what Mark is going to do, so I creep over to the closet and I've got a bunch of crap in there. It's mostly dumb stuff like a box of papers and tests I did good on and some dumb stuffed animals that I don't want to get rid of. There are also old shoes, a couple of notebooks I wrote some poetry in, a plastic bag full of golf balls (I don't know how I got those), and a bunch of other stuff.

It takes like five minutes to move it all from the closet to next to my desk, but I'm working quietly and I'm thinking it's kind of hot in the house and humid too. On Andrea's side, it's pretty cleared out. She's really organized and don't like clutter too much.

Anyway, it turns out the hole is big enough even for me, and I crawl through into her closet. I'm wearing a gray sweatshirt and sweatpants (not ones I'd wear to school). Our closets got those folding doors that got slats in them so you can see out. Anyway, apparently, I'm just in time because I see Agent Mallory and Mark walk in.

When the door closes, Mark calls Agent Mallory a cocksucker.

"Don't start with me right now, Mark," Agent Mallory says.

"You actually let them think their kid's still alive."

"We don't know for certain…"

"Oh, don't give me that. She is dead as dead can be. I can't believe you didn't tell me. I can't believe I didn't figure it out before we got here. I don't read the papers or watch the news, and I know about Vandergeest. You're sure he got this girl?"

Mallory nodded, "It was him. She was seen talking to someone who looked like him at the gas station, we have a receipt from a card he was using from that gas station, and Vandergeest kept trophies of the girls he took. We haven't made that last part public knowledge."

"Then what you've done here is wrong, Bill." Mark takes both hands and rubs his face. "You damn well know that she was tortured and is lying in a grave somewhere."

"That's why you're here."

"I told you I didn't want to do this anymore. Only cases where the victim is alive, I said."

"This is important."

"It's a body, Bill! And the guy who killed her is already dead!" Mark's face is contorted, like he doesn't know what to feel.

"Quiet down."

"She's dead and yet you want me to do this," Mark whispers loudly, "and you know what this does to me. How hard this is."

"Is it any harder than what those folks out there have to go through every day?"

"You asshole," Mark says, "if you were honest with them, they'd know she was dead and could start moving on."

While they're talking, I feel tears running down my cheeks. It's sad tears but kind of relieved ones too. I mean, I know that Andrea's dead and that she's not joined some cult or anything. I know that. But everyone's been talking to me the last two months like I can't, I dunno, like I can't deal with it. I mean, at least these guys are honest now. And it's not like I didn't know in my heart. It feels good a little to hear someone say it out loud. I don't know yet what to think about what Mark said about Andrea being tortured. I whisper to God that I hope she didn't get tortured.

"You're being selfish." Agent Mallory says.

"Selfish? Me?"

"You could try some sympathy for these folks."

"Sympathy? Sympathy is all I am." Mark makes that waving his hand gesture again. "I'm here, and we both know I'm going to do this, so let's get it done. I'm smoking though, so I'm opening this window and you go find something for me to use as an ashtray."

"I'll get a bowl or something. I'll tell the parents it's part of your ritual."

"Tell them whatever you want."

Agent Mallory leaves and Mark goes to the window and opens it. A warm wet smell gusts into the room. He pulls a pack of Camels from the pocket of his windbreaker and takes out a cigarette. He fumbles around his pants until he finds a book of matches. He lights his cigarette, takes a deep puff, and exhales out the window.

I don't much like the smell of cigarettes but oh well. He smokes for a minute and begins dropping the ashes into his other hand. The door opens and Agent Mallory and the other two FBI agents come in. The other two are wet and they're carrying stuff. The guy has an easel and the girl a large pad of paper that artists use, like one I used one art class this year. Agent Mallory has a white bowl from our kitchen and he puts it in the window.

"Where do you want me to set up the easel?" The other guy FBI agent says.

Mark turns around and looks at the room. "Right there," he says, pointing at the middle of the floor. "Facing the window. I'll use that chair."

They put the easel down. Luckily, I can see it if I get real low. The girl agent puts the paper on it and folds the cover back so a blank page is facing the window. The other agent pulls a chair up near the easel and they stop and watch Mark smoke his cigarette.

He stubs it out in the bowl and you can tell he's thinking about lighting another one up, but he decides not to and he goes to the chair and sits.

Mark looks up at the man FBI agent, who is standing next to the easel. "I need something personal," he says. He points to Andrea's bed, which has a pink bedspread on it and a few stuffed penguins. "We can try one of the stuffed animals or the pillow. Pillows usually work."

"I have something," Agent Mallory says and he gestures to the girl FBI agent. She pulls a clear plastic bag from a box on the floor that also had the pencils. Inside it is a keyring. I gasp but no one notices. It's Andrea's. I can tell because she got this attachment on it that shows pictures. It's about two inches square and pink. I got it for her when she turned sixteen last year. I downloaded all these photos to it of me, her, Mom, Dad, and Smoky the Cat. It cost me $30 which was more than she spent on me, but I knew she'd love it and Andrea thought it was the best thing she got for her birthday.

"I still don't think we should be doing this," the girl FBI agent says but she opens up the plastic bag.

"Don't touch it," Agent Mallory says. "Just give the bag to Mark."

She does and Mark holds the plastic bag in his lap, open. He doesn't reach in for a minute. "I wish I couldn't do this," he said at last.

"I know," Agent Mallory says and he sounds like he's sympathetic.

The man named Mark reaches in the bag.

Chapter Twenty-Seven
Monday, November 7, 2016

About half a mile away from work, Mark pulled over to a deserted parking lot and all, but fell out of the car. He could barely see the pavement in front of his car. It felt like the reality before his eyes was overlaid with a different reality, memories from the events he had lived, from those horrible times of being someone else for a small spell.

In his mind's eye, he could see a basement, a figure huddled in the corner just visible in the light from the door behind.

Then it flipped, and Mark looked up a deep slope. The hiking path he had just fallen from was hidden from his eyes. He looked down at his mangled leg, the shin bone poking out below the knee.

Another flip and Mark saw the fear in a pretty blond girl's eyes looking at him from a trunk.

Then the real world, a world made definitely from memories, faded away and Mark could see that he managed to stop the car only a few inches away from a light pole.

"And it's only fucking Monday," Mark said aloud. He cussed a little bit more. One thing he did not want to do was think about the weekend. Not Saturday night.

"Duuuude," Lawrence said as Mark opened the door to the IT room, "How did Saturday night go?"

Mark grunted. "Don't you have a serial killer targeting your house to worry about?"

"Number one, thanks for bringing it up. I really need to be reminded of that," Lawrence said. "And number two, there are more important things. Like, you sent me a very mysterious text message on Saturday night that seemed to indicate you were on your way to Ms. Hapke's apartment to have the sex. Considering that you are, well, you, this is pretty momentous news. Now, did you get laid? I have to know."

Rather than respond, Mark sat at his desk and proceeded to check his e-mail.

"I am going to guess that you did not."

Mark turned toward Lawrence and regarded the floor for a long moment. "We did, I think. Have sex, I mean."

"Okay, let's pause for a second. People who get laid usually know it. So, let me ask you: Mark, dost thou know whence your manly parts are supposed to go whilst one is engaged in heterosexual intercourse?"

"Yeah, I know," Mark said irritably.

"Because the internet is filled with many helpful videos in that area. Was it just very bad sex?"

Mark didn't reply, merely stared at the ground.

"Okay, the sex was bad," Lawrence said soothingly. "Actually, given your proclivity toward not touching another human being, how exactly did it happen? I mean, I don't usually care much about straight people sex, but I'm curious here."

"It was Happy's idea. I used a condom, obvious. There was some other protection that I used. In order to make sure there wouldn't be any skin-on-skin touching." Mark made an awkward gesture. "I'd rather not explain."

"This sounds like a Dear Penthouse letter. Dear Penthouse, my lover and I cannot touch skin, so I used a condom and other kinds of protection."

"Do shut up," Mark said.

Lawrence tried to stop smiling but he couldn't. "Sorry, Mark. I know I shouldn't laugh. That's totally not cool. Here you are trying something new and I should not mock that. It is kind of funny, though."

"Imagine your sex life," Mark grumbled, "if every time you touched Joe, he got horrible waking nightmares."

"I know, I know. Just tell me, how bad was it?" Lawrence waited a few seconds. "Seriously, did she run away screaming?"

"Have you ever blocked out a memory?"

"Oh shit," Lawrence oohed. "That bad?"

"Probably. Everything was kind of a blur."

"Did you call? I mean, like on Sunday?" Lawrence asked.

Mark shook his head. He explained that he had come home after the, err, encounter (which caused Lawrence to give him an exasperated expression). Sunday, Mark continued, consisted of video games, cleaning the house, reorganizing his books, and buying groceries (which caused Lawrence to, in order, mutter "oh really," throw up his hands in the air, roll his eyes, and finally close his eyes for four long seconds).

When finished with how he spent Sunday, Mark ventured, "Do you think I should have?"

Rather than answer, Lawrence planted his forehead into his hand. "Dude, you are so bad at this."

"I know."

"Luckily, Happy's pretty chill, so you aren't dead." Lawrence seemed to think of something. "Well, let me ask, do you want to keep seeing her, in a romantic sense?"

"That's not such a simple question," Mark answered. "I mean, yeah, I want to see her. I really, really like Happy. But she makes my life more complicated. Before Happy, I never worried about the mechanics of having actual sex. It was never an issue."

"Madam Hand was always down for some fun?" Lawrence teased.

"Don't laugh but yeah, and it was, I don't know, safe. Imagine spending almost your entire life, at least since you were a kid, in a small room. Imagine how scary it is if someone opened the door to that room and tried to shove you outside. You've seen it all through a window but never thought you'd be out there." Mark looked at his hands. "I wasn't ecstatic with my existence, but I had a nice routine going. Now…" He trailed off.

"You have women problems."

"Exactly."

"And a psychotic killer who may be trying to murder you."

"Everybody's got problems," Mark smiled as he spoke. "I can't even think about Vandergeest right now. Do you think I should call her?"

"Speaking as your friend," Lawrence said earnestly, "I want you to do what makes you happy. I mean it. I can joke about whatever freaked out sex you and Happy are contemplating, but at the end of the day you got to do what brings you the most happiness. The natural assumption would be to get yourself in a relationship. I mean, it's what our culture kind of expects. But people aren't all like that. Some people aren't meant to have a girlfriend. Some people are meant…"

Mark interrupted "…to stay in their rooms."

"Safe in the womb. It ain't cowardice for you to be you."

Mark stood up, ran his gloved hands through his thinning black hair. He paced to one end of the room and back again. "I don't suppose," he began before stopping and pacing the room a few more times. "I don't suppose it would hurt to talk to her." Mark picked up the phone.

"You should go talk to her in person," Lawrence suggested.

"I'd rather call. Or e-mail, actually."

"You should go talk to her in person."

"Fine."

Lawrence cocked his head when his friend got up. "You're not going alone. You need all the help you can get."

Mark opened the door and almost ran into Kyler Rankin, who had apparently been waiting outside the door. Stumbling back a few steps, Mark felt his heart thump in his chest. "What do you want?" Mark asked, his voice sounding tinny.

"Just trying to stay in touch," Kyler said. A couple of his friends, students Mark didn't recognize, laughed.

A few months ago, Mark might have felt fear. But when one has a serial killer after you, high school bullies don't seem that important.

"Oh, I thought you wanted to know about all that stuff I found when I remotely checked your computer," Mark said, standing up.

Kyler's body language shifted. "Huh?"

"I'm going to give you a break," Mark continued, feeling his confidence grow, "this time. But if I check again and see that kind of stuff on your computer again, I will contact the principal."

"I wasn't looking at no porn," Kyler said, looking at his friends.

"It's okay to be curious. I know you have to look tough for your friends, but there is nothing wrong with the stuff you were looking at. I mean, it's unusual, but you have to be yourself."

One of Kyler's friends snickered, "Dude, what were you looking at?"

"It's nothing," Mark said in what he thought was a soothing voice. "Kyler, I want you to know a lot of people find adults wearing diapers to be interesting in that way. You are not alone."

"Dude," another of the friends pointed a finger at Kyler, "sick."

Kyler himself sputtered. He seemed ready to throw a punch.

"You know," Lawrence said stepping between Kyler and Mark, "I think it's time you folks went to your class. Go on."

When they had left, Lawrence gave Mark a grim look, "Kyler's an asshole and a bully, but, dang, that's dangerous talking like that to a student."

Mark shrugged confidently. They walked together downstairs to the 100 wing. It was 7:54 a.m. and students were hurrying to class. A small cluster of students gathered around Happy's door.

"Clear a path," Lawrence said and the students shuffled aside. The door was locked and they could see through the small rectangular window that the room was dark. Lawrence turned to Mark and said, "Maybe you could leave a note?"

Lawrence didn't have his key, so Mark used his to get into the room. The students filed in behind them. When Mark turned on the lights, his thoughts were on what he wanted to say. An apology first, then maybe a suggestion that they could meet after school for coffee? Not that I drink coffee, Mark wrote in his head.

"What is that?" one of the students asked.

Mark felt Lawrence grab his arm. Lawrence's arm was pointed at the board, at the message written there.

"Hi Mark," it read, "I have her."

Chapter Twenty-Eight
Monday, November 7, 2016

"Here is what the cameras captured." School Resource Officer Carlson's finger hovered above the enter key. A broad-shouldered man, he clearly felt crowded by the number of people in his office. In addition to Carlson, the room held Mark, Lawrence, Principal Chester, a sergeant from the Omaha Police Department, Bill, and Bill's superior, Special Agent Parmero.

"When is this happening?" the sergeant asks as the video begins to play back. Taken from down the hall from Happy's door, it began with a darkened hallway leading to the back entrance. The lights, triggered by a motion sensor, light up.

"At 2:35 a.m. this morning."

A figure, dressed entirely in black, opened the door and walked straight to the alarm panel next to the door. The figure looked at a card and entered a number into the panel, undoing the alarm.

"What ID did he use to unlock the door?" Chester asked.

"Um, he didn't." Carlson shrugged his shoulders. "That particular door has had some issues. It doesn't really lock."

"So, anyone can just walk in?" Parmero's tone was icy.

"It's a large public school, not the White House. We have an alarm system too. Anyway, I know that maintenance knows about the issue. They hadn't gotten around to it."

"Our support staff is stretched pretty thin," Chester explained.

"What about the alarm?"

Chester said, "All the staff knows how to disable the alarm. We gave them a card explaining the procedure."

"He probably got it off Ms. Hapke," Bill suggested. "He could have used her ID card as well." The principal shot Bill a look of gratitude.

"Okay, so he walks down the hall here to the stairs." Carlson's deep voice narrated the figure on the screen. "He comes out here from across Ms. Hapke's room. She's a real nice lady, you know. Always friendly."

The figure in black emerged from the stairwell with a key in its hand.

"Can we tell how tall this guy is?" Bill asked.

"The camera is pretty far away, and he looks to be hunched over." The sergeant chimes in. "Ballpark, I'd say in the six-foot range."

"This is crap video," Bill said, "and there is no way you can estimate the guy's height."

"We're on track to upgrade our security systems next summer," Chester said.

Parmero turned to Bill. "We need to get a copy of this to the Digital Evidence Library."

"I know the person to send it to," said Bill.

Mark pointed at the image on the screen. "It looks like he's wearing a cloak."

"That's odd. There anything in the case file to suggest that Vandergeest ever wore a cloak?" Parmero asked.

Bill shook his head. "I'd remember that. Probably, I'd say, looking to disguise his appearance."

"It's not like we don't know who took her," Mark said. "Why did he need to disguise himself?"

"Maybe," Lawrence had been silent until then, "something is wrong with him. An injury. Like he has an artificial leg or something."

"An artificial leg?" Bill mocked. "What is this? The Fugitive?"

"Or something," Parmero growled. He pointed back at the SRO's screen. "So Vandergeest goes into the room and closes the door, presumably to write the note, but he doesn't leave for almost ten minutes."

Carlson fast-forwarded the video. He stopped when the time stamp hit 2:47:20. The same figure emerged from the door and, without looking toward the camera, stepped into the stairwell again. Ten seconds later, the figure in black appeared at the top of the stairs and walked to the doors. He stepped through them into the night.

"What about the parking lot cameras?"

"Camera," Carlson said, "there's the one for the back lot."

"What about the parking lot camera?" Parmero said through slightly clenched teeth.

"Well," Chester piped up, "that one apparently is also broken. We really were hoping to get an upgrade this next summer."

Parmero took off his glasses and rubbed at his moustache. "Perfect."

"I told those maintenance guys that they needed to fix that shit," Carlson said.

"I'm sure you did." Parmero's voice had all the warmth of a glacier. "Since we don't have that evidence, let's see what we do have. Folks, how long do you think it would take to write a note on the board? A minute?"

"He wrote it in sharpie," Carlson offered, "and we haven't found the marker. He must have taken it with him."

Parmero continued, "Doesn't that strike anyone else as suspicious? He didn't have a large to-do list."

"I see two options," said Bill. "Either he was looking for something or leaving something."

Parmero looked at Mark for a long second, then asked everyone to leave but Bill and Mark. Carlson tried to sputter for a second about it being his office, but Parmero shot him a look that suppressed any further words; Carlson left like a meek puppy.

When they were alone, Parmero asked Bill if there were any other agents available.

"Dylan's in the room, helping the lab guys from OPD."

"How much have they done?"

Bill got on his phone and walked to the door to talk. Parmero sat behind the desk, Mark stood in front of the desk, looking and feeling awkward.

For a few seconds, Paremero worked on a text message, his head down. A bald spot the size of a silver dollar sat at the back of his scalp. Mark checked his phone, half-expecting some kind of contact from Vandergeest. He could only assume that the serial killer would have his number.

"So," Parmero said, drawing Mark's attention back, "this Ms. Hapke is, what, your girlfriend?"

"Well, it's kind of… yes. She is." Mark said.

"You've been helping us for twelve years now. They've brought you in for about 60 cases, correct?"

"I think that number is at 63," Mark replied.

"Indeed." Parmero's expression implied that he'd known exactly how many cases Mark had work on. "Now, Agent Mallory tells me that you did not wish to work with the FBI anymore."

"It's gotten too hard."

"He said that. He said you suffer from nightmares. That these bad dreams seem to be interrupting your daily life. Is that correct?"

Mark felt a burst of anger, raw emotion he had been storing back since he'd seen the note written on the board, spew forth and he glared at Parmero. "I don't have bad dreams, sir. What happens is that I sometimes close my eyes and find myself in the body of a young woman getting stabbed to death. I die, Special Agent Parmero. I don't have a bad dream and feel better once I'm awake. I die. They are not bad dreams."

"We can find help for you, Mr. Peter."

"I don't like feeling like this."

Paremero said, "I don't blame you. Maybe with the right combination of medication and therapy, you might consider coming back to help us out. You have been an invaluable resource."

Mark let out a sharp bark of a laugh. Aside from Bill, who cared, the FBI saw him as nothing more than a resource, a poorly paid one at that. A tool that they could call up and deliver to a crime scene. One who could grasp some object and point them in the direction of a kidnapper or killer. Of course, Parmero would care little for what effect it would have on someone like Mark.

Parmero continued, "What if we could find some medication that could, say, allow you to touch other people? Unofficially, your friend has been speaking with a psychiatrist." Mark looked at Bill sharply. "It's all anonymous. Based upon the ways your gift manifests itself, Dr. Kucera suggested we might try to take up a regimen of Amisulpride. It's a drug used to treat schizophrenia, social phobias, and depression. I could make that happen, Mark. And, maybe, if the drugs and therapy prove effective, maybe we could take you off the drugs for short periods of time so that you could help us with major cases. The bad ones. You could live a normal life, Mark."

Mark leaned back in his chair. "I've never been to a psychologist before. I mean, I'm not a germophobe or OCD or anything. I'm just built differently. What's the catch?"

"No catch. We'll help you. A reward for over a decade of sacrifice. Of course, we'd still expect your help in the future. Perhaps even with catching Vandergeest, and rescuing your girlfriend."

"I'll help with this," Mark said. "I don't really have a choice."

From the corner of the room, Bill, who had been speaking quietly with Dylan, let out a burst of expletives. He hung up and looked at them. "They found something in one of Happy's desk drawers. Mark," Bill suppressed a spasm of coughing, "don't freak out, man. It appears to be one of her toes."

Vandergeest had put the toe in a plastic baggie, which he placed into a cooler the size of a shoebox, surrounded by cylinders of dry ice. Mark had not seen the toe personally, and he did not want to. Yet he had, of course, volunteered to use his gift one more time to find Happy.

"You are not moving it yet," Parmero was saying to one of the paramedics.

The argument had been going on for a few minutes. "That is not up to you. This toe needs to be preserved and reattached," the paramedic said.

"For one thing, there is no foot at present to reattach the toe to. Second, a toe can last for several days when properly cooled. It is already in a plastic bag and properly refrigerated. There is literally nothing more anyone could do."

"Still, we need to be ready," she persisted. "This toe needs to be at the hospital."

Parmero put up his hands in a placating gesture. "And it will be, but we have to run a few tests on it first. A half-hour, at most. I promise." He began to shoo the paramedic towards the door of Happy's classroom.

208

"I really feel that I should stay with the appendage," she said. "What tests do you need to run that I can't be here."

"A radio-spectrum apperception test. Very useful for determining trace elements left on the toe." When the paramedic had been shown the exit and the door closed (the small window in the door had already been covered), Parmero turned to Bill and Mark. "We have about half an hour. Do you have everything you need?"

Mark sat at the student desk and remembered how uncomfortable the things were. No wonder students can't sit still. A piece of computer paper sat in front of him, and Bill stood ready with other sheets of paper. "This isn't how we usually do this," he said.

"We don't have the materials. No time to get them." Bill looked back up at Parmero. "You staying?"

Parmero seemed to consider the question. "To be honest, I've never seen Mr. Peter here employ his gift. I've always thought it better to have plausible deniability. However, under the circumstances, I think I will watch.

Dylan opened the cooler with a steady, neutral expression. If she felt any revulsion at seeing a severed toe, Dylan did not show it.

However, Mark had no compunctions. He about threw up when Dylan lifted the cooler's lid. The toe sat there on the ice, a small drop of ruby-bright in the baggie as well. Dylan, also wearing gloves, opened the baggie in such a way as to allow Mark to touch it.

"Are you ready?" Bill asked.

"I am. I don't know if this will work. I've never tried to find someone I know. Also, I've never touched a body part. Do you think it will be different?"

"You act as if I could possibly know that. All I do know is that this is the first time you have ever, in the decade that we've been partners on this, said you wanted to do it."

"Yeah, well, it's important to me."

"We'll find her," Bill said, "trust me."

Mark took a few deep breaths. "Let's do this." He reached out and touched the severed toe.

For a few seconds, Mark seemed frozen. Parmero began to talk, "Bill is this..." before Mark spasmed. Then the left hand flew up and began to draw.

The background of the drawing received only a few cursory shades before Mark's hand moved onto what appeared to be a face.

"I think that's his hair," Parmero said, approaching to stand behind Mark. "Wait, that does not look like Vandergeest at all."

Indeed, it didn't. For one thing, the hair was sparse and looked gray. The man in the image could not have been younger than 55 years old. Deep lines flared out from the nose to the corners of the man's unsmiling lips. He had black eyebrows and black, thick brow line glasses.

"What is this?" Bill muttered. "What are you giving me here, Mark?"

In response, Mark said nothing. His head hung slightly to one side, eyes closed, his lips slightly parted.

"Is he sitting there?" Dylan asked. "Looks like the old dude is looking off into the distance."

The sketch continued. "I think it's in a basement," Parmero said. "Mark's drawing, I think those are cinderblocks. It could be a basement."

"There's a pipe," Dylan added.

Mark made a gesture and Bill swapped out the piece of paper for a new one. "It's not finished," Bill said as he looked at the picture of the old man, "but we have a face. I don't know if this is a suspect or another victim or what."

Dylan said, "It could be a relative. Most of the time he touches objects. Who knows what happens with detached body parts? Mark could be receiving info about where she is, but he might not. This could be, I don't know, her grandpa or something."

Parmero said, "This next one, I think, will be about the kidnapping."

Continuing his silence, Mark's next drawing seemed to consist of a white rectangle that was open at the bottom. Using the flat of the pencil, Mark began to shade large swaths of the paper.

"It's a…" Bill began. "I think it's a dark room. That's a door there in the middle."

Mark kept sketching furiously, his head still lolled to the side. It became more and more apparent that it was a darkened room, the only light coming from the doorway in the middle of the image. They could see shadows of objects, boxes perhaps, but nothing distinct, nothing that gave them any indication of where the image came from.

"Do you think this means that she's still alive?" Dylan asked. "Is this now?"

"No idea, Dylan," Bill said, his frustration showing. "Mark, come on, stop drawing the shadows."

As if he heard him, Mark waved his hand to indicate he needed another sheet.

The third drawing is again dark around the edges. Bill cursed quietly when he sees the dark shading, thinking that maybe it will be a second darkened window. A line appeared about midway high, running vertically across the entire piece of paper.

"I think this is something," Bill said.

More shading. Another line running horizontal on the left side of the page. A second horizontal line, broken up.

"Those, those are fingers," said Dylan.

Parmero added, "Somebody is holding a sign."

"Maybe Happy is writing to us," Bill suggested.

Everything outside the rectangle became darkness. Inside the box, the sign, Mark began to write letters.

The FBI agents began to say the letters as they appeared. "That's an M. An A, I believe. Is that… It is, an R."

They fell silent. The third image did not take long to draw at all.

It read:

"Mark,

You'll Never Find Her. Now I'm Coming For You.

- Eric"

Mark fell out of the chair, unconscious.

Chapter Twenty-Nine
1996

When I was really young, like six, my mom took us down to Kansas City for the weekend. Back then, I really loved trains. As in, all I talked about was trains. I drew pictures of trains, made trains from little wooden blocks. Mom took us to this train restaurant. Toy trains delivered the hamburgers to the table on this track up near the ceiling and deposited the basket onto a tray which lowered down to where Mom could grab it.

It was an amazing day. Mom and Stacy were both very happy, no one fought. We went to Worlds of Fun the next day, so everyone was looking forward to the adventure.

I thought about that day. It would be so easy to think about it again, and think about other days. When Stacy took me to the movies on my birthday last year, we saw Jurassic Park. The times when I played with my friends.

It would have been so easy to just stop.

Easy.

But some small voice spoke softly into my ear, whispered to me, "Don't give up, Mark. It's going to hurt but you can escape."

Out loud, I replied, "I can't." At least, I tried to, as my throat felt so dry.

"Your handcuffs are loose," the voice said. "You can get out."

I pulled against the cuffs; I could not get out. Maybe the right hand one was a little wabbly. "It's not loose enough. I can't do it."

The voice, it sounded like the voice of God, whispered back, "It's going to hurt to pull your hand out. It's going to hurt a lot."

I could hear the groan of the water pipes. The angry man was in the shower. "I hurt all over."

"I know," the voice said.

"He's been hurting me."

"I know."

"I hurt too bad."

"I know. You can do this. You can take the pain. All the pain. Pull now."

"I can't."

The voice no longer whispered. It screamed, "NOW! NOW! NOW!"

I pulled at the handcuffs. The right cuff came further up my hand, but I couldn't pull it out of the cuff.

"I can't get it off!" I screamed.

"You'll have to hurt yourself," the voice said, steady and somber. "You will have to break something in your hand."

The very thought of breaking my own hand should have made me stop. I was not the kind of kid who handled pain very well. Yet, oddly, for whatever reason, it felt like I was being offered a choice. For the past few days, since being shoved into the locker, really, I'd had things done to me. *I could do this*, I thought. My head grew clearer. If I was going to die, I'd at least die trying to escape.

How long would he keep showering? I wondered. It couldn't be long.

I pulled again. And again. My hand wouldn't fit. Every part of my body screamed in agony. The third time I pulled, my vision began to darken and I had to stop.

"You have to escape now. You don't have long."

I wanted to scream at the voice that I already knew it. I could vaguely hear the sounds of water rushing.

I pulled again, holding the chain with my left hand. Nothing.

The pipes clunked again. The angry man had turned off the shower. I had no more than a few minutes, five to ten, before he finished drying and putting on fresh clothes. Maybe he had to do other stuff, I had no way of knowing, but he probably was excited to kill me.

Frantic with animal energy, I planted my feet against the wall. The pain had not gone and blood still trickled down my legs, but I did not notice the pain anymore. It had receded to a far corner of my mind.

In my head, I could see the angry man drying his hair and his puffy belly. I could almost feel his anticipation though wood and plaster, pipes and wires separated us.

My left hand wrapped a length of the handcuff chain around.

Once more, one last time (for how much did I have left) I pulled. The metal handcuff bit into my skin and stuck there. Yet I did not stop.

My eyes registered the muscles of my thin legs popping out in exertion, shaking. When some part of my hand cracked, I barely gasped at the new pain. I landed back onto the mattress, my head bopping against the concrete floor.

For a sickening second, the world wavered.

The Angry Man. Coming for me. The angry man. Coming for me. He's coming. He's coming. Get up. Get up.

I couldn't hear anything from upstairs. He's coming.

I staggered to my feet. Blood at the back of my head. The chain still through the ring.

"Twist the handcuff, work it through the ring."

Done. I Staggered off the bed. The white sheets covered in stains. Mine? Didn't know. Not important. Find a way out. Up the stairs before. The angry man coming.

The sound of loose handcuff dragging on the ground, I walked around the mattress out the door.

A sound a sound any sound upstairs. A creak, a groan of wood floor. Silence. I move toward the stairs.

The sound of walking from upstairs. No, no, no, no, nonononononono! Look around. Main room clean, a couch, a barred window. No closets, a washer/dryer. I could hide there, but he is coming. The Angry Man is coming. Oh god no, please. Step back

Look around.

"LOOK!" Voice is angry. Angry Man coming for me. To kill to kill.

Don't wanna go back into the room. He's coming to kill me.

Back in. Close the door. It's so heavy. No lock. Creaking on the stairs. Step down. Step. Step.

Angry Man says I'm back.

Look around at table. A gun.

Grab the gun. Don't know if it's loaded, but point point point point! Only way he's killing coming to…

Angry Man's eyes widen. Gun's loaded

His lips move, but I hear nothing except the roar in my ears

I pull the trigger. Nothing happens. Safety off. He takes a step with his hand out. His face, a little smile on it his face. A flash on his face. He steps away. Flash. He turns away. Stagger. I fall against the wall. Flash. Flash. Angry man up the stairs. Flash. Walk to stairs. I see red on stairs. Is it my red blood? My blood did not walk on stairs. It's his. It's his. Walk up the stairs. Need to get out. Gun in my hand, at my side.

Get out. The useless hand tries to grab the rail. Fall down, get up, fall down, get up, up, up. Step, step, step. One more step to go.

Chapter Thirty
Tuesday, November 8, 2016

ylan knocked on Mark's door. "We need to get going."

Behind the door, in his bedroom, a muttering curse is overheard. "I'm still packing."

"We need to get to the safe house. Just pack clothes for a few days."

Mark's voice dripped with sarcasm. "What does one wear to protective custody? I simply cannot decide between this camisole and this floral frock dress."

"First," Dylan responded, "you have no idea what you're talking about when it comes to women's fashion, and I have neither the time nor the inclination to set you straight. Second, a highly dangerous serial killer has let it be known that you are his next target. We cannot let you hang out at your house waiting for him."

"I can defend myself you know. I do work out."

Dylan snorted. "One bag, that's all you need. Some clothes, toothpaste, deodorant, a few books. That's it."

Mark stood next to his bed, the bag he used whenever he travelled on FBI business (he did not travel for vacation, preferring to spend his precious vacation time at home) open, a scowl on his face. "Are you going to be watching my house while I'm gone?" he asked.

A pause from outside his door. "Would you like me to tell you the truth?"

"If possible."

"Then OPD will be coming by more often on patrols. But, more than that, no."

"Wonderful."

"This sucks all the way around. We are doing everything we can."

"Exactly what are you doing?" Mark asked.

"We are analyzing physical evidence. We've gone over Happy's house with a fine-tooth comb. We don't know where he took her from, although we assume her home. The door was unlocked."

"Fingerprints?"

"No, but he was always good at erasing physical evidence. His face is all over the media. I'm not going to lie; it's an absolute shit storm out there. We're getting hundreds of calls an hour on the hotline. If you ask me, that's how we find Vandergeest. Somebody gives us a solid tip and we get him. The problem is separating the solid tip from that old lady who thinks the elderly black woman walking down the street is our average-height, blond-haired, Caucasian serial killer."

Mark decided that he'd had enough with packing, threw a copy of Patrick O'Brien's Desolation Island on top of the clothes, and zipped everything up. As he finished, a headache, a real whopper, descended upon his head like an anvil from the sky in some Wile E. Coyote cartoon.

The sheer power of the pain made him sit down on the bed.

In the hall, Dylan, her patience rapidly deteriorating (she'd rather be working on the case than shepherding Mark around), knocked again.

"Hey," Mark called. His voice sounded weak, "would you mind getting me some Tylenol? Bathroom mirror. Behind."

"What now?" she asked, irritation dripping into her voice.

"Headache. Bad one."

Dylan bit back further response. She'd been working with Mark long enough to know that if he had a petty little request, it was far easier to give in. Otherwise, he'd bitch and moan. She went to the bathroom. Like every other part of the house, the room was meticulously clean. The smell of Pine-Sol hung like a second shower curtain. *Better*, she thought, *than most bachelor pads. Such a fussy little man.*

She opened the mirror above his sink and saw his finicky ways in the organization of the medicine cabinet. Each of the two shelves were subdivided by clear plastic bins. On the bottom shelf, one bin seemed devoted to antacids while the other contained a variety of allergy medicines.

The top shelf bins held pain killers and old, outdated antibiotic bottles. She grabbed the bottle of Tylenol and rolled two pills into her hand. She closed the cabinet door and saw a figure behind her in the doorway.

"Shit," she said, "Mark, you asshole."

"Heh, heh," Mark laughed. "I forgot I needed water too."

"Asshole," she repeated.

They didn't talk much on the way to the car; Dylan kept her eyes moving from place to place, looking for threats. With the button on her keyring, she opened the trunk, but Mark shook his head. He got into the car, hugging the piece of luggage as if he were a three-year-old with a teddy bear.

"Fine," she muttered. "Just get him to the motel, let the old guys do the rest." Two retired agents, including a former agent named Gordon whom Mark was always comparing her to, waited to hang out with Mark while Dylan went back to work.

"So, how long will I have to stay at the motel?" Mark asked as Dylan pulled onto Pacific Street.

"Well, until we catch him, I suppose," Dylan answered. A red minivan had also turned right onto Pacific Street. It had also taken a left with them from Mason Street onto 60th. The Elmwood Golf Course rolled past with Mark staring out at the lone golfer on the first fairway.

"Do you golf?" he asked.

"Uhhh, no."

Something in the way she answered caught his attention.

"What is it?" he asked.

Mark started to turn around but Dylan hissed at him to stop and look forward.

They stopped at the intersection of 72nd and Pacific, the minivan two cars behind and in the left lane.

"It's probably nothing," Dylan said before explaining about the car that may or may not have been following them.

"A minivan?" Mark asked, leaning a little to peer out the side mirror. "Kinda wimpy isn't it?"

"Well, they're not bad vehicles for transporting, you know, bodies. Also, most people don't pay much attention to minivans. They kind of disappear from your consciousness."

"Oh."

At the green light, Dylan drove at a normal pace, her eyes darting to the rear-view mirror.

"So, if he is following us, what do we do?" Mark asked.

"Well, the first thing we do is to make sure that the van is following us. I'd rather not rain hell on some soccer mom. If it turns out we are being followed, I call it in. I'm going to assume he has a police scanner and will bolt if I make him, so I will make my way toward the motel like everything's kosher while unmarked police vehicles converge around our poor, unsuspecting Vandergeest. Then we catch the son of a bitch."

"What if he makes a move on us first?"

"Makes a move?" Dylan asked. "What, like he tries to cop a feel? You do know that I am trained FBI agent. If Vandergeest should say, try to force my car off the road, I am more than prepared to engage him. What is it with people thinking this guy has some kind of superpower? He's a man who likes killing women, that's it. He's not Hannibal Lecter or some expert marksman. He's only a man."

Annoyed, she switched lanes and turned left on 78th. The minivan went into the lane as well, turning.

"Is this the plan?" Mark asked, looking over his shoulder.

"Shut the hell up."

Dylan gunned it and turned left onto Pierce Street. She screeched to a stop and put her hand on her weapon. The red minivan drove past, the man at the wheel not even bothering to look at them.

She exhaled, put the car in park. "Well, that was interesting."

"I don't think that was standard operating procedure," Mark said, rubbing his eyes.

"Well, now we know." Dylan's hand drifted toward the gearshift.

Mark looked back over his shoulder. "Dylan, wait."

She looked at him then back over her shoulder too. "What?" she asked, looking the other way.

Taking the .38 revolver, which had been resting in the front pocket of the luggage, Mark lifted the gun to Dylan's head and fired a bullet. The bullet blew through the driver's side window, leaving a smattering of brains behind.

"That was fascinating," Mark said.

Chapter Thirty-One
Tuesday, November 8, 2016

To be honest, and don't tell anyone, Skylar would rather have gone to school.

Not because she loved school. Not that at all. She inherited her mother's quick, decisive intelligence and an inability to use that intelligence in a formal setting. For Skylar (as it was for Stacy), her brains were a key too complicated for the lock that was public school.

She also inherited her mother's looks, a combination of youthful beauty and boobs that caused boys to hover like flies around roadkill. Unlike her mother, Skylar had no intention of getting pregnant before the age of twenty just because some guy didn't like the way condoms felt.

The reason Skylar did not want to be home on Tuesday, November 8 was that her house had police around it 24/7. She would not, for instance, be able to go to Emmy's house. She would not be able to sneak away from Emmy's house with Emmy to Nick's house. Skylar liked Nick, and he certainly seemed to like her, except he got a little vague when putting a label on it. This kind of pissed Skylar off because if you want to get your hands under Skylar's shirt while you are sitting on a couch in Nick's basement, you'd better be ready to hold Skylar's hand at school.

"What are you staring at," Stacy said to her daughter.

"Huh," Skylar answered, still thinking about Nick and how cute he was when he was flirting. "Just looking at the police outside."

Stacy walked to the living room window and looked out at the black and white cruiser parked in their driveway.

Skylar asked, "How's Grandma?"

"Napping." Stacy looked upstairs at the approximate place where Grandma would be. "She knows something's up. She took her pill, though, so she should be good for a few hours."

"Are you going to do any work?" Skylar asked.

Stacy worked as a freelance graphic designer now, so most days she worked from a small room in the basement that held her desk, chair, and an elliptical machine Stacy spoke of as if it were a distant friend that she needed to catch up with one of these days.

"I tried but I'm too distracted. All I do is flip over to the news sites, seeing if there's been a break in the case. Mark is worried sick about his girlfriend. She's nice."

Nice was not a word Skylar used to describe Ms. Hapke (she could not think of her civics teacher as "Happy"). Sarcastic, perhaps, uncaring to personal circumstance. The kind of teacher who took your phone away even when your mom was texting you about after school pick up. Not nice. Ms. Hapke did know her stuff, and once or twice she did shut down Colt Kinnerson when he was being a complete dumbass. She dated Colt last year and regretted ever kissing the dumbass.

Skylar's reply was lost in the sound of the phone ringing.

"Maybe they caught him," Stacy said as she picked up the phone. A beat later, she said, "Bill" in a flat tone that conveyed depths. Skylar noticed her mom's expression change, become concerned. "Slow down. What happened? Bill, tell me what happened."

Stacy never panicked, never lost it. Instead, she became laser focused, her face set and hard. It became so as she listened to Bill. She let the FBI agent talk for nearly a minute.

"You cannot find him," she said, more a confirmation than a question.

"And the agent died. And the car burned. Was it Mark's? Do you know for a fact that he was in the car when…"? Another spate of listening.

Skylar twisted a lock of her hair, a nervous habit, and asked only one question about what was happening. Her mother ignored the question, never even heard it. Skylar knew she could probably hit her mom in the arm and would still receive no notice.

"Have you heard anything from Vandergeest? A ransom?" Stacy asked. "I see. No, Bill, I will tell her." There was another pause. Stacy interrupted him, "I know all I need to. Fuck you, Bill. Eternally." And Stacy hung up the phone.

"Mom?" Skylar asked. The finger looped the hair, tugged, released, then repeated.

"Mark was taken by Vandergeest. He's gone."

Neither of them spoke. Skylar coughed and the cough became tears, hard, moaning tears.

"Another FBI agent was transporting Mark to a safe house. I guess they thought that Vandergeest…"

Stacy remembered a day, 21 years before, when she had come home to find her mother in a panic. The moments of that day flowed before her eyes as if her daughter disappeared. They had lived in that house even then, and a younger Stacy (then a senior at Eastside) went to work at Pizza Hut after school. Her manager came to get her about eight and told her to go home. Didn't say what was wrong, just said go home.

Her mom's panic, demanding Stacy go out in the neighborhood to look. "Use this," Mom had said, thrusting a dim-wattage flashlight into Stacy's hands. The police crowding the kitchen, and then one or two neighbors.

"What about Grandma?" Skylar managed after a while. "What are we going to tell her."

Saying nothing, Stacy gathered up her daughter into an embrace. "We're going to let Grandma sleep."

Chapter Thirty-Two
Thursday, November 10, 2016

Adam "Cooter" Kovanda stared for a long moment at the can of Fresca sitting on his scratched and burnt coffee table. Cold condensation dripped and made a ring around the can, which had been opened but only sipped. In the fridge, Cooter knew, sat a 12-pack (11-pack, actually) of Fresca. He could not remember, when had he gotten Fresca nor why. Cooter did not like Fresca, he was a Coca-Cola man (preferably with Jack). He did not have the money for such extravagant purchases.

Taco Bell only paid out once a month, on the 15th, which totally sucked. Luckily, he'd made some arrangements with the folks at Apple Creek to pay his rent on payday rather than the first. Had it in his lease and everything. If he didn't pay his rent right on the day he got his monthlies, Cooter had argued to that asshole at the apartment office, by the time the beginning of the month came around there'd be nothing left.

Cooter being Cooter.

After rent and whatever utilities he had to pay that month (Cooter had a system by which he'd only pay his electric bill after they'd turn off his lights – "If I died tomorrow," he liked to say, "I don't want my last thought to be 'Hey, at least my electric's paid up till the end of the month'"), then the first thing Cooter did was head over to Luke's.

Luke, who lived a few buildings away, knew that Cooter got his paycheck the 15th, and always made sure to have the party waiting when Luke sauntered over with his cash money and a hunger for the spiciest weed. After smoking a bowl or three, Cooter called that Thai restaurant across 144th and ordered Garlic Chicken to go.

Maybe some folks lived better lives, but for a few days after the 15th of each month, Luke lived like a king. Around the 20th or so, Luke started eying that bag of weed, wondering if maybe he'd smoked a little too much. By the end of the month, man, Cooter started feeling the need to, you know, build a wall around his dwindling reserves. It was the economic rule of scarce weed; you got to serve yourself first. Catch Cooter on the 17th, he'd smoke you out for free. Around about the end of the month, and the Cooter be shut for casual inquiries. Especially Gina, who was always calling asking if he'd share a spliff. Gina was cool and everything, but the once or twice a year she had some, it was always weak-ass ditch weed.

On October 30, he'd shown up at Luke's unannounced, which cause his buddy to open the door with a machete in his hand. A few "What the hell, man" later, Cooter explained that he'd come into some unexpected cash and would like as much high octane weed as $100 would purchase.

"How'd you get $100 bucks? Your birthday's in July, Cooter," Luke asked.

"Providing sexy time for old ladies, motherfucker. You really care?"

Luke shrugged. "What about your car? Thought your muffler was broke."

"Law of economic scarcity, mi amigo."

"What?"

"It means I already got a car. I don't need another. The scarce resource in the microcosm of my life is that wonderful marijuana," Cooter began (he pronounced it mary-ju-anna). "So, I am putting my resources, this hundred bucks, toward the resources of greatest paucity. Now, gimme some."

"Where did you learn that?" Luke asked. "You fall asleep watching PBS?"

"Nah, intermediate macroeconomics with Professor Gross."

"I have a tough time believing you went to college."

Cooter shrugged, a gesture he performed with absolute efficiency. "I know, right? It's weird, life is. One day you're studying economics at Creighton, the next you're slinging tacos and lightin' up some home grown. Fuckin' A."

So, Luke sold the weed and Cooter spent the next six days having himself a little party: smoking out his friends and even almost having the sex with Julie, who closed up with Cooter on Saturday and said "hell yeah" to a little post-work fiesta of chalupas and green goodness. There they were, on the couch, high as kites, and Julie got all "This is so confusing" and talked about Cooter as if they were boyfriend-girlfriend and not just hooking up on his yellow couch at 2 a.m.

So, Julie left.

Cause Cooter got to be Cooter.

But on the November 10th, Luke called at 10 p.m. and said he had some hash and wanted someone to try it out with him. Now, Cooter might have been dumb but he wasn't stupid, he knew that Luke wanted to sell him some of that hash, thinking maybe since Cooter already had an extra $100 maybe he had a little more. Cooter didn't, but Luke didn't offer free drugs any old time. It was all about opportunity cost, with the x axis the quantity while the y axis the price and… whatevs.

So, Luke came over, they smoked some of Cooter's weed and Luke's hash (which made Cooter feel like his head was expanding so much that he lost his balance and tripped over the coffee table and cut his arm, which bled like a motherfucker).

"Dude, there's a lot of blood," Luke said in a very chill tone. Luke was pretty tall and had long blond hair. Between his looks and his drugs, he did pretty well with the ladies.

"Gimme that napkin. Asswipe."

"It's red." Luke giggled. "Red wine."

Cooter rolled his eyes, reached over and grabbed the napkin. Luke was so gone he was Gandhi. Some of the blood had spilled on the carpet but that didn't matter. Cooter knew he wasn't getting his deposit back, known it since that time he'd lost that bag of mushrooms and punched a hole in the bedroom wall. And that, folks, was why his Megadeath poster (respect the golden oldies!) was so low on the wall. Not that anyone asked.

So, the evening was kind of quiet. They'd been watching some kind of British baking show on Netflix and it had started making Cooter hungry, so he turned it off. He didn't have money and didn't know where to get anise-infused sponge cake at 1:30 a.m. Didn't even have flour in his kitchen to try to bake something.

At some point, Luke had fallen asleep. Every now and then Luke's eyes would kinda flap open. Disturbing shit, in Cooter's book.

Only thing in Cooter's fridge, really, was that 12-pack of Fresca, which he had bought that evening along with a Tostino's frozen pepperoni pizza. If he could only remember: why Fresca?

Cooter wanted something to eat. He got up to check if he had any chips when he heard a noise outside. He wasn't the paranoid type, figured that the police didn't have time to waste with potheads like him, so he didn't think too much of it. But all his neighbors were pretty quiet; they didn't stay out until 1:30 on a Thursday morning.

Maybe it was a raccoon or something. So, Cooter looked around for a weapon and found this 20 -pound weight that he'd bought at some garage sale a few months back (and sometimes lifted whenever he needed a little exercise). He picked it up, shit was heavy, and walked to the door.

He got to the door, his hand raising up to the handle when the door goes BOOM, like somebody lit an M-80 right outside.

Time seemed to slow down for Cooter. On the easy chair, he saw in his peripheral vision Luke jerk upright, brought awake by the boom. A crack appeared in the center of the door, like something heavy had run into it. A thought crossed Cooter's mind, thinking maybe this was some kind of home invasion.

Someone outside the door yelled "POLICE!" real loud.

Leaning forward, Cooter cocked his head and got as far as "What the fu-" before the door came flying in and smashed him in the nose.

The next few seconds seemed to leap by in a cacophony of angry yelling and the kind of pain that only comes when an apartment door breaks your nose while a 20-pound weight drops right on your big toe.

When those first confusing seconds had receded, Cooter found himself on his stomach, his hands cuffed, and the taste of blood spilling into his mouth. "My node, my ucking node!" Cooter yelled, adding to the shouting.

Luke was also on the floor, but he seemed determined to make the cops earn their money. Four officers were on top of him, yanking Luke's arms and legs into position for cuffing. "Stop fighting!" one of them, a muscular dude, kept yelling.

In a part of Cooter's brain untouched by drugs or the pain of his broken nose and toe, it began to register that all of the cops seemed a bit overdressed for busting up a couple of guys smoking hash. *Shit's illegal and all*, said rational brain, *but damn you don't need the SWAT team or anything*. His brain processed that this was the SWAT team, and they were searching his apartment like he was the head of some

Columbian drug cartel. Like he'd be living at the damn Apple Creek Apartments if he had more than $60 in his bank account.

"It's all clear," said one of the cops coming back in from Cooter's bedroom. "only these two numbnuts."

The cops all started asking him shit, about some delivery.

Cooter didn't quite understand. "I work at Taco Bell," he said. "I don't do deliveries."

"Who gave you the box to deliver, asswipe?" said one of the cops.

"What box?" Cooter said, but as the words left his mouth, he realized what the guys were talking about. "You mean the birthday present?"

Two of the cops exchanged looks. "Yeah," said the first one, "the birthday present."

"Some dude wanted to surprise his brother, told me to take the box to Eastside. Gave me a hundred bucks. I would have stolen it but the dude wrote down my license plate number. I thought that shit might have been drugs, but I didn't ask. You know, plausible deniability and all that. Easiest hundred bucks I ever made."

The cop who kept calling Cooter names called him a dumb motherfucker. "What did the guy look like? The one who gave you the package to deliver."

"It was a dude. I don't know. Kinda average."

This black guy with a long face, who was dressed in a suit, said hold on. He gave Cooter fuck eyes, took out his phone and started looking for something. The black guy found it and stuck the phone in front of Cooter's face. "Is this the guy?"

Cooter looked. "Nah, dat wadn't him. The guy who gave me the box had dark hair and his hair was receding. Looked like a total nerd. Had glasses, too."

"Like a nerd?" said the black guy.

Cooter nodded. "Can I get some ice for my node?"

The black guy started looking through his phone again. A minute later, he bent down, held out the phone and showed

Cooter a picture of the black guy dressed in shorts and a polo shirt. Next to him…

"Yeah, dat's the guy. Standing next to you. Glasses, receding hair. Did he give me drugs or what?"

The black guy stepped back, fell into a long racking cough. Cooter didn't have a clue what any of it meant.

Chapter Thirty-Three
Friday, November 11, 2016

Transcript Excerpts of FBI Interviews
Investigation Pertaining to "Omaha Strangler" Murders
FBI Office
4411 South 121st Street

Interviews Between:
SA – Special Agent (FBI)
and
1. LC – Lawrence Chang
2. TK – Dr. Tracy Kucera
3. WM – William Mallory, FBI Agent

1.
SA: Mr. Chang, thank you for coming in… are you okay?

LC: Not really. I'm not certain what's going on. Does this have to do with the walkie-talkie thing? I spoke to an agent about that already.

SA: It does, in fact. As you know, we have been working nonstop on finding the person who Mark Peter spoke to on Wednesday.

LC: The one who threatened to kill me on my way home from work?

SA: Yes. And, as you know, another of your colleagues, a Daffodil Hapke, disappeared yesterday.

LC: We all call her Happy. And so did Mark. Disappear, I mean.

SA: Do you know where Mark Peter is at this moment?

LC: Man, I don't have a clue. Didn't Vandergeest kidnap both him and Happy?

SA: One second. (pause of about five minutes) Mr. Chang, I will speak honestly with you. We have some reason to doubt that Both Mark and Happy were kidnapped.

LC: Okay.

SA: We found the person who dropped the package off at the school. The one carrying the walkie-talkie you saw Mark use to have a conversation with Vandergeest. The man who delivered the box is named Rich Hartman, a part-time employee at Canfield's Sporting Goods.

LC: That's good. Did you arrest him?

SA: No, we didn't. We don't think he committed any crime. What is interesting is that Mr. Hartman said the man who hired him was short, dark-haired, balding, and wore gloves.

LC: What the fu-

SA: Exactly.

LC: But I heard someone else talking? He was talking to someone else.

SA: You weren't, actually. After we spoke to Mr. Hartman, we searched Mark's car. In the trunk was a heavily modified computer that was hooked up to a walkie-talkie. Our tech team is still examining the device, but it looks like he used it to stage a conversation with someone that was meant to be Vandergeest.

LC: I don't. I don't. The threats Vandergeest made? My husband took our son to Kansas City because I thought Vandergeest would be coming after us. It was all just Mark?

SA: Yeah, I understand.

LC: This doesn't make sense. Mark is my friend. We've been friends for years.

SA: It doesn't make sense to us. We're hoping that you can help us make sense of it.

LC: What about the murders? Do you think Mark killed those girls?

SA: Quite frankly, we don't know yet. This information changes things.

LC: He couldn't have. I know him. He might be, I don't know, fucked up, but he's not a killer.

SA: This is why you're here. To help us understand why Mark Peter would fake a conversation with a notorious serial killer. What could he gain? Do you think he was looking for attention?

LC: Mark? God no. He hated attention. He didn't even like it when people looked at him.

SA: Were there any issues at work that might have caused undue stress.

LC: There were, but not anymore. We had this issue with this woman named Shit about this ICW software. But it wasn't…

SA: Tell me. We need to know everything.

2.

TK: I'm not entirely certain how much help I can be to you. I've never actually met Mr. Peter. The only information I have is what Agent Mallory told me.

SA: I understand, doctor, but given those limitations, I was hoping that you might at least try to provide some possible reasons for Mr. Peter's behavior.

TK: Are you asking me if Mr. Peter has suffered a psychotic break?

SA: Something like that.

TK: I couldn't say. The one thing I think is most clear about Mr. Peter is that he has been under a great deal of stress. Some of that may come from work or family pressures, but I believe that he also uses what might be termed a psychic ability to help the FBI catch murderers…

SA: Something like that.

TK: That alone makes anything I say suspect. Everything I've ever known about the human mind screams that there are no psychics. Yet Agent Mallory, and now you, are telling me that Mr. Peter can indeed handle an object and be able to know events related to the object's owner?

SA: I believe the term is psychometry.

TK: I know the word. I don't want to give credence to the legions of con artists who claim psychic abilities to defraud old ladies who want to talk to their dead husbands.

SA: Here. We recorded some of the sessions where Mr. Peter exercised his gift. This was several years ago with the original Vandergeest murders. This is a recording of Mark touching the pillowcase of Andrea Hawkins.

(Video is shown)

TK: I'm sorry. Excuse me.

SA: You're not the only one to do that, doctor. The images are pretty disturbing. It's why I put the wastepaper basket next to you.

TK: It was his voice. This is real?

SA: Everything you saw. These drawings led us straight to where Vandergeest buried Andrea.

TK: Are you sure that Mr. Peter didn't commit the murders originally?

SA: Mark has rock solid alibis for at least five of the victims, including Andrea. And we have found no evidence that he ever even met Eric Vandergeest.

TK: This, this ability that Mr. Peter apparently seems to have makes any kind of diagnosis impossible. It's like asking where a hit golf ball would end up but telling me that the golf ball had rockets attached to it.

SA: All I ask is for your opinion.

TK: Fine. Okay, let me start with something you mentioned earlier. You spoke of a psychotic break. That makes it sound unnecessarily violent. Psychotic breaks from reality is what happens when someone with an underlying mental illness like schizophrenia, schizoaffective disorder, bipolar disorder or several others experiences difficulty distinguishing what is real and not real. This break can lead to a person having a belief that the government is out to get them or they might hear voices telling them to do things. People who have psychosis don't just grab a gun and start shooting up schools. Most often, people suffering from psychosis are the victims of violent crime, not the perpetrators. However, if you are wondering if Mark is suffering from some kind of psychosis, I could not tell you. You need to ask people who know him. Did he withdraw socially in the time leading up to the murders? Did he voice suspicious or anxious thoughts? Did he change his routines? Those are the things you should be looking for.

SA: We've been interviewing those close to Mark, and I don't think… (sound of flipping pages) … Would you mind taking a look at these reports that Agent Mallory submitted?

(Interview break of about two hours)

SA: Does anything jump out at you?

TK: Mr. Peter appears to be socially awkward, but he has a supportive social structure. Let's see. There are a few things that jump out to me. One is that he suffers from nightmares. Do you know if they are common?

SA: I don't.

TK: And there is this part about the sensory issues. He always wears gloves. Part of this obviously has to do with this extrasensory ability he has. However, there seems to be a psychological need, a need to be wearing the gloves in order to function. It isn't obsessive-compulsive, or at least I don't see it. Frankly, part of me wonders if this is a symptom of hyperarousal. It's not textbook, but Mr. Peter seems wound pretty tight. Having the gloves on appears to deaden his ability to sense the world. It's also a way to avoid the stress caused by this ability. It's a classic sign of PTSD.

SA: Would that cause him to commit violence?

TK: Number one, I am not diagnosing Mr. Peter with anything. I am merely speculating. Number two, PTSD does not cause violent behavior. Certainly not kidnapping and murder. If this was a domestic violence case, a lawyer might bring up the PTSD. But not this. I'm not sure I'm much help.

SA: You've been invaluable, doctor. One last question, do you see in those files any clue as to where Mr. Peter is right now.

TK: No. Sorry, but I haven't the faintest.

3.

SA: Do you know where Mark Peter is at this moment?

WM: No sir, I do not. Do you?

SA: Do you know if Mark Peter owns any property outside of his home?

WM: No sir, I do not.

SA: Has he mentioned any places where he spends a great deal of time outside of his home, his mother's home, or place of employment?

WM: No sir.

SA: Do you know anything that can help us in locating Mark Peter?

WM: No sir, I do not.

SA: How long has Mr. Peter worked for the FBI in an unofficial capacity?

WM: About a dozen years. He has been an invaluable asset.

SA: I'm sure he has. Did you see any signs that Mark Peter had become mentally unstable?

WM: Mentally… No, I have not seen any signs. I don't think that Mark…

SA: Do you know the symptoms of PTSD, Agent Mallory?

WM: Yeah, it's, uh, you can't sleep, you are triggered very easily. There are others.

SA: Did Mr. Peter exhibit any symptoms of PTSD?

WM: I don't recall him talking about insomnia.

SA: Do you know where Mr. Peter is?

WM: No. Do you suspect me of helping Mark?

SA: We don't know what to think. We do know that you are the closest link we have to him. We know he has been under great stress. We are operating under the theory that Mark is experiencing a psychotic episode.

WM: He isn't crazy.

SA: Are you sure? How well does anyone know Mark?

WM: How well does anyone know anyone? Mark said that to me a few weeks ago.

SA: He said that to you? I think we need to start at the beginning.

WM: We've been here for an hour.

SA: Okay, let's start with how you met Mr. Peter.

Chapter Thirty-Four
Saturday, November 12, 2016

Parmero stopped and put his arm in front of Bill. "Officially," Parmero said, "you are not allowed anywhere near this house."

"I understand," Bill replied. His allergies had gone into overdrive.

The two men stood in the driveway of Mark Peter's house, the only light from a streetlight down the street. The KMTV van, the last of the local news, had left ten minutes before. All four stations had broadcast that evening from Mark's house, breathless speculation about Mark Peter, Eric Vandergeest, and the murderer-at-large. They'd received their information from someone at OPD.

"I get it," Bill said again.

Bill knew he might be a suspect in aiding and abetting his friend murder at least three different women. The original Vandergeest cases had not yet been reopened, but the thick files on each of the nine known victims were at that moment being scrutinized by a hastily formed special task force of the Omaha Police Department.

"The only reason you're here right now is because you might be able to help us catch your buddy, and there might be some kind of clue in there that we missed. Do you understand?"

"What have you guys found out?" Bill asked.

"Are you familiar with what being off the case entails?" Agent Parmero gave Bill a long look then seemed to relent. "We found he had a computer program wired up to the other walkie talkie along with a series of pre-recorded responses. All Mark had to do was stick to a script and it would appear to any observer that he was having an actual conversation with Vandergeest. The whole point of the walkie talkie thing was to have Mr. Chang witness the exchange. Very clever, actually.

"If you hadn't caught the guy who delivered it to the school," Bill agreed, "and if Cooter hadn't been able to remember Mark in his addled mind, you'd be looking for some tall blond dude who died six years ago."

"Well, I don't know," Agent Parmero drawled out, "that Vandergeest is for sure dead. Maybe he and your buddy were working together? Maybe Vandergeest crawled out of the Mississippi River, gave ol' Mark Peter a call, and has been chilling in Mark's basement for the past few years, plotting revenge?"

Bill snorted. "That's pretty far-fetched."

Paremero put his hand on Bill's upper arm and gripped it. The agent had strong, powerful hands. "This case, Agent Mallory, is so far from anything we've ever seen that we cannot afford to discount any hypothesis. We cannot say for absolute certainty that Vandergeest even committed these crimes to begin with."

"That's a load of…"

"Nothing is off the table. Nothing. Hell, even you are under suspicion."

Bill willed himself to not shout out. "If that is the case, why am I here?"

"Because believe it or not, I don't think you have anything to do with this. Several of your fellow agents believe otherwise. Because I don't think you had anything to do with this, you are being given a chance at redeeming yourself, at helping us find Ms. Hapke. Of bringing in Mark safely."

A dark sedan pulled into the driveway and two people got out, a woman and a man. "These two folks are from Omaha Police Homicide," Parmero said by way of introduction. "They have graciously allowed you to examine Mr. Peter's house to see if there is anything that you can find that might help us locate either Mr. Peter or Ms. Hapke."

"This was not our idea," the woman said, taking the lead. She wore her hair short and radiated disdain. "Are you going to play by the rules?"

"What rules?" Bill asked.

Parmero spoke up. "Officer Karnes, I didn't get to that part yet. Bill, because of your connection to Mark, you are not entirely clear of this investigation. However, I was able to convince their boss to let you help us."

"You want me to prove that I'm not helping Mark."

"Something like that. However, these detectives will make sure you do not take any materials from the house and will be watching you while you search Mr. Peter's belongings."

"We've already searched the house, but it's thought that you might see something we missed. At least, that's the explanation we've been given," said Karnes.

Something seemed fishy about this entire setup but Bill knew better than to think too hard on it. He nodded and the four of them clustered by the front door. Karnes took a key from his pocket and opened the door; the four of them ducked underneath the yellow tape to go in.

Whoever had conducted the search of Mark's house had done a shoddy job of putting everything back. Mark's living room couch, for instance, lay upturned in the middle of the living room.

In his mind, Bill Mallory made a mental checklist.

One, it appeared that his friend had in fact murdered multiple people. This first point alone almost could not be conceived of in its entirety. Bill had known Mark for years, knew Mark as well as he knew anyone in the world. Yet this did not guarantee anything. Dennis Rader (the BTK Killer), Gary Ridgeway (the Green River Killer), and numerous other serial killers had spouses who knew nothing of their husbands' murderous activities. So, it was entirely possible that Mark Peter could keep four murders (if not more) from his friend.

Bill only gave a cursory examination to the living room. By its nature, living rooms tended to showcase the homeowner's public face to the world. If Mark left clues to his location, they'd not be there.

Two, why would Mark kill anyone? Would his past (the kidnapping and sexual abuse, the inability to touch others, his stunted romantic life) cause such strain over him that Mark would break and begin to murder young women? Mark always spoke of the horrible nightmares he had from the objects he touched. Bill wondered if perhaps these nightmares wrecked his sanity. He knew the women had been found in water, perhaps the crimes contained elements of the other killers Mark had helped capture.

"Where have you looked?" Bill asked. "For Mark?"

Karnes deliberated before answering. "We've gained access to his computers and have people looking at those. We are also seeing if he or his family owns property that he might have access to. We've gone through his office with a fine-toothed comb. If he had anything at school, we'd know about it."

"What about land belonging to Ms. Hapke or her family? She'd probably tell him."

"I'm sure we're looking into that as well," Karnes said.

Bill walked into the kitchen and was struck by how all the cabinet doors were open. "That seems so odd," he murmured.

The thing was, Bill thought, you would think an FBI agent would be able to spot a serial killer in a friend. Bill Mallory was no dumb, bulled-over housewife who didn't think twice when her husband came home at four in the morning with bloodstains all over his shirt.

Again, things had been gone through in such a way as to disrupt the order Mark had so scrupulously arranged. The spices, for instance, no longer were separated by cuisine (rosemary, oregano, and basil in the Italian section, cumin, turmeric, coriander in Indian). The various kitchen tools in the drawer nearest the fridge no longer all lay in even horizontal lines. The small area in the corner which held the bills, checkbook, mail, and coupons had been taken away, presumably for closer analysis.

Bill opened the fridge. As with every other part of the kitchen, it showed evidence of slightly disturbed order.

"He has a pot roast in here," Bill said over his shoulder to the two detectives.

"Are you hungry, or is there a symbolic importance I'm not seeing?" Karnes asked.

"Well, Mark loved pot roast." Bill stood and showed one finger as if a list were forthcoming. "He always cooked these things on his slow cooker. It was one of his specialties. It's a big enough pot roast to feed an entire family."

Karnes smirked. "Should we be hoping Mark is going to have a heart attack from eating too much beef?"

"I know Mark. He's a planner. Why would he buy a pot roast with enough for several meals left over?" Bill knew in some part of his brain that he sounded foolish but cared little.

"Okay, if I'm understanding you correctly," said Karnes slowly, "we should disregard neutral testimony that says Mr. Peter sent a package to the school designed to make people think Eric Vandergeest was still alive and active. Other witnesses saw someone who matches the physical description of Mr. Peter leaving the scene of Agent Mannion's murder.

Alone. And this is based on what Mr. Peter got on his last trip to Hy-Vee?"

"I didn't know about the other witnesses."

"We canvassed the shit out of that neighborhood, Agent Mallory." Karnes gave him a thin smile. "Better police work than your psychic bullshit."

Bill closed the door and left the kitchen, not bothering to wait for the detectives.

"How much longer is he gonna be?" said the male detective, the first time Bill had heard him speak.

If Parmero responded, Bill did not hear. The bedroom had been searched more thoroughly than any other room. He spent a few minutes there but saw nothing out of the ordinary. That left the basement and the hobby room.

In most houses, this would have contained another bed for guests, but Mark did not have guests over for the night. That was what hotels were for. Instead, his spare room contained a few bookshelves, a walking treadmill, two fifteen-pound weights, and his miniatures. Bill started with the bookshelves.

The three shelves, all taller than Bill, still held some sense of organization, although Bill knew they'd previously been ordered according first to genre and then by the author's last name. Science fiction, from Asimov to Zelazny, comprised the entire first shelf. The second shelf held fantasy and crime fiction. The third shelf general fiction, non-fiction, and odds and ends.

For several minutes, Bill perused the shelves. He had occasionally borrowed some novels from Carl Hiaasen or Alan Furst, but not often. Mark did not like to lend his books and would only lend them to Bill on condition that he read them whilst wearing gloves. Bill always did, even though he suspected Mark might not have known otherwise.

That detail, small detail, caused tears to well in Bill's eyes. His poor friend.

"Shit," Bill said aloud.

"You almost done?" Karnes asked from the door.

"A few minutes, then downstairs."

The third bookshelf's top half was filled with the kind of fiction Mark liked. The complete set of Patrick O'Brien's Aubrey-Maturin series (which Bill had never gotten into). The bottom half held a dictionary, a Whole Earth Catalogue from 1993, some Eastside High School yearbooks (the last six years and then one from 1996, separated from the others by a thick piece of cardboard), Strunk and White's thin books on grammar, an atlas, several books by Bill Bryson, and a few textbooks on psychology.

Bill took out one of the textbooks and thumbed through it. It was new, no underlines, notes in the margins, or highlighting marks.

"We looked at those, too," said Karnes.

Something knocked about in Bill's mind as he went over to the miniatures table. Although he rarely did so anymore, Mark at one point had a group of friends who played Dungeons & Dragons. They had more or less broken as a group (marriage, kids, jobs in other cities), but Mark once remarked that he loved the miniatures and would sometimes sell the figurines on e-bay. Not that he needed the money.

The figurines on the table all were slate gray, the finished ones were arranged downstairs on display cases which lined the basement's main room. On the desk's shelves sat a few cans of primer, a staggering variety of enamel and acrylic paints, and rows of small brushes.

"Have you seen the stuff downstairs?" Karnes asked. "This kid was pretty big into this stuff. Whatever, but he must have put a lot of money into it."

Bill, who had been leaning over and examining one of the figures (an ogre of some kind) stood up straight. "What is it?" Karnes asked.

"My back," Bill lied, and put his hand to his lower back to sell the lie. "Messed it up a few days ago. You ever sleep wrong?"

"You're sure?"

"Yeah, it's the worst," Karnes said but Bill could feel her eyes boring into him.

Bill hesitated (deliberately) before turning and saying, "I was wondering if there could be any way of looking at the psychology books. Maybe seeing if the books fell open to any spots in particular. I don't know, probably wouldn't help."

Karnes stared for a second longer before she said that was interesting and would have someone follow up on that. "You ready to check the basement?"

Bill nodded and followed her out of the room, although he didn't care about the basement at all.

The thing that had been rattling around Bill's head had grown into a thought. Parmero noticed something in Bill's expression. "You either have to take a shit or you are having a thought. If it's a shit, there's a gas station down the street. I don't want you messing up my crime scene. If it's a thought, you'd better talk."

"I was thinking," Bill began slowly. Then, he rushed on, "You have to try to save him."

"He killed an agent," Parmero said flatly. "We'll try to keep him from harm, but a lot of people aren't going to care about that."

Bill knew that his boss could give no better answer. He decided to continue, "If there's anything Mark cannot abide having anything in his house, it's old, used stuff."

"His OCD has been noted."

"He has yearbooks in his bedroom. Most are recent, one for each year he's been working at the school. There's one old one, from 1996. That was before he was in high school. I doubt they were someone else's, so that meant that yearbook has never been owned."

"I don't follow," Parmero said. "You think an old yearbook on his bookshelf is a clue? Like an actual Agatha Christie novel kind of clue?"

"I think Mark left it there." Bill looked out at some invisible point on the wall, deep in thought. "I think he left it there for me, because I know him best. He separated the 1996 book from the others because he could not stand having it in the house. It's a cry for help. I think he needs help from Vandergeest. I don't know how it happened, but I believe Mark is trying to get the FBI to free him from Vandergeest."

Parmero's face darkened. "Vandergeest is dead. He died five years ago."

"This situation is fucked up," Bill agreed, "but that yearbook is a clue."

"And what does this clue mean, do you think?"

"There's an old, never-owned yearbook sitting on Mark's shelf. There's only one place he could have gotten it."

"From the school?" Parmero asked. "We searched the school."

"Everywhere?"

For a second, Parmero drummed his fingers against his leg. "Perhaps not. What do you suggest?"

"Personally? I would talk to the custodians," Bill said, "they know where the hidden places are."

Chapter Thirty-Five
Saturday, November 12, 2016

Parmero and Bill stood outside the main doors of Eastside High School and banged on the door. The lights were on, so someone should have been there. After a few minutes, a man shambled out from a hallway and squinted his eyes at the darkness where Bill stood. In his mid-fifties, the tall, crouched man had a face with close-set eyes and an uneven beard. The custodian did not appear to think very quickly but eventually he went to let the two men in.

"You police?" The janitor's mouth seemed incapable of closing all the way

Parmero showed the janitor his badge. "FBI. We're looking for Mark Peter."

"Didn't you guys already search the building?" The custodian sounded vaguely resentful, as if more FBI agents meant for a longer shift.

"We did, actually," Bill interrupted. "Were you here?"

"I'm here every night. I was when you had police all over the place."

"Did they miss anything?" Parmero said, looking at Bill. Stop asking questions, Parmero's expression said.

"I don't know. They seemed in a hurry." Although the custodian seemed dumb as a board, something in his expression turned almost sly. "They probably didn't look everywhere."

Parmero noticed the look and shifted his tactics immediately. "What did they miss? Bet no one thought to ask you."

"Probably didn't miss anything. They wanted all the keys but didn't ask me. When they gave the keys back to me, the policeman about threw the keys back in my face. I asked 'em if they looked in the boiler rooms and he said yeah. But I looked and they hadn't."

"Boiler rooms?" Bill asked, unable to help himself. "More than one?"

"There's the boiler room in the basement. They probably looked there." The custodian shrugged. "Then there's the old boiler room, just off the gym. We haven't done much with it in years. A lot of old crap in that room. Door doesn't look like much."

"You don't think they checked there?" Bill asked, again getting a look.

"Sully said they didn't," the custodian said, "and he was around the gym. But I don't know. Usually there's a rack of volleyballs blocking the door. Ain't blocking the door now."

Parmero's lips thinned. "Let's come away from the building," he said, pulling out his cell phone. When they were across the drop off lane, in the parking lot, Parmero looked up from the call. "Bill, would you mind waiting in the car?"

"I do, actually. He's my friend."

"He's a suspect."

"Vandergeest is behind this."

Parmero shook his head, listened for a second before addressing Bill, "Vandergeest is dead, as I said before. If you are his friend, let us do our job. We are professionals; we'll do our best to not hurt Mark."

The way Parmero spoke stabbed Bill deep. The use of "we" to exclude Bill, the little dig about professionalism. He still was employed by the Federal Bureau of Investigations, but Bill felt like he had already been fired.

However, true soldier that he was, Bill went to the car. He did not sit down but instead stood next to the passenger door. Parmero looked over but decided not to press the issue. Not long after, unmarked cars and a S.W.A.T. truck arrived in complete silence. Men and women huddled not too far away from Bill, but he could not hear their conversations.

The years of faithful service felt, in Bill's eyes, like so much of a Missouri River beneath a pedestrian bridge where Eric Vandergeest held off an entire police department. The water flew by beneath the bridge, uncaring to the drama above. When Vandergeest pulled the girl with him over the edge, Bill had screamed in frustration.

All the years, all the cases. His marriage ending. Children he barely saw. All the sacrifices. Water beneath the bridge. Now Mark too, about to be thrown into the river. All his sacrifices. Water beneath the bridge.

A phalanx of armored police rushed through the front doors. Police everywhere, their cars dark and quiet.

The quiet of the evening wore on. The phone in Bill's pocked buzzed, his ringer silent. A text message. Bill took the phone and, holding it low so that it would not be noticed, looked at the message. It came from an unknown number.

"A lot of police for one tiny room."

From inside, Bill could vaguely hear a muffled boom, a deep bark. "Who are you?" he wrote back.

"Come alone," came the reply. "Don't bother replying. This phone is gone."

Chapter Thirty-Six
Saturday, November 12, 2016

"She was there," Parmero said when he finally returned to the car. Forensics vans sat idling by the front doors. "Along with cameras, a router, computer… He's hacked into the security cameras. We think he's watching everything on a website. Maybe we'll get lucky and find him through that. It's going to take a little while. Take this car home, Bill, and I will call you tomorrow."

Bill could feel his cell phone in his pocket but he did not take it out. Something in Parmero's angry expression, in the fury of the police and FBI agents around him. They wanted blood for Dylan, for making them look like fools. They wanted a body to wrap up the case, nice and neat and without a trial. Bill did not know for absolute certain that it wasn't Vandergeest. He hated the idea that Mark had done any of this. Therefore, Bill's phone remained in his pocket, its cryptic message unread by anyone else.

Rather than protest, Bill acquiesced and got into the car. The second he did, Parmero clearly moved on to other things. Someone, Mark or Vandergeest, wanted Bill to be the one to find him. Yet he had no idea where Mark or Vandergeest was. All he had was an Eastside yearbook from 1996, an abandoned boiler room, and an overly clean house.

How was Bill, of all people, supposed to find Mark / Vandergeest?

Bill drove straight from the school to a Scooter's, ordering a large cup of coffee. He felt so tired. Not just physically tired but soul-deep tired. He pulled away from the drive-thru and into a parking space in the all-night Hy-Vee. The coffee felt good burning down his throat. If I'm tired, Bill thought, how weary must my friend be.

It was difficult to imagine the kind of things that kept Mark up at night. Mark had described reliving the worst crimes, getting chased or choked. No wonder Mark hadn't had a good night's sleep in years.

"Decades, probably," Bill muttered. Probably since 1996…

Bill's eyes widened as a thought struck him. He knew where Mark was.

The dark house sat at the end of the street, half-hidden by overgrown mulberry bushes and untrimmed pines. There had been talk of destroying the home, but apparently nothing had come of it. The home owner apparently decided to remodel. Bill had not been by the place for many years, but he'd found it as easily as he could have found the home he'd grown up in.

Was Mark in there? Was Happy? Was she alive? The windows reflected no light that Bill could see, but he wondered if perhaps he saw a light peeking through from a basement window. Bill got out of his car, put his hand to his phone. One phone call and the police would be here within minutes.

The old porch creaked as Bill's heavy shoes walked to the front door. Gun drawn, Bill looked through the curtainless window. There, in the back of the kitchen, he could see a faint glow. Probably from the basement.

Knowing he was making a stupid, stupid mistake, Bill tested the door. Unlocked and it swung open without a hint of protests from the hinges. One step inside and the floor groaned. Anyone downstairs knew that Bill was there.

In a fit of sanity, Bill took out his phone and sent a text message to Parmero. After the address, Bill wrote, "Mark is here. Send everyone. I'm going in."

After the message sent, Bill felt a jolt of relief. His fate was sealed, wedded to whatever he found below. A half-dozen steps to the back of the kitchen and the stairs to the basement. He did not even feel his phone buzzing with phone call after call. His non-FBI-issued .44 caliber Smith and Wesson 629 revolver in hand, Bill began to walk down the stairs.

A step down the stairs. Another. The light seemed to come from some farther room. Bill remembered that farther room as the place where Mark had been tortured. Old boxes, some falling apart, lined the walls of the main room. An old, broken television and couch sat in the middle of the floor. The only light came from the room beyond, and the light from the door cast massive shadows in which a person could easily hide.

Bill peered into the dark spaces of the room but could see nothing. It did not seem likely, to Bill at least, that Mark would attack him from behind. That is, if Mark really were behind all of this, which Bill still did not wholly believe.

It was not as if Mark were free from his oddities, Bill thought as he began to inch toward the door. The gloves, the touching, the constant headaches, the paranoia. His strange attitude toward cleaning his house. Any man who loves vinegar that much is not normal, Bill thought and almost chuckled. He felt ashamed of almost laughing, considering where he stood and what had happened. Trying to shut down all of those feelings and memories, Bill took another few steps toward the door.

Finally, he stopped outside the far room, his back against the concrete wall, his shoulder almost touching the cool metal doorframe. Bill took a few deep breaths to calm himself and pivoted to peek into the room.

He saw a large room, almost completely empty. At a student desk (one in which chair and desk were one) in the center of the room, Mark's girlfriend sat. Rope lashed Happy's feet to the legs of the desk and a thick leather strap of some kind wrapped around her waist secured her to the desk's back. Her hands appeared free, but the lower half of Happy's face was covered in some kind of mask. It must have allowed Happy to breathe but probably kept her from speaking. Her head hung down but her chest rose and fell.

Behind Happy, at a similar 1960s style desk, sat Mark. He was looking at a computer. From what Bill could see, Mark had no ropes around his feet or waist, although the hands were not visible. Mark could move freely, it would seem. Bill's heart sank.

"I've been watching you for the last five minutes," Mark said aloud, not taking his eyes off his computer. "Cameras in the living room and kitchen. You may as well come in, Bill."

So much for any element of surprise. Bill swiveled and half-appeared in the door, his revolver pointed at Mark. "Put your hands up, Mark." Bill's voice wavered when he spoke and he felt tears running down his face.

Mark shifted his position and Bill could see a gun in Mark's right hand, the one that had faced away from him. He could see it pointing at Happy's head. "Can't do that at this point in time. Would you mind lowering your weapon?" Mark asked.

He didn't have a good shot, not with Happy in his way, so Bill entered the room and began to step to his right to open up the space between them. He took a few steps when he heard Mark pulling back the hammer of his pistol.

"Stop, please," Mark said. He sounded like Mark, the man Bill had known for... Bill shook his head and forced those thoughts down. "You know I'll shoot her."

"No, you won't. You won't. You wouldn't hurt a fly," Bill said. "I know you."

"How well do you know anyone, Bill? Not me, I assure you. I myself have killed..." Mark stopped off, blinked furiously for a second. "This gets semantically confusing. Let's just say I've killed at least three and perhaps as many fifty people."

"Mark, you didn't."

"I did. At least three. Like I said, semantically confusing. It's a long story."

"Tell me," Bill implored, "I'm your friend. Tell me."

"Your claims of friendship are somewhat dubious, Billy. Bill-a-roon-o. Billy Boy. For one thing, you've kind of fucked me here. Lastly, you want me to tell you a story? How long before the police or the FBI or the National Guard gets here? I saw you send a text. You should have seen the activity at the school. We probably only have a few minutes. It's a long story."

Some part of Bill's training kicked in. "If I have done you wrong, Mark, if I have betrayed you, I apologize. I'm the only one here. Just you and me. We got a long time, as long as you want. Tell me your story, Mark, I want to hear it. I'm interested."

If Mark knew he was being manipulated, he gave no sign. "So, what, you want me to lower my gun, let her go, and then you'll kill me?"

"No," Bill said, "no, I do not want that. I want you to be the Mark that I've been friends with for so long. The person I consider my best friend in the world. You dying? I couldn't live with myself."

"I want you to back the hell up," Mark spat out.

"I'm moving back," Bill said. "I'm lowering my gun. I can't put it away but I'm lowering it. Are you okay? Does anyone need medical attention?" Bill phrased it so that the second part would include Happy, who still appeared to be asleep.

"Everybody's fine," Mark replied, his voice cruel. "She's doped up."

"So, what happened?" Bill asked. "Did Ms. Hapke there try to hurt you?"

"She's fine. We had sex. Something got messed up and our skin touched." Mark shrugged and said, "She started screaming about how I killed all those people and I knew I couldn't let her go. Maybe I wanted that to happen. I took her here. Doctored the security footage. That's the story. End of story. That's it."

Bill spoke slowly. "I get that."

"Do you?"

"I do. She knew too much, so…"

"You don't know shit," Mark said.

"You're right. I don't know what it's like to be you. To have those memories…"

Mark interrupted. "They're not memories. I see murder whenever I close my eyes. It's fantasies. I…" He stopped, unclear. "I don't know how to explain this."

Happy's head moved a little, enough for Bill to see she was awake. "It's tough to explain?"

"You could say that."

"Are you Mark?" Bill asked.

At this, Mark smiled. "At this point, not really. Think of it like, I don't know. Imagine living your life in a room split in half. Half of the room is behind a glass wall. And behind that wall it's filled with water. And swimming in that water are monsters that want to eat you. Every year, every time you touch some teddy bear or pillow or cheap piece of jewelry, you see someone get hurt or someone get murdered. And the water rises and more monsters start swimming back and forth
258

behind that glass. More water, more monsters. And then the glass starts to crack. A little water starts spilling in, but you're not hurt. But you know that wall's gonna break at some point. Then it does."

"The wall broke?"

"Yeah, whatever. It broke into, like, a million pieces." Mark's hand trailed off into the air. "I'm drowning in a room with all these monsters and one day not long after I find myself choking some girl to death and throwing her body in a lake."

An image popped into Bill's head. In it, he's walking with Mark in Fontanelle Forest. They're both much younger. Mark's in college and they just took a walk. And they're standing at this overlook, looking at the Missouri River, when a butterfly comes out of the sky and lands on Mark's head (he had a full head of hair, although a few strands of silver seemed to be poking through). The butterfly, gray with little orange bursts on the wings, sat there as if Mark were the most beautiful flower on earth.

"Maybe," Bill began before swallowing hard. He started again, "Maybe you didn't do it. Not the real you, Mark. You go to court, we explain how your gift works, maybe get counseling." That wasn't what he should say in a hostage situation, Bill knew, but...

"You don't understand," Mark hissed. "Forget the glass wall. Maybe it's like a wrestling match. Or a dance. Or maybe like a tapeworm. Or something. It doesn't matter. I did it. I killed those girls. And boys. Men, women, I killed Mark's cat. You ever smell a cat shit itself when it dies? I have. I did it."

"I haven't. It must be difficult," Bill agreed.

"No one in the world knows what this is like."

"Yeah," Bill agreed, "Your gift is unprecedented.

"I liked killing those girls. All three of them."

"Three?" The police had only found two bodies.

"Yeah," Mark said, "three. It made me feel happy, like I'd exploded."

"Do you want to feel like that again?" Bill asked.

"Yeah but not the rest, not the other parts," Mark said.

"So, what would you like me to do? A helicopter? I can make that happen."

Mark chuckled. "No, you can't. The marksman would shoot me the second I gave them an open shot. I'm not leaving this house alive. I didn't before, all those years ago. Not really."

"Hey," Bill said softly. "Hey, Mark. How often have you been over to my house for dinner? How many times have I eaten with your family?" He trailed off.

Some small part of Mark's face twisted and he actually gave a genuine, if rueful smile. "Pretty often. I loved your wife's enchiladas. Wish you hadn't divorced," Mark said in a small voice. "We had some good times."

"You remember when we were in that forest, looking for that autistic boy who got lost? In Arkansas, I think."

"The wasps," Mark whispered.

"Yeah, yellow jackets. I was in front, you right behind me, and I about walked right into the damn nest. I thought it was part of the tree."

"We had to take off running."

"You remember that deputy that was with us, the fat one? He cleared a path for us through the brush like he was a bulldozer."

"Then we jumped in that pond," Mark said.

Bill looked away, thinking of how they waded, jumped, and swam into the nasty greenish pond, each of them got stung by at least fifteen wasps. "I can count on one hand the times I've been in more pain."

"The kid died though," Mark said after a minute.

"Yeah," Bill replied, "he did. Exposure. We did the best we could."

"I felt his fear. It's part of me now. That and I can't have my food touching each other on the plate now. That's the thing, Bill, is that even the good memories usually involve pain and suffering." Mark's face froze again in that unfamiliar stare. "I don't even know what I want. Too many things, I suppose. And they're all at odds with each other. I'm like an army of voices."

"What are they fighting about?" Bill asked.

Mark jerked his head toward the computer. "I think the cavalry is here."

That was quick, Bill thought. He felt the buzzing of the phone. "It's Agent Mallory," he told Parmero, who had the brains to be quiet. "I'm with Mark Peter. Daffodil Hapke is also here. She appears to be okay. Is that right?"

"She is unharmed."

"Mr. Peter has told me that she is unharmed. However, he has asked that you stay outside the house for the time being," Bill continued to yell, "but I will contact you in a short while."

Mark looked at the monitor for a second. He took a pair of headphones from the desk next to him and, with one hand, put his ear to the one of the speakers, never taking his eyes off of Bill.

"The one guy up there is not very fond of you. I think he's cussing a lot." Mark looked at Bill. "This is not standard FBI procedure, huh?"

Bill shook his head. "That it isn't, Mark."

"I'm glad that it's just you and me. You're the person who fucked me up. I'm kind of hoping all three of us die tonight."

"I'm not concerned for myself. I'm concerned about you and Happy. Why do you want us to die?"

"I don't think I do," Mark said, "It's really hard to explain."

"Yeah?" Bill prompted. "How?"

"I have to. I don't want to, but I have to. Like I don't really get a choice in the matter. I don't know. Mark is feeling really tense right now, Bill, like I want to pull the trigger and kill her."

"Her?" Bill asked. "You mean Happy? Your girlfriend?"

Mark shook his head. "I don't want to do this. I have to. I'm being pulled toward it. Like this strain comes from all these monsters in Mark's head. All these monsters telling me to pull the trigger, to lick her blood, to cut her whore eyes out."

"It sounds like you have a lot of conflicts going on in there," Bill echoed.

"You don't understand. It's an army in Mark. And she has to die."

"Mark," Bill said, "you are in control here. I understand that you have some anger toward her. But there's probably more than anger going on with you. Is that right?"

"I'm not angry. I don't know."

"That's understandable. Human emotions are complex." Bill tried to keep his voice slow and measured.

"She's so beautiful," Mark said wistfully.

"She is," Bill agreed. "You don't have to hurt her."

"I won't shoot her in the head. Mark made us promise that." Mark looked up although his eyes seemed to have lost focus. "Not in the head. Won't mess her up for the coffin."

"That's good. That's a good start." Bill saw Mark shift his gun to the left of her spine.

"We'll shoot her in the heart," Mark said, and fired.

Happy's eyes and mouth opened wide, but Bill only heard the sound as if it were from a long, long way away. The gun in Bill's hand rose up in a long smooth arc, the barrel appearing in his vision like a pointed arrow.

The space around Mark darkened and he seemed to grow. In slow motion, Happy slumped to the ground and Mark's hand began to extend toward Bill. Then the .44 revolver in Bill's hand leaped in a flash of light. The gun's roar seemed deadened as well. Bill fired again, and Mark dropped the gun, which floated down, hit the back of Happy's desk, and cluttered out of sight.

Mark's hand came up and covered his throat, his eyes wide and his mouth in the shape of an O. He tried to stand up but instead seemed to kick himself to the side; Mark's legs working independently of one another and he fell on his back on the ground.

Spurts of blood squirted from between Mark's fingers. Somewhere behind him, Bill could hear shouts.

When he got to Mark's side, he knelt beside his friend. Bill's knee grew wet with blood.

"I'm sorry," Bill cried.

In response, Mark's mouth opened once, twice. No words came out. Maybe he mouthed the words thank you, maybe Bill wanted Mark to say that. Out of the corner of his eye, Bill saw Agent Parmero screaming something, holding his gun on Mark, but Bill did not care.

Mark closed his eyes and Bill saw his friend, his best friend, die.

Chapter Thirty-Seven
1996

Officer Bill Mallory stamped his feet when he got out of the cruiser, his eyes on the darkening evening skies. The meteorologist said that it would be a cold night for September, 40 degrees or so, and the skies promised the kind of nasty spitting rain that made for miserable nights.

He stepped inside the Conoco gas station, ignoring the squawking radio chatter. A few hours earlier, a man named Garrett O'Neill had walked onto the pedestrian bridge overlooking Dodge Street at 60th, taken off all of his clothes, and proceeded to give every west-bound driver a little show. The first few officers had only approached from the Memorial Park side of the bridge, which led to the naked O'Neill (it turned out that aside from getting naked in public, O'Neill ran marathons) racing onto the University of Nebraska-Omaha campus at a spirited six-minute-mile clip. The naked man led the officers (by then around ten) across field and through building, where he managed to dodge several tacklers and one taser (which struck another officer). About twenty minutes after the first officer responded, nearly a dozen Omaha Police Officers had joined the chase.

One student happened to have a video camera on hand and recorded part of the chase, which she turned around and gave to KMTV.

My legs give out at the top of the stairs and I fall to the ground like some stuffed animal that's been thrown to the ground by a temper-tantruming kid. I'm covered in blood, big smears of it. My right hand is on fire, flopping against my chest. I don't even want to look at it. I'm holding the gun in my left hand.

The Angry Man is right over there. In the kitchen. It's filthy and it smells like moldy bread. He got blood over himself too but he's not moving. I know I have to get past him to get to the door but I don't wanna move. Everything hurts so bad. Maybe the Angry Man is dead but I don't know. He might be faking it. Might be dead, might be alive, don't know. Don't wanna move.

His foot twitches maybe. Sweat in my eyes. Have to move. Gonna close my eyes soon and if he's alive he might hurt me hurt me. Have to move. I keep my hand close and get up on my knees. Can't walk. I go on my knees toward the Angry Man blocking the door to the rest of the house. Gotta move.

The call, when it comes, is for a noise complaint on Bleaken Street. It's in the area of one of Omaha's frequent flyers.

They called him Rat Tail John, and those in the department regarded him with something like amusement. He was known for two things: getting into incredibly physical arguments with his wife and a rat tail that stretched half way down his back. About once a week Rat Tail gets into it with his wife and the police get called.

The noise complaint said it sounded like fireworks, which sounds like Rat Tail, blowing off fireworks in October. He takes the call and guns the engine.

I get closer and closer and closer. Angry Man doesn't move. I get closer and I reach out my hand. My hand shaking. My hand touches his bare foot.

Suddenly I'm the Angry Man. I'm cowering behind a couch while my dad beats up Mom. My dad telling me I'm a pussy. Me in the woods near my house, seeing a rabbit caught in the trap I made with my own hands. Me peeling apart the rabbit's skin while it screamed. I see this and I see my left hand, finger extended dipping into the blood, and I'm drawing little pictures in blood of the rabbit spread eagle on the ground.

The Angry Man is looking at me, dazed.

I get to my feet, never mind the pain, and I run toward the door.

Bill is driving down the street, Rat Tail's house is at the very end amid a broken-down fence and two busted lawn mowers in the front yard. He almost does not see the naked boy sprint into the street. The tires squeal, and the car stops a foot away from the emaciated looking child.

For a fraction of a second, Bill stares wide-eyed at the child standing in the beams of his headlights. His training kicks in, and Bill reaches for the radio to call for backup, lots of backup. Every officer in Omaha has been looking for Markie Peter.

He is out of the car and, gun out, next to the child. He asks the kid if he's okay, where's the man who took you. Markie points at a white ranch home, well-lit and normal. Bill orders the kid to stay there and he sprints up the cement walkway. He points his gun through the door and sees a man in a bathrobe sitting against a fridge. The man is covered in blood. When Bill checks, he finds no pulse. Bill notices the markings on the floor, as if the boy had tried to draw something in blood.

Bill checks the rest of the first floor before racing back to the kid, still standing in the headlights. People are coming out onto their porches.

The kid looks so lost, so disorientated. Bill goes to the trunk and finds the heavy blanket all police cars have there for situations like this. He wraps it around the kid, keeping his eyes on the house. Officers from all over are on the way, angrily slicing through traffic.

Markie looks at Bill and reaches up a hand, touching Bill's hand. Bill sees what Markie has gone through. The ear flicking, the locker, the journal, the kidnapping, the torture. It flows through Bill's head in an instant.

"Good Jesus," Bill says to Markie. "I'm so sorry. I'll protect you." It's the only think he can think to say, so Bill says it again. "I'll protect you, Mark. Always."

Chapter Thirty-Eight
Sunday, November 20, 2016

He hated the smell of hospitals. Not that this is unusual. If hospitals smelled pleasant, you could find car air fresheners in the shapes of tall white buildings and smelling of antiseptic and death fear.

The evening sun cast low yellow lights across the lobby, giving everything a long, evil-seeming shadow. A few people milled about, each one with a tale. That one perhaps visiting her uncle who'd had a stroke, this one hurrying past could not take another minute with his mother looking like that.

He did not wear a badge or a gun, not anymore and probably never again. There were hearings left to be endured, interviews with the women and men from the Office of Professional Responsibility. Already there was talk of him quitting, leaving voluntarily, which was fine with the powers that be.

Whatever drove Bill during his career as member of the law enforcement community had fallen along with Mark there in the basement of Bleaken Street.

That past four days had blurred past.

And now he wandered into the gift shop thinking about flowers. Some noise caught his ear and he looked up. A second later, Bill took a step to move behind a rotating rack of small stuffed animals.

Mark's sister and niece walked past, neither of them sparing a look in Bill's direction. Their faces were set in a kind of permafrown. Bill ambled to his left, watching Stacy and Skylar move toward the massive revolving door. They walked with, Bill noted, the same gait, the same sway of hips. And if they had seen Bill, Stacy and Skylar would no doubt have accosted him in the same angry tone.

"And I would have deserved it," Bill murmured, loud enough for a teenager nearby to hear it. They made eye contact, and the boy fixed Bill a strange look. Bill turned and left the gift shop without buying anything.

To be honest, Bill did not quite know how he felt about anything. He felt sadness and regret, of course. A sense of betrayal, perhaps. Guilt. Shame. Embarrassment, self-pity, bewilderment, a kind of projecting anger which blames others to avoid the idea of blaming one's own self. Perhaps even a smidgen of relief that something difficult had ended. Then guilt at that smidgen of relief.

Bill took the elevator up to the fourth floor. He took the slip of paper from his pocket, the one with the number written on it. He looked up at the room numbers and directions and stepped right. A hundred feet later, he turned left.

4125, 4127, and then 4129. Bill stopped outside the frame of the door. His allergies were killing him. Every lungful of antiseptic air made him want to double over in coughs.

Happy lay on her back, staring at some stupid reality show. He took another step into the room and finally Happy pivoted her head to look at him. She said nothing, although Bill was certain she recognized him.

Bill cleared his throat, found words hard to come by. Decided upon the easiest thing to say. "How are you doing?"

In response, Happy looked away.

"You are lucky you know," Bill continued, feeling as if his words were sliding down the face of a vast cliff. "The situs inversus. If your heart had been in the, uh, normal position, you would have died instantly. I mean, you still suffered a lot of internal damage and…" He trailed off. No doubt she knew all that.

Although he cared about Happy's well-being, at least as much as he could for someone he barely knew, Bill had a few specific questions. He decided to ask. "Did Mark," he began. "Did Mark know about your condition?"

Happy rotated her head toward Bill, her eyes red and wet. In the background, the ping of the heart monitor began to race up.

"I was thinking that maybe if Mark knew about your condition, then maybe he didn't…"

He trailed off again, as Happy's eyes bugged out. She wheezed her breath and began to speak. "Don't talk to me… about Mark…" Each phrase came out in short bursts. "I don't want… to talk."

Tears began to flow down her cheeks. After a second of indecision, Bill took a box of Kleenex from the table and handed them to her. Happy dabbed her eyes.

"Happy, I cannot begin to understand what happened to you, what Mark did to you, but I do know what it is like to touch him. I did so, years ago. It was a very unpleasant experience."

Happy began to wheeze again. "He didn't touch me… He held me… For hours…" She reached and punched at a button next to her hand.

For hours… Bill bent over and closed his eyes. "I'm so sorry. Mark, I don't know, that wasn't Mark. He faced so many horrors."

"I know that…" Happy got up on one elbow to face him, the effort causing her face to redden. "…you made him."

"No," Bill began, defensive. "I never forced him."

"Mark held me… I know… you made him." Happy collapsed back onto the pillow. The heart monitor pinged faster. "The last straw was that little girl. Quinn. I see… I see her dying. It broke him. He started to become Vandergeest after." A pause. "Vandergeest and all the others."

A nurse came in, crossed the room to Happy's side. "Are you okay?" she asked.

"He broke my Mark," Happy hissed in her wheezy voice. "Make him leave."

The nurse turned, her face stony. "Sir, please leave this room." She took a step. "Now, sir."

Bill straightened. "He only wanted to help. I know this. He was my friend."

"You ruined him…" Happy said. The nurse began to maneuver Bill toward the door. "…and me."

He heard this last, faint but clear, as he left the room. He walked a few steps down the hall, thinking of things he wanted to say to her. Happy did not know Mark, the real Mark. Mark's sister never liked me. We solved so many crimes together.

By the time he reached the elevator, Bill felt these responses congealing around him, a protective coating. He coughed heavily into his sleeve. He had done the right thing, Bill told himself. He had. He had.

He had.

Chapter Thirty-Nine
April 23, 2012

"Okay, okay, okay." Mark reaches in with his right hand, he's got a pencil in his left. He picks up the keyring and pushes the bag off his lap.

He's still. I thought he might start jerking around or something, but he doesn't move. No one else talks, and the only sound I hear is the rain outside which is muffled and hard to hear. Something is pressing against my left leg. It hurts and I want to move it, but I think they'll hear me.

When Mark talks, it's usually quick, like he thinks at twice the speed. Which is why it's surprising when he speaks up. His voice is lower and slower. "Oh yeah," Mark says, "there it is."

His left hand, holding a pencil, shoots up and starts to draw. It's heavy paper, so even though he's drawing fast the pencil doesn't catch and tear the paper up. Within a minute, a picture starts to emerge. I can see Andrea's car parked at the Kum n Go and she's still in it. Mark is a beautiful artist. He is drawing quickly, but I can tell that's her Ford and he got her crazy hair right.

For a minute Mark keeps drawing, but his hand jerks away and he waves it. The guy FBI agent leaps forward and rips the piece of paper off, and Mark starts drawing again.

This time it's of Andrea's face. Mark seems less like he's drawing and more like he's some sort of computer printer stuck in a person's body. As Andrea's face emerges from his pencil, I look at him and his face has a huge smile on it. I don't want to think about what that means.

The way he's drawing her is beautiful. Andrea's got this smile on her face and her head cocked a little bit like maybe she got asked a question. He takes about three or four minutes and then, even though the picture doesn't look done, Mark waves his hands again and the paper is ripped off.

The next drawing starts with a rectangle that takes up most of the sheet. He shades in part of the top left then shades the bottom left and so on and I don't know what he's supposed to be drawing. He still has that smile on his face, though. If anything, it's bigger. "Now, that's a pretty sight," he says in that low voice. The hair on my head prickles up and I feel like I want to pee.

He keeps drawing and drawing and it looks like nothing until it suddenly doesn't. I see legs and they're tied up with rope. Behind her, she's got her hands tied up too. I want to be sick because that's Andrea in the trunk and he's moving to the right in the drawing toward her face. I close my eyes because I don't want to see it.

But when I close my eyes, I think about that last day and how it is that if I'd hadn't been a fat girl then Andrea wouldn't have wanted me to feel better. There's a sound of paper ripping, but I don't look back. Then she wouldn't have been at the Kum n Go and she wouldn't have been seen by that Vandergeest and everything would be horrible and normal. But Andrea'd be alive. And I'm a horrible, fat, horrible girl and it should have been me because who would have noticed if I'd gone?

I lift up my eyes and look through the shutters of the closet door. Mark is drawing and he's got that smile on. Even worse, he's got a boner too. It's like he pitched a little tent in his pants. Then he starts talking and with the hand that's holding the keys he kind of starts rubbing himself a little bit.

"I know you want this," he says.

"This is fascinating," he says.

And what he's drawing is Andrea. At least I think it's her because the top of the paper ends at her neck. I don't think it's because Mark's being nice because I don't think he's all the way Mark anymore. I think that it's somebody that he's drawing, but it's really Andrea. The drawing isn't beautiful like the one in the parking lot of Andrea's face it's like… like Mark is drawing faster and Andrea's naked and I think about what maybe he's seeing because maybe he's seeing things from Vandergeest's viewpoint—and maybe Vandergeest had a boner too.

I crawl backwards feeling the puke coming up my throat. I don't care if I make any noise, but I get out of the closet, I grab my waste paper basket, and I throw up into it. I throw up a couple more times and I rest my head against the rim of the basket. It smells like puke but I think I'm done.

It's a time before I want to hear anything from that room. It's quiet and I don't think I hear much. I hear Agent Malloy say something at one point, "Do your job, dammit."

Then, after a while I start to feel better enough that I don't have to sit here on the floor wondering if I'm going to barf again. But I don't want to see what Mark is drawing next, but I need to see it because I need to. So, on all fours, I crawl into my closet and shimmy through to Andrea's closet and I scrunch up on the floor.

Mark is still drawing, but it's real slow, like he's tired. He's got a blank face on and there's a wet spot on his pants. I feel a little sick again, but it passes after I close my eyes.

Agent Mallory is watching the drawing. He doesn't have any expression on his face, but the other two FBI agents do.

Both the man and the woman are looking at Mark like he's something that crawled in dog poop.

Mark's pencil is drifting up and down, and I think it looks like a tree. Or a bunch of trees on the left side of the picture. It's kind of dark and I think maybe Mark is seeing this at night.

"It's outside," Agent Mallory says quietly. The other agents join in with quiet voices as Mark keeps drawing.

"What's that? I think those are grain silos."

"Those aren't commercial silos."

"That's a farm."

Mark keeps drawing but doesn't hear the agents. I look at the drawing, and I get this bad feeling starting to form in my tummy. I think I know the place he's drawing. On the right side he draws a rectangle, and it's an abandoned building. It don't have a roof. I see him drawing a tree that grew up inside of it, and I know it's the Tvurdy farm, about two miles from here.

I don't even think about it, but I run out of my room. Only this time I don't care about being quiet. I run out the back into the open field and I'm running. I'm a big girl, but I can run. Maybe I hear Mom yelling at me but I don't turn around.

About halfway to the Tvurdy's I get a pain in my side so I slow down so that I'm only walking fast. I use the railroad tracks because it's the easiest way and the Tvurdy's ain't too far. I know that tree because in the fall I took a picture of it for my photo journalism class which turned out really good. So, I'm walking fast and the world is kind of muzzy, I'm crying, and my nose is running. I wipe it with my sleeve.

Mark's drawing is burned in my head (actually, all of them are, and I think they will be forever), so I know I'm looking for a spot where the main farm is in back of the abandoned building with the tree growing out of it.

I see a bunch of trees near a little stream that isn't too far from the road, and whatever bad feeling I got in my stomach gets worse. The pain in my side has gone away and I run up to the bunch of trees.

Although I don't know what I'm looking for, it doesn't take me but a minute to find a patch of ground that looks different than the rest, all churned up. I look around and see if there's anything I can use for digging. I don't even think about going back for the FBI. I caused Andrea to die and I figure I should be the one to find her.

It takes a few minutes but I find this flat rock nearby that I can grab with both hands. I start digging, and I don't know how long I dig. It's like I know it's not long, but I don't even think about it or how dirty I'm getting or how sore I'm going to be tomorrow.

I smell something. It's kind of low in my nose, but it makes me want to barf again. I look down at the ground and I see something there. It's getting toward dark and it's hard to see. With my hands I brush away the dirt and see it's Andrea's dance team jacket. I think that Vandergeest threw Andrea into a hole after he got done with her and threw her clothes on top.

I don't dig anymore because I'm crying so hard and I don't want to anymore. I want to lie down and sleep. I feel a hand on my shoulder. It's Agent Mallory and behind him are the other FBI agents.

My face is all gross and blubbery, and I figure he's going to be real mad at me, but he ain't. Agent Mallory squats down and looks me in the eye and says real nice, "Janelle, thank you. If it wasn't for you, it would have taken us a long time to find Andrea. Why don't you come back here and warm up a little bit?" Now that Agent Mallory says it, he's right. Although the rain stopped, it's gotten cold and I'm wet and shivering.

I stand up and we walk back to the road where there's a lot of cop cars.

"Do you drink coffee?" Agent Mallory asks. I nod and he hands me a cup, making my hands warm. I take a sip and ask him what's going to happen now.

"We are going to dig Andrea up and process the crime scene. The people are very respectful, Janelle, I hope you know that. We are going to treat Andrea with the utmost respect." I nod and Agent Mallory smiles a little. He says a few more things and walks back to where Andrea is. My parents aren't here but I think they will be soon.

I see a motion to my right and I turn and see Mark. He's looking at me and I must have glared at him because he says quickly, "You saw, didn't you? It's not me, I hate it. I hate that I can do that." I can smell his breath. It smells like beer.

Mark's eyes are real big and his skin is white, like he's scared or something. "So, you can see through them?" I ask. "The guys who kill?"

"I live it," he says, and the way he says it makes me feel bad for him. "Sometimes I'm the victim, sometimes the killer. It's awful, either way."

"What does it feel like?"

Mark shrugs his shoulders and quick reaches out and with one finger touches my hand. And then I'm in Mark's head and also in there is every person he's ever touched.

It only lasts a second it's over and I stumble a bit and drop my coffee. "I shouldn't have done that," Mark says.

I don't say anything and he doesn't make a move toward me. If he had, I would have screamed and run.

"It gets lonely," he says, "that I don't have anyone to touch. I shouldn't have done that, but you're lonely. Sort of like me…" Mark kind of squints and shakes his head violently and I think maybe his name is Mark. Maybe it's only partly Mark and partly something else.

He points and says, "I see your parents over there. You should go to them. I think you should go."

I don't need telling two times so I get up and run over to where Mom and Dad are. They are looking at the bunch of trees and we're hugging. They're crying and I'm crying too but not as hard.

It's because Mark gave me a little of Vandergeest and he don't feel sorry at all.

- End -

About Your Author

Photo credit: Derrald Farnsworth-Livingston

Andrew Kanago was born and raised in American Midwest. In the fourth grade, Mrs. Arent had to quiet him down because he was laughing out loud while reading Judy Blume.

In his twenties, Andrew worked as a political aide, small-town journalist, telemarketer, senior customer finance administrator, janitor, and warehouse loader. He finally hit upon the idea of becoming a teacher, both at the high school and college level.

He wanted to be a writer since high school but sadly lacked the discipline for many years. It was only after meeting his wife, Heather, that Andrew began to develop the discipline needed to embark on a writing career. He spent several years writing a 210,000-word Magnus opus that lacked a plot or any recognizable characterization. It was the best writing education he could have received.

Andrew currently resides in Nebraska with his family.

www.andrewkanago.com

Other HellBound Books Titles
Available at: www.hellboundbookspublishing.com

Mother Legs

A giant, telepathic spider befriends a small boy, seeing the world through his eyes, with murderous intent... When Blake Turner's addict mother disappears in rural Canada, he assumes she's simply relapsed. But, when his search for her uncovers evidence of a terrifying monster and the sinister conspiracy to hide its existence, he must decide just how far he is willing to go to protect his loved ones. With only a depressed park ranger and a local reporter to aid him, Blake delves deeper into the mystery to discover what the creature is, and why it wants to start a family.

The Devil's Hour

A new and altogether awesome anthology of all things horror!

Seventeen spine-chilling tales of the darkest terror, most unpleasant people, and slithering monsters that lurk beneath the bed and in the blackest of shadows…

Satanic Panic

An incredible homage to 1980's horror!

Satanic Panic, a mass hysteria created in the nineteen eighties, has returned to a small college town in the Midwest.

Ritualistic murders and the presence of the occult have bled below the surface of the town in the form of icy accidents and other coincidences.

And when three lifelong friends find themselves on the radar of a killer—and leader of a satanic cult—they must fight for what's good without being seduced by the evil that possesses their campus.

The Toilet Zone

RESTROOM READING AT ITS MOST FRIGHTENING!

Compiled and edited by the grand master of 80's schlock horror, Bret McCormick, each one of this collection of 32 terrifying tales is just the perfect length for a visit to the smallest room....

At the very boundaries of human imagination dwells one single, solitary place of solitude, of peace and quiet, a place in which your regular human being spends, on average, 10 to 15 minutes - at least once every single day of their lives.

Now, consider a typical, everyday reading speed of 200 to 250 words per minute - that means your average visitor has the time to read between 2,500 to 4,000 words, which makes each and every one of these 32 tales of terror - from some of the best contemporary independent authors - within this anthology of horror the perfect, meticulously calculated length. Dare you take a walk to the small room from where inky shadows creep out to smother the light and solitude's siren call beckons you?

Dare you take a quiet, lonely walk into… The Toilet Zone

Invasive Species

A monster has come to Maldus, Arkansas, and the residents of the small mountain town are too busy to notice. With the monster comes something even more terrifying and threatening than gnashing teeth or razor-sharp claws.

The monster has brought change.

The residents of the small mountain town are too busy to notice at first. Busy with things such as addiction, racism, work, or land deals. Unnoticed, the change the monster brings in its insidious wake spreads like wildfire.

Unnoticed, the town of Maldus falls prey to an Invasive Species.

Tremble

Widow and single mother, Rebecca Noland, wants nothing more than to rekindle the passion with her overworked fiancé, Detective Dan Slaviche.

Expecting to surprise him by slipping into his apartment before he comes home from work, her curiosity gets the best of her when she discovers the key to unlock his desktop. What she finds there is a nightmare that sends her, along with her seven-year-old son, running for their lives.

Terrified and broke, her only option is to flee to her family's estate in Tremble, Tennessee where memories of her mother's violent death still haunt her childhood home.

But bad memories aren't the only thing that await her.

As Dan abandons all morals in his attempt to locate his bride-to-be, Rebecca struggles to make the house a home for her son while growing closer to her next door neighbors.

Her sanity comes into question when she realizes the entity responsible for her mother's murder is lying in wait, intent on destroying anyone who tries to come between it and the object of its deadly obsession… her.

**A HellBound Books LLC
Publication**

http://www.hellboundbookspublishing.com

Printed in the United States of America